Praise for *Riders of the Realm: Across the Dark Water*

"A story with both wings and heart, Across the Dark Water
is a breathtaking ride into a rich and dangerous world. Animal lovers
and thrill-seekers alike will cheer for Echofrost and Rahkki at each
of the many twists and turns. Clever, epic, and wildly imaginative!"
—Kamilla Benko, author of The Unicorn Quest

"An epic adventure that moves at the speed of flight.
Thrilling, compelling, and completely enchanting. I fell in love
with the Storm Herd, and one particular winged steed that
Pegasus himself would fall for!"
—Kate O'Hearn, author of the international bestselling Pegasus series

"Exhilarating! A well-woven tale full of loyalty, bravery,
danger, and love. Readers will be delighted!"
—Lindsay Cummings, New York Times bestselling author
of the Balance Keepers series

"A riveting, richly imagined epic tale of loyalty, bravery, and friendship
that will make your heart (literally!) soar—a pulse-pounding adventure!
Jennifer Lynn Alvarez is a true master of her craft."
—Kristen Kittscher, author of The Wig in the Window
and The Tiara on the Terrace

"Getting swept up in Jennifer Lynn Alvarez's rich world of flying steeds,
Landwalkers, giants, and spit dragons was the most fun I've had all year.
It's like How to Train Your Dragon meets Watership Down.
But with pegasi. A fantastic read!"
—John Kloepfer, author of the Zombie Chasers series
and the Galaxy's Most Wanted series

"Honor and courage soar on every page of Jennifer Lynn Alvarez's books!"
—Jenn Reese, author of the Above World trilogy

"A beautiful tale of loyalty, adventure, and bravery. Readers will want
to soar through the clouds with Echofrost and befriend kindhearted Rahkki.
Across the Dark Water is a captivating opener to the Riders of the Realm trilogy."
—Jill Diamond, author of the Lou Lou and Pea series

"Gorgeously detailed and with heart-wrenching conflict, *Across the Dark Water* is a breathtaking read sure to please new fans and old. Jennifer Lynn Alvarez's fantasy world is richly developed with a cast of characters readers will be sure to love, both winged and human. I read it as fast as a pegasus can fly and am already longing for more."
—Mindee Arnett, critically acclaimed author of *Onyx & Ivory*

Praise for the Guardian Herd series

"From page one, Jennifer Lynn Alvarez weaves an epic tale of a doomed black pegasus foal named Star, whose race against time will lift the reader on the wings of danger and destiny, magic and hope. It's a world I did not want to leave, and neither will you."
—Peter Lerangis, *New York Times* bestselling author in the 39 Clues series and of the Seven Wonders series

"Perfect for fans of *Charlotte's Web* and the Guardians of Ga'Hoole series."
—ALA *Booklist*

"Chock-full of adventure and twists, making it difficult to put down. Readers will be clamoring for the next book."
—*School Library Journal*

"Alvarez's world is lush with description and atmosphere."
—*Publishers Weekly*

"Will prove popular with both animal-lovers and fantasy fans. A good choice for reluctant readers. The clever resolution will get kids psyched for more tales from the Guardian Herd."
—ALA *Booklist*

"Filled with fantastical action, and rich with description. A well-paced and engrossing story. Alvarez has created a series that will be beloved by readers."
—*VOYA*

RIDERS of the REALM

3

BENEATH THE WEEPING CLOUDS

BY

JENNIFER LYNN ALVAREZ

Also by Jennifer Lynn Alvarez

Riders of the Realm 1: Across the Dark Water

Riders of the Realm 2: Through the Untamed Sky

The Guardian Herd: Starfire

The Guardian Herd: Stormbound

The Guardian Herd: Landfall

The Guardian Herd: Windborn

Riders of the Realm: Beneath the Weeping Clouds
Text copyright © 2019 by Jennifer Lynn Alvarez
Illustrations copyright © 2019 by David McClellan
All rights reserved. Printed in the United States of America.
No part of this book may be used or reproduced in any manner whatsoever without written permission except in the case of brief quotations embodied in critical articles and reviews. For information address HarperCollins Children's Books, a division of HarperCollins Publishers, 195 Broadway, New York, NY 10007.
www.harpercollinschildrens.com

Library of Congress Cataloging-in-Publication Data

Names: Alvarez, Jennifer Lynn, author.
Title: Beneath the weeping clouds / by Jennifer Lynn Alvarez.
Description: First edition. | New York, NY : HarperCollins, [2019] | Series: Riders of the realm ; 3 | Summary: "Storm Herd will have to join forces with the humans they have long-feared to save Rahkki and defeat the giants"— Provided by publisher.
Identifiers: LCCN 2019009523 | ISBN 978-0-06-249441-2 (hardback)
Subjects: | CYAC: Horses—Fiction. | Animals, Mythical—Fiction. | Giants—Fiction. | Adventure and adventurers—Fiction. | Fantasy. | BISAC: JUVENILE FICTION / Fantasy & Magic. | JUVENILE FICTION / Action & Adventure / General. | JUVENILE FICTION / Animals / Horses.
Classification: LCC PZ7.A4797 Be 2019 | DDC [Fic]—dc23 LC record available at https://lccn.loc.gov/2019009523

Typography by Catherine San Juan
19 20 21 22 23   PC/LSCH   10 9 8 7 6 5 4 3 2 1
❖
First Edition

FOR HORSES,

WILD AND TAME,

WISHING YOU PEACE

TABLE OF CONTENTS

Neither friend nor foe
Where giants go.
Deep, deep in the jungle keep.
Neither man nor beast
Where giants feast.
Deep, deep in the jungle keep.

—Fire Horde song

SANDWEN CLANS

Humans

BRIM CARVER—animal doctor of the Fifth Clan

KOKO DALE—age fifteen; head groom of the Kihlari stable of the Fifth Clan Sky Guard

MUT FINN—age fifteen; leader of the Sandwen teens, kids too old for games but too young for war

OSSI FINN—caretaker of Brauk Stormrunner. Sister to Mut Finn

WILLA GREEN—Daakuran merchant, operates a tent at the trading post

KASHIK HIGHTOWER—operates a food kiosk at the trading post. Mother to Tuni Hightower. Nickname: Kashi

TUNI HIGHTOWER—Headwind of Dusk Patrol, member of the Fifth Clan Sky Guard. Kihlara mount: Rizah

HARAK NIGHTSEER—Headwind of Day Patrol, member of the Fifth Clan Sky Guard. Kihlara mount: Ilan

JUL RANGER—age fourteen; Meela Swift's apprentice

BRAUK STORMRUNNER—Rahkki's brother, Headwind of Dawn Patrol, member of the Fifth Clan Sky Guard. Kihlari mount: Kol

UNCLE DARTHAN STORMRUNNER—rice farmer of the

Fifth Clan. Uncle to Brauk and Rahkki on their mother's side

RAHKKI STORMRUNNER—age thirteen; Rider in the Sky Guard army. Kihlara mount: Sula

REYELLA STORMRUNNER—past queen of the Fifth Clan, supplanted by Lilliam Whitehall. Mother to Rahkki and Brauk. Kihlara mount: Drael

MEELA SWIFT—provisional Headwind of Dawn Patrol. Kihlara mount: Jax

GENERAL AKMID TSUN—commander of the Land Guard army. Deceased

PRINCESS I'LENNA WHITEHALL—age twelve; eldest daughter of Queen Lilliam. Crown Princess of the Fifth Clan. Kihlara mount: Firo

PRINCESS JOR WHITEHALL—age five; youngest daughter of Queen Lilliam

PRINCE K'LAR WHITEHALL—newborn son of Queen Lilliam

PRINCESS RAYNI WHITEHALL—age eight; middle daughter of Queen Lilliam

QUEEN LILLIAM WHITEHALL—leader of the Fifth Clan, prior princess of the Second Clan. Also referred to as *Queen of the Fifth*. Kihlara mount: Mahrsan

QUEEN TAVARA WHITEHALL—leader of the Second Clan. Mother to Queen Lilliam

TAMBOR WOODSON—age fifteen; Mut Finn's best friend

Places

DAAKURAN EMPIRE—across the bay from the Sandwen
Realm is the empire, a highly populated land of commerce,
academics, and magic. Common language of the empire:
Talu

SANDWEN CLANS—seven clans of people founded by
the Seven Sisters, each ruled by a monarch queen. Clan
language: Sandwen

Sandwen Clan Divinities

GRANAK—"Father of Dragons," guardian mascot of the
Fifth Clan. Sixteen-foot-tall, thirty-three-foot-long
drooling lizard called a *spit dragon*

KAJI (sing.), **KAJIES** (pl.)—troublesome or playful spirits

THE SEVEN SISTERS—the royal founders of the seven
Sandwen clans

SULA—"Mother of Serpents," guardian mascot of the Second
Clan. Forty-two-foot jungle python

SUNCHASER—the moon

☙ KIHLARI ❧

(KEE-lar-ee) (pl.), Kihlara (sing.)
Translation: "Children of the Wind"

Tame pegasi of the Sandwen Clans

DRAEL—Queen Reyella's Chosen stallion. Small bay with black-tipped dark-amber feathers, fluffy black mane and tail, white muzzle, four white socks

ILAN—white stallion with black spots, black mane and tail, dark-silver wings edged in black

JAX—gold dun stallion, dark-orange wings at the mantle changing to midnight-blue toward the ends, black mane and tail, white snip on muzzle

KOL—shiny chestnut stallion with bright-yellow feathers, yellow-streaked red mane and tail, white blaze, two white hind socks

MAHRSAN—Queen Lilliam's Chosen stallion. Blood-bay with sapphire-blue feathers edged in white, black mane and tail, jagged white blaze, four white socks

RIZAH—golden palomino pinto mare with dark-pink feathers edged in gold, white-and-gold mixed mane and tail

TOR—Drael's identical twin. Belonged to Uncle Darthan Stormrunner. Deceased

CꝏƆ STORM HERD Ꙭ

Wild pegasi from Anok

DEWBERRY—bay pinto mare with emerald feathers, black mane and tail, thin blaze on forehead, two white hind anklets

ECHOFROST—sleek silver mare with a mix of dark- and light-purple feathers, white mane and tail, one white sock

GRAYSTONE—white stallion with pale-yellow feathers each with a silver center, blue eyes, silver mane and tail

HAZELWIND—buckskin stallion with jade feathers, black mane and tail, big white blaze, two white hind socks

REDFIRE—tall copper chestnut stallion with dark-gold feathers, dark-red mane and tail, white star on forehead

SHYSONG—blue roan mare with dusty-blue feathers edged in black, ice-blue eyes, black mane and tail, jagged blaze, two hind socks

GORLAN HORDES

Giant Folk

Living in the mountains in three separate hordes—
Highland Horde, Fire Horde, and Great Cave Horde. They
stand from eleven to fourteen feet tall. All have red hair,
pale skin, and a double set of tusks. Language: Gorlish, a
form of sign language

PRINCE DAANATH—prince of Highland Horde. Father to
Drake, Fallon, Krell, and Miah

RIDERS

of the

REALM

3

BENEATH THE WEEPING CLOUDS

SANDWEN

Mill

Darthan's Farm

Barn

Beach

Jungle

Rice Fields

Brim's Hut

Fallows

FIFTH CLAN

Ruk

Horse Pasture

Farmland

Horse Arena

Supply Barn

Kihlari Training Yard

Fort Prowl

Kihlari Barn

Jungle

Rain Forest

Leshi Creek

Sandwen Clan Travelways

River Tsallan

FOURTH CLAN

SIXTH CLAN

Lake

To the THIRD CLAN

Southern Mountains

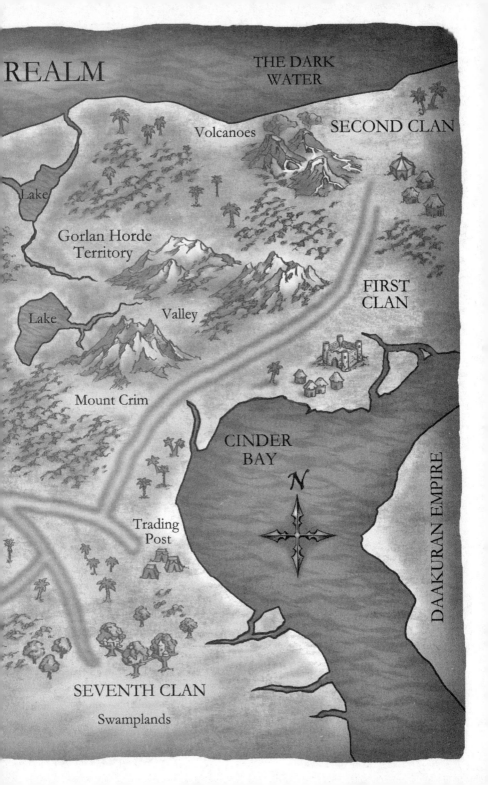

THE DARK WATER

SECOND
CLAN →

Volcanoes

Fire Horde Warren

Sandwen Clan Travelway

MOUNT CRIM

FIRST
CLAN →

Highland Horde Camp

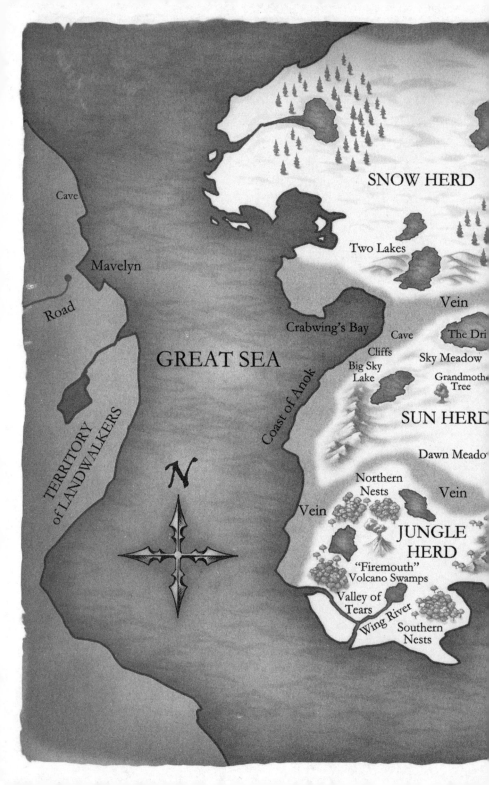

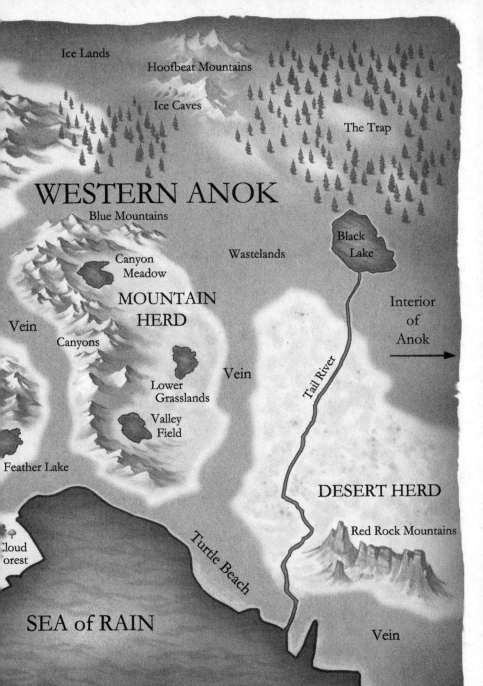

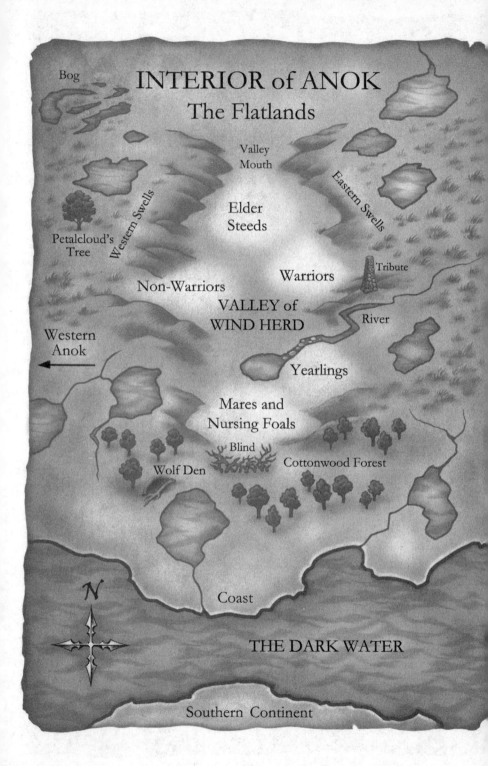

RIDERS
of the
REALM

3

BENEATH THE WEEPING CLOUDS

1

THE SOUP

"LET ME GO," RAHKKI SIGNED. HIS MOTHER HAD taught him the silent language of the giants when he was a toddler, and he was grateful for it now. The Highland prince had captured him and was taking Rahkki to his soup cauldron—whether to feed him or eat him, Rahkki wasn't sure.

The prince ignored Rahkki's plea as they traversed a weed-strewn plateau aboard an elephant. Rahkki peered over the bull's head. Jagged peaks sawed the skyline that surrounded the Highland encampment, which was a flat mesa sliced across otherwise rugged terrain. Beyond the camp, tame elephants foraged in a trampled clearing and the sky spanned overhead, a smear of blue between the mountains.

"I saved your life," Rahkki mumbled. The giants didn't understand his Sandwen language, but just yesterday Rahkki had saved this Gorlan prince from being eaten by a snake. *He* should be grateful!

The prince's blue eyes narrowed. His breath whooshed in a rumbling snarl.

Highland Horde had just returned from war with Rahkki's clan over the release of the wild Kihlari steeds. Queen Lilliam had dispatched the Fifth Clan armies to rescue the rare animals so she could sell them. However, the wild herd had escaped during the battle and flown away. Rahkki was glad about this. His Flier, Sula, was finally free.

But the wild herd's freedom was the only good thing that had come from that battle. In the middle of it, civil war had erupted between the Sandwens loyal to Queen Lilliam and the rebels who were loyal to her eldest daughter, Princess I'Lenna. I'Lenna's side had lost and Harak had arrested her after killing her most loyal supporter, General Tsun.

Rahkki sighed. Everything had gone wrong and he had to get home. He turned his golden eyes toward the

Highland prince. *"Let me go,"* he repeated. *"Please."*

The prince chuffed, sounding to Rahkki like a jungle tiger. They entered the Highland camp and giants approached from every direction when they spied their prince. They beat the mossy stone and roared like thunderclouds, gesturing to one another in rapid Gorlish.

Rahkki flinched, and sparkling pain shot through his injured ankle. Fire Horde giants had fractured it when he'd tried to protect I'Lenna from them, and Sula had been injured too. She'd taken an arrow meant for Rahkki. Truly, nothing had gone as he'd expected.

He scanned the patchy blue skies, hoping Sula's injury wouldn't prevent her from leaving the Realm with her wild herd. His belly tightened with worry.

Trailing behind Rahkki and the prince were wounded Highland warriors and their elephants, straggling into camp. Several giants ran to help their hordemates while the prince continued on with Rahkki. Soon they arrived at the massive cauldron of soup that simmered over a low flame. A huge shade structure loomed above it, protecting the broth from rain and sun.

"Daanath! Daanath!" the giants signed in Gorlish. Rahkki didn't know what the word meant, but understood that it was the Highland prince's name or title, or both.

Daanath curled his lips, showing the full length of his yellowed tusks. His horde gathered closer, growing silent and expectant. Some drooled, others licked their lips. Rahkki, who had been raised on Fifth Clan warnings, feared the worst.

Be home by dark or the giants will eat you.

Take your bath or the giants will smell you.

Go to sleep or the giants will hear you.

Next, the Highland king emerged from his tent and a hush fell over the encampment. Rahkki knew from listening to his brother, Brauk, that Gorlan princes led raids and commanded warriors under the watchful eyes of their kings. Kings also enforced horde laws.

Prince Daanath dipped his head toward his gigantic sire, and Rahkki's eyes drifted up the king's wide girth and thick chest, to his graying red hair. The Highland leader plodded across the flat mesa, tusks bared, and sank his heavy body onto a seat that had been carved from a great boulder. He turned his attention to the soup.

Bubbles popped on the surface of the broth, releasing a scent that, surprisingly, wasn't awful. *How will it taste with me in it*, Rahkki wondered. A light breeze ruffled his hair, carrying the faint scent of rain.

The horde passed stacks of empty bowls to one another,

forming a circle around the cauldron. The toddlers, some as tall as Rahkki, leaped up and down, rumbling happily and clutching their bowls to their chests.

They're excited to eat me, Rahkki thought. Fresh pain erupted from his injured ankle and crackled up his leg. He flopped over and vomited all over the prince's callused fingers.

The Gorlander swapped Rahkki to his cleaner hand and wiped the dirty one on his loincloth. But he continued stomping toward the soup.

"*Stop*," Rahkki gestured.

They reached the rim of the pot. The chuffing and roaring ceased.

"*Help me*," Rahkki signed, throwing the same words at the prince that the prince had used when the python had attacked him.

Daanath didn't respond.

Land to skies! Rahkki had saved countless lives—both human and giant—during the day's battle. He'd shot the giants using darts treated with powerful medicine. He'd fooled everyone into thinking he was a mighty warrior by putting Gorlan warriors temporarily to sleep. This had prevented much bloodshed, and when the quick-acting sedative wore off, the giants had risen, unharmed.

But, as usual, Rahkki's plans seemed to have back-fired. His clan had called him a *Deathlifter*, the most terrifying type of sorcerer, and they'd abandoned him. And now this horde wanted to eat him. It didn't seem fair, honestly. *Don't wish for life to be fair, Rahkki*—this was one of his uncle's favorite sayings, and Rahkki sighed because he couldn't stop wishing it.

The youngest giants grew restless and began slapping their hands against the bottoms of their carved wooden soup bowls, creating a unique and complicated rhythm. The beat swelled as each member of the horde drummed, adding to the song until it culminated in a deafening cre-scendo that abruptly ended. The giants plopped down all at once.

Just get it over with and toss me into the soup, Rahkki wanted to shout. Large logs glowed red beneath the caul-dron and the steady heat warmed his face.

Prince Daanath finally set Rahkki down. Rahkki peeked at the rain forest that surrounded the mesa. If his ankle weren't busted, he'd run for it.

Six lanky Gorlanders approached the cauldron, wield-ing ladles. They dipped them into the soup and then trod around the circle, filling the bowls.

Rahkki stared at his human-sized serving, exhaling in

relief and horror. They weren't going to eat him; they were going to feed him. Neither option was ideal. Green and brown lumps floated on the surface of the yellow broth. Rahkki couldn't make out if the lumps were flesh, roots, vegetables, or all of that. What if there were Sandwens in this soup? His belly shrank, but his mouth watered. He'd missed lunch, after all, and the soup's scent was surprisingly good.

The prince motioned toward his mouth, and Rahkki recognized the Gorlish word *eat*. His mother had used it often when Rahkki was young.

He shook his head. *"No, thank you."* Perhaps if he refused it, they'd offer him something else. Something less . . . disgusting.

The prince snarled at Rahkki so loudly that the boy covered his ears. *"Eat,"* he repeated.

Rahkki's blood drained toward his toes. Suddenly he understood why Queen Lilliam had refused her portion when the Gorlanders had come to parlay for their ancient farmland. Maybe it *wasn't* because Lilliam didn't speak Gorlish, maybe it was because the soup was bloody disgusting and she didn't want to be a cannibal! *"No eat,"* he signed, wishing he knew their language better.

The prince slammed the mesa with both fists. The

black cauldron rocked and the horde screeched. Rahkki scooted away from Daanath, crawling like a three-legged crab.

Signing fluidly, the prince spoke to him while the horde waited. Rahkki stared at the prince's fingers, trying to understand. Around him stomachs grumbled and drool seeped, but not one Gorlander touched the soup. It dawned on him that the horde would not eat until he did. *They're trying to honor me,* he realized.

Rahkki knew his mother, Reyella Stormrunner, the past Queen of the Fifth, would never refuse this honor. He inched closer to his bowl, glancing up at Prince Daanath. The beast curled his lips again, showing the full length of his sharp tusks. Was he smiling or snarling? *Did it matter?* If Rahkki didn't eat the soup, the horde would only get hungrier waiting on him. They might change their minds and toss him into the pot after all.

"Okay," he said, breathing through his mouth. He lifted the bowl to his lips, and the entire horde leaned closer and excited grumbling buzzed around the circle.

Warm soup flowed toward Rahkki's throat. He slurped a mouthful, chewed the lumps, and swallowed. He'd expected to vomit, but instead wonderful flavors burst across his tongue, making him gasp.

The horde exhaled in a collective sigh of satisfaction.

Rahkki drank more. Delicate seasonings spiced the savory broth and it slid smoothly down his gullet, causing his eyes to roll with pleasure. Never in his life had he tasted anything so good, so comforting.

All around him the giants roared their approval and tipped their bowls to their mouths.

The more Rahkki drank, the more he wanted, and his entire body hummed as the nutrition flooded his bloodstream and raced through his limbs. The pain in his ankle subsided and contentment filled him. He finished the entire bowl and then licked the side. When he was finished, he reclined on the stone, lost in a stupor of satisfaction.

The horde also finished and then broke their circle to return to their camp duties. The children gathered around Rahkki, breathing loudly. He recognized the prince's flame-haired daughter. She and her brothers had attended the Sandwen parlay with their sire. That peace negotiation had failed as miserably as I'Lenna's more recent one.

Rahkki shifted his attention back to the prince. *"I go home now?"* he signed.

The giant shook his head. *"The three hordes are meeting to discuss your clan. You will attend the meeting."*

Rahkki didn't catch every word, but he understood well enough and melted into the stone. "*Why? When?*"

"*Soon,*" the prince answered without further elaboration.

"*But I can't wait.*"

The prince slammed down his fist. "*You can wait.*"

Rahkki narrowed his eyes. Why did the hordes want to meet with *him*? He had no power, nothing to say.

Daanath's clawed hand swept toward him and, moments later, he deposited Rahkki into what appeared to be a Gorlish healing tent. Everything inside was Gorlan sized—the tools, the containers, the cabinets, and the wooden cots. Rahkki recognized special herbs hanging from the ceiling and rolled bandages, supplies similar to those used by Brim Carver, the Fifth Clan's healer. Wounded warriors lay strewn on cots and across the floor. They grunted at Rahkki, not quite as accepting of the Sandwen boy as their unscathed hordemates.

The healers, two old Gorlanders, one male and one female, nodded receipt of Rahkki, and Prince Daanath exited the tent, leaving the boy alone with them. The male giant scooped Rahkki onto a huge gurney, felt his fractured bone, and then gathered cloth wraps from a bin, cutting them into boy-sized pieces.

Rahkki sat up, confused and curious. It seemed the giants were going to treat his wounds. But why? So far, their behavior was shocking and unexpected—it went against everything he had been taught about giants. Rahkki still wasn't sure he could trust their kindness but saw no profit in rejecting it. Through an open tent flap, he watched the sun drop fast in the western sky, casting the clouds in scorching hues of orange and pink. Outside, the Gorlanders went about their evening business, grunting and stomping and playing reed pipes.

As the healer splinted and wrapped Rahkki's ankle, Rahkki remembered Sula's bravery when she'd taken Harak's arrow to protect him. She'd been using Rahkki to save her friends from the hordes—he knew that—but he'd never guessed she truly *cared*. She'd proved she did when she risked her life for his. Rahkki clenched his fists, hoping she was safe.

The Gorlan giant had just finished casting Rahkki's ankle when a ruckus outside startled all of them. Giants beat the ground and rumbled. Rahkki's medical cot shook. *This is it*, he thought. *They're coming to kill me.* He tensed, waiting.

Another flap swept open and two giants carried a feathered creature into the massive tent. Fresh claw marks raked her gold-and-white flank and an arrow jutted from her throat.

"Rizah!" Rahkki scrambled out of his cot and crawled toward the Kihlara mare. This was his friend Tuni Hightower's Flier. A young Sandwen soldier had shot Rizah after Harak ordered Tuni arrested during the Sandwen uprising. The soldier had been trying to scare Rizah off, but his aim was poor and his arrow had pierced her throat.

Rahkki stroked the golden pinto's forelock. "Shh, Rizah," he whispered to the mare. Her green eyes, glassy with pain, met his and brightened with recognition. She tried to nicker and her throat rattled. "Shh," he repeated.

He studied the claw marks in her flank and exhaled dizzily. A jaguar had attacked her, drawn by her weakness, no doubt. The giants must have found her and carried her to their camp. More unexpected kindness! Everything Rahkki thought he knew about the giants swirled in his mind, a confusing jumble when compared to what he was witnessing firsthand. He couldn't wait to tell his uncle and his brother, Brauk, about it.

The female healer prepped an awl and sinew and set about removing Rizah's arrow and treating the wound. The male healer cleaned the claw marks on her flank and dressed them in salve. Rizah's eyelids flickered as she lost consciousness. When they'd finished treating her, the healers layered a bed of furs on the floor and gently placed the golden pinto on top of them.

Rahkki curled beside her. "You're going to be okay," he whispered. Her breathing was shallow and marked by wheezing. He doubted she would have survived another moment alone in the jungle. Rahkki's heart swelled, overcome with gratitude. He grunted to draw all the healers' attention. "*Thank you*," he signed, and they nodded.

But Rahkki remained suspicious. *Was* this kindness, or were the giants healing him and Rizah for a darker purpose? His mother had believed that the hordes could be allies, and maybe she was right, but his mother was gone.

Rahkki rolled onto his back, feeling drowsy. All the Fifth Clan's troubles had begun eight years ago when Lilliam had attempted to assassinate Reyella and failed. His mother had reached the docks of Daakur, very pregnant with her third child and traveling with two Sandwen guards, but there her trail had gone cold. No one knew where she was now, or if her unborn child had survived.

Eyes watering, Rahkki turned his thoughts toward Sula. He and his mount had Paired and now she was gone. As glad as he was for her new freedom, the pain of it stabbed his heart, sharper than any arrow. He imagined her soft gray muzzle, her dark eyes, and her powerful wings. They'd worked hard to understand each other. She'd accepted a bit and armor and let him ride on her back. She'd reminded him that he did love to fly! Rahkki could feel the pleasant looping sensation in his belly as he remembered her sharpened hooves pushing off the grass, her nose angled toward the clouds, and her agile purple wings shaping the wind. Sula—his Flier, his protector.

From the first moment he'd spotted her wild herd flying above his territory, hopes and dreams had blossomed within him. Clan elders had taught him that no wild Kihlari existed anymore, but they'd been wrong, and maybe they were wrong about the giants too.

As the Gorlanders rumbled and chuffed around him, and the crickets launched into their evening chorus, Rahkki snuggled tight against Rizah. He dreamed of his own mount, wondering where Sula was and if she missed him half as much as he missed her.

2

THE FIFTH CLAN

HAZELWIND, REDFIRE, AND GRAYSTONE CARRIED Echofrost by her wings and tail, flying her just above the treetops. The Storm Herd steeds glided beside her, casting nervous glances at their silver friend. Harak's arrow had slid neatly between a gap in Echofrost's armor and pierced her lung. Beside her, pregnant Dewberry panted hard. The round weight of her belly drew down her hindquarters, causing her to fly at an almost upright angle.

Echofrost moaned. "What happened to Rahkki?" she whinnied.

"Don't speak," Dewberry nickered. "We're far from your Landwalker friend."

Echofrost's eyes slid toward the pinto mare's stretched

belly and pinched expression, and she guessed Dewberry had entered the early stages of labor. She glanced back toward Mount Crim, the home of the Gorlan giants. The massive ranges reached toward the clouds, forming a barrier around its plateaus and valleys.

Her Rider, Rahkki Stormrunner, was trapped somewhere in those mountains. She imagined his golden eyes and gentle hands, his chattering voice. Rahkki's people had abandoned him to their enemies, the giants. Her heart walloped with familiar fury and disappointment. How could they leave such a young cub behind? She tossed her mane. Actually, she *did* know how they could do it.

When she was a weanling in Anok—her homeland across the Dark Water ocean—she'd been abandoned too. A foreign herd had stolen her and another colt because they'd trespassed. Her herd had decided not to risk a war to rescue them. Eventually, the foreign steeds had let her go, but Echofrost had suffered horrific bullying from their yearlings.

And after crossing the Dark Water and landing on this continent, the Fifth Clan people had captured the roan mare named Shysong. Hazelwind and the others had decided not to risk Storm Herd in order to save her, so Echofrost had gone back to rescue Shysong on her own.

She didn't understand the point of a herd or a clan if they didn't fight to save each member. One might as well live alone! But now Hazelwind had promised that they would stick together, all of them. She gasped for air, afraid she'd pass out again in the heights.

Below her dangling hooves, the palm trees swayed and the jungle creatures quieted as the winged shadows of Storm Herd passed over them. The static-filled sky had darkened, the clouds once again piling high and threatening rain.

Still dressed in the Sandwen armor Rahkki had given her, Echofrost knew her body was heavy. "We're almost there," she nickered, encouraging the friends who supported her.

"I see it," Hazelwind whinnied through a mouthful of feathers.

Ahead, the Fifth Clan village rolled into view. Small torches brightened the Sandwen settlement like fallen stars. The Landwalkers had carved the chaotic jungle into organized pathways, built stone dens, corralled animals, grown food in perfectly aligned rows, and tamed an ancient herd of pegasi, turning them into flying warhorses.

"Are they going to attack us?" Graystone asked,

glancing nervously at her and Hazelwind's wounds. Harak's arrows had punctured each of them.

"I don't think they'll hurt us," Echofrost answered, "but they might try to catch us."

"What's the difference?" Dewberry huffed.

"You're right, we'll land in the jungle," Echofrost decided. "Brim will have to come to me."

Her friends were carrying Echofrost to Brim Carver, the Fifth Clan's healer. It was Shysong's idea. The roan mare had lived with the Sandwens long enough to know that Brim was a talented and gentle healer, and she was one of the few Landwalkers Echofrost and Shysong had learned to trust. Storm Herd had quickly agreed, hoping Brim could repair the hole in Echofrost's lung.

"I'll fetch her," Shysong nickered. "Brim knows me."

The pegasi quickly descended and landed outside the settlement. Beneath the wind-brushed jungle canopy, singing insects, calling parrots, and hooting primates performed their daily chorus. Hazelwind, Redfire, and Graystone lowered Echofrost as gently to the soft soil as possible. Still, she grunted on impact.

"Sorry," Hazelwind nickered. He anxiously swiveled his ears, and Echofrost leaned against her best friend.

"I'll set up a perimeter to look out for predators," Redfire said.

Hazelwind nodded. "And we need to keep our eyes up. The Sky Guard flies all day and most of the night."

Redfire and Graystone assembled Storm Herd and assigned jobs. They'd lost twelve steeds in the battle against the giants, leaving one hundred and thirty pegasi.

Shysong nuzzled Echofrost. "I'll be back soon, with Brim." The roan folded her black-edged blue feathers and trotted into the darkness, her tail swishing confidently.

"That mare is much stronger than I first thought," Echofrost whispered to Hazelwind.

He flipped his long forelock off his face. "You're strong too." He raked his gaze over the brand on her shoulder, the armor she wore, the saddle on her back, and the bit in her mouth. "I can't believe what you've endured to save Shysong and Storm Herd. . . ." He pressed his forehead hard against hers, unable to finish his thoughts.

"I'm sorry I underestimated the danger here," she nickered.

He pulled back, arching his neck. "Storm Herd believes in you, Echofrost. *I'm* the one who's made mistakes."

They let their feelings flow between them, felt but

unspoken. Dewberry, whose mother was a medicine mare in Anok, worked nearby, assessing the jungle plants and collecting a few herbs and leaves. She chewed and spit, chewed and spit, muttering comments: *Nope, that's no good; Gah, my tongue; Ah, bitter!*

"Don't poison yourself," Hazelwind warned.

"Ahh, this is the one," Dewberry nickered, ignoring him. She chewed the chosen leaves into a pulp. Using her agile wingtips, Dewberry wiped the mixture around the plunged arrows that stuck out from Echofrost and Hazelwind like porcupine quills.

Echofrost didn't trust any jungle plants, but she trusted Dewberry, and as the pulp soaked into the wound, her pain eased. "It's working."

"I figurrrred ith would," Dewberry said. "Ith nuuumbed my thongue." Next she inspected Hazelwind's injuries more closely. "They'rrrre not therious," she said, and before he could object, she bit the arrows' shafts and yanked them out.

She let the holes bleed, and then applied a different mixture to clean the wounds. "Ith's turmeric," she explained, having recognized the yellow plant from her mother's teachings. Afterward, she again applied the chewed leaf pulp that had numbed her tongue.

Redfire returned from assigning patrols and admired Dewberry's salves. "Maybe we don't need this Landwalker healer named Brim," he nickered.

Dewberry preened her stained feathers. "Hathelwind willlll be fine, but Ethofost neeeeeds more help."

Wingbeats startled them. Shysong arrived, coasting between the trees with an old Landwalker woman riding on her back. The roan touched down near Echofrost. "I've got Brim," she nickered. "I don't think anyone saw us."

The woman slid off Shysong's back. "Oh my," she cried, her cheeks bright. She smoothed her cloak and fixed her hair, swaying a bit unsteadily. Then she stilled, observing the herd of wild pegasi that surrounded her. They rustled their hooves and a few rattled their feathers, most having never been so close to a Landwalker.

Swallowing hard, Brim clutched her satchel against her chest. "Oh my," she repeated.

"You're scaring her," Echofrost nickered to Storm Herd. "Lower your wings, don't stare at her."

The wild steeds did as she asked and Brim heaved a breath. Her eyes found Echofrost tucked into a thicket with an arrow jutting from between her ribs. "I'm here for you, aren't I?" she asked, her blue eyes shining in the dark.

Echofrost didn't understand Brim, but she lifted her wing, inviting the woman closer. Brim knelt, examining the wound, and then she began removing Echofrost's armor and tack. At the sight of the chewed-leaf poultice, she froze. Glancing around, her gaze fell upon Dewberry, taking in her green-stained lips and her yellow-stained wingtips. "Oh my," she said a third time, and then she opened her medical bag and began to work.

3

TRIAL

"MY NAME IS I'LENNA WHITEHALL AND I AM the Queen of the Fifth Clan."

"Wrong." I'Lenna's mother, Lilliam, squinted at her from aboard her winged stallion. Her newborn baby, Prince K'Lar, lay curled in a sling across her chest. "*I am the queen, I'Lenna.*"

The sun glided west overhead, floating like a blazing bubble toward the horizon. Three days had passed since the battle with the giants. I'Lenna's uprising against her mother had failed and Harak had arrested her. Now, back at the Fifth Clan village, I'Lenna twisted, restrained by two Land Guard soldiers.

Her hair hung loose and her feet were bare. A light cotton shift covered her body. Behind her lay the clan's Sunstone. If she didn't renounce her claim to the crown, the Borla would lash her to it and leave her for three nights to be judged by the clan's guardian mascot, Granak, the Father of Dragons.

I'Lenna glanced desperately at the Fifth Clan villagers. They grimaced, wanting to help her, but Harak's soldiers menaced them. I'Lenna and her personal guards had wrested the queenship from Lilliam right after the armies left to fight the giants. In a quick, private ceremony, the Borla had coronated her.

I'Lenna had left the clan then and flown to the battlefield to negotiate peace with the hordes, and that had been her mistake. She couldn't prove what had happened at home. Harak had accused her of lying and arrested her. When they returned to the clan, he immediately freed her mother from the Eighth Tower, the prison tower, and locked up the rebel army.

Lilliam and her Borla had promptly denied that I'Lenna's coronation had ever occurred. It was a bald-faced lie, everyone knew it, but the villagers who spoke out were immediately arrested. I'Lenna had spent three days locked in the prison tower, and now Lilliam wanted "justice."

I'Lenna writhed, furious and embarrassed. She'd let her people down, and she'd let down Rahkki Stormrunner, her best and only friend. She'd lied to him—about everything—but in spite of that, he'd forgiven her, even kissed her! Her belly fluttered, remembering.

"Relinquish your claim," the Borla screeched at her.

I'Lenna drew a ragged breath as her eyes rolled toward the Land Guard soldiers. *Never show your feelings to your subjects*—Lilliam had drilled this into her, and so she addressed them with practiced confidence. "I command you to release me."

"The princess is mad, yeah," Harak said to the armies. "Queen Lilliam never surrendered her throne. Why would she?"

"You weren't even *here*," I'Lenna growled.

Murmurings erupted from the Sandwen villagers. Several adults stood, their eyes scanning the crowd for support. Harak noticed their clenched fists and darting eyes. He nodded to the Sky Guard and the warriors flew down on their winged horses to push the villagers back.

Lilliam fixed her dark-blue eyes on I'Lenna's face and

said nothing, her body as still as a mountain.

The villagers fell back, defeated. The first thing Harak had done upon returning from Mount Crim was to send his soldiers from hut to hut, confiscating all blades and bludgeons. Stealing their weapons went against Clan Law, but who could stop him? Lilliam had named Harak the acting general of the Land Guard and Sky Guard armies. And the sad truth was—whoever controlled the armies controlled the clan.

I'Lenna's teeth dug into her lips and several angry tears escaped her eyes. She'd never give up—*never under the bloody sun!* She'd taken the throne to *protect* the Fifth Clan. Three moons ago she'd discovered a terrible secret and the real reason why Lilliam had assassinated Reyella Stormrunner. It was not for personal glory, it was to steal from the Fifth Clan!

A tremor rolled through I'Lenna's body just thinking about it. Her grandmother, Queen Tavara Whitehall of the Second Clan, had sent Lilliam and a bevy of guards to oust Reyella and gain control of the Fifth Clan's treasury. One moonless evening, while sneaking around the fortress, I'Lenna had witnessed a handoff between Lilliam's treasurer and a woman disguised as a "merchant."

I'Lenna had hidden behind a door, listening to their voices.

"The bag feels light," the merchant had said, handling a sack that clinked with coins. "Is that all there is?"

"Yes, that's it," snapped the Fifth's treasurer. "Queen Tavara has been taking too much. I have to keep enough coin to run the Fifth Clan smoothly or folks will start asking questions."

"Tell Lilliam to stop spending so much on herself."

The Fifth Clan treasurer crossed her arms. "I cannot control that woman."

The other smiled, eyes glinting, and lowered her voice. "Just keep the deposits coming or Queen Tavara will replace Lilliam with one of her other daughters."

The false merchant tightened her cloak, mounted her Kihlara, and vanished into the star-spangled sky.

Once I'Lenna had gotten over her shock and anger, she'd realized that both her mother and the Fifth Clan were in grave danger. She'd spied on the treasurer for another moon and witnessed two more exchanges, then she'd confided in General Tsun. They'd founded the rebellion against Lilliam together, but Tsun had promised to keep Lilliam's treachery a secret. If the Fifth Clan knew, they'd execute I'Lenna's mother. Queens did not abuse their own people, Clan Law forbade it. It was an abomination that required yanking out by its roots. I'Lenna had hoped to banish Lilliam peacefully, but she had failed and now General Tsun was dead.

"Look at me," her mother said, dragging I'Lenna back to the present.

She raised her eyes. Queen Lilliam nudged her winged stallion closer and leaned over his neck. "You want to be like me, don't you? To sit on my throne, command my armies . . . control my treasury?" She dismounted, cooing at her princeling son. I'Lenna's baby brother mewed and stretched in his sling. "Leave us a moment," Lilliam commanded the guards, wiping her hand as if to erase them.

The guards and the Borla stepped back, allowing Lilliam and I'Lenna their privacy. Lilliam lowered herself to I'Lenna's face and whispered to her daughter, her expression softening. "Renounce your claim, Len, and I'll release you from this trial by dragon. You can leave for Daakur today."

I'Lenna's heart snapped in half. By Granak, what no one understood was that she loved her mother *and* her clan! Everything she'd done had been to protect them both.

She stiffened, deciding it was time to confront Lilliam. "I know you give half our tithes to grandmother in the Second Clan," she whispered. "I've witnessed the secret handoffs. If the Fifth Clan finds out, *they will kill you.*"

Two bright spots of color appeared on Lilliam's cheeks.

I'Lenna continued. "I've kept your secret, but you have to stop stealing. You're ruining this clan, and if they find out, they won't stop at you. They'll feed *all* the Whitehalls to the dragon." She glanced pointedly at Prince K'Lar. "Just go, return to grandmother in the Second and leave the Fifth to me."

Lilliam hunched, working her jaw. Her voice hardened. "What do you think Tavara will do to me if I lose this throne? I can't go *home.* I can never go home."

"But you can't keep robbing this clan," I'Lenna argued, desperate. She understood why her grandmother had orchestrated the fleecing of the Fifth. The Second Clan was shamefully poor and jealous of the others, but it had to stop before a larger war broke out between them. The clans had never fought one another before; it would destroy their society.

"So no one knows about the stealing but you?" Lilliam summarized.

I'Lenna realized she'd backed herself into a corner and shook her head in dismay. "If you tie me to that Sunstone and call the dragon, I *will* tell on you."

Lilliam blanched. "Our family has a good thing going here, I'Lenna, and the Second Clan is no longer starving. If you tell, and anything happens to your sisters and brother, it will be on your head. Think about the ramifications of what you're doing."

"What *I'm* doing?" I'Lenna sputtered.

"Enough," Lilliam said, swallowing hard. "You've disappointed me, Len. You're disloyal to your family. You spy and steal from the clan."

"What—"

Lilliam shushed her. "I know you take candy and medicine and give it away for free. You think you're better than me." She scoffed. "You *are* me."

Tears welled in I'Lenna's eyes. In a different life, perhaps she and her mother could have been friends. But that was not to be. Tears slid down her cheeks, as hot as blood. She'd been bluffing anyway. Telling on Lilliam would put her three siblings at risk, just as her mother had said.

Lilliam leaned over her a final time. "I gave you a chance to renounce the throne and you did not. I cannot change Clan Law." She withdrew and called for her Borla. "Granak will judge my daughter."

"No!" I'Lenna cried.

Without a backward glance, Lilliam boarded her stallion, secured K'Lar's sling, and flew away, her red robes fluttering behind her.

The Borla spoke to the gathered clan. "I'Lenna Whitehall has lost her challenge for the throne. Clan Law requires I place her fate upon the Father of Dragons." His eyes searched the jungle, as if Granak were there right now, waiting for the dinner bell to clang. Then to I'Lenna he said, "If you survive three nights, you will spend the remainder of your life in exile. Be thankful your mother is merciful."

The villagers exhaled in a collective gasp. "She is just a child," one woman argued. The Borla ignored her.

The guards snatched I'Lenna's arms and lashed them to the Sunstone.

Stunned and helpless, the villagers wrung their hands. The Sunstone was cordoned off and no Sandwen would be allowed near the princess until her sentence had passed. Three armed soldiers guarded the perimeter.

I'Lenna faced the sky, her back pressed against the

rough stone. A warm breeze tickled her nose and her gut seethed. How was she supposed to get past three armed guards? How was she supposed to get free at all?

As the Borla's apprentices began beating the drums, calling Granak from the jungle, I'Lenna watched the golden sun vanish, leaving the Fifth Clan settlement in darkness.

4

THE WARREN

RAHKKI WOKE TO HOT GORLAN BREATH IN HIS
face and four sets of blue eyes blinking at him. "*Sa jin!*"
He tried to stand, but his fractured ankle screamed in
complaint. He felt for his dagger. It was gone. He and the
mare Rizah had been recuperating for three long days
inside the medical tent.

The four young giants staring at him pushed closer,
shoving one another, and Rahkki recognized the siblings—
they were Prince Daanath's offspring. They'd traveled
to his clan with their sire to attend the parlay. Rahkki
braced when the smallest one leaned into him, her big face
a hand's breadth from his.

"Ay, there," he greeted in Sandwen.

The giantess chuffed. A neat row of baby teeth lined her black gums, and he spied a gap where two had recently fallen out. Her immature tusks were thin and sharp, like fangs. Rahkki swallowed, his heart speeding. The four young giants, one girl and three boys, were each taller than he. The biggest one reached for him.

Rahkki raised his fists.

But the Gorlander merely slid him a bowl of warm soup. "*Eat*," he signed. Small bones pierced the young male's eyebrows and earlobes and, like all Gorlanders, he was barefoot. A half-filled skin of goat's milk dangled from his waist.

Recognizing hospitality when he saw it, Rahkki signed back "*Thank you*," and this caused the children to growl happily. Then a rapid conversation ensued as their fingers danced in their language. Rahkki became transfixed, but he understood so little. They needed to slow down. He reached into his memory for words that would explain he didn't understand them. "*I . . . I stupid*," he gestured.

The giants roared louder and their snarling blast rippled through Rahkki's bones. Their breath reeked of goat's milk and the delicious soup, a nauseating combination.

"No, not stupid," Rahkki corrected in Sandwen,

shaking his head. He'd learned that word from Brauk. His older brother had used it often when they were kids. Rahkki tried again. *"Talk slower. Please."*

The tallest male, whose rounded muscles and sprouting chest hair indicated he might be a teenager, nodded his comprehension. Rahkki smiled, flashing his own small teeth, and this set the kids into another fit of terrifying Gorlish laughter.

When they finally settled down, the little giantess spoke to Rahkki, signing as slowly as she could, *"If you eat, you'll feel better."*

Rahkki lifted the bowl, and the soup's delicious scent made his belly clamor. The healers had also fed him soup, but he still felt guilty eating it. The Gorlan kids flicked their eyes from Rahkki to the broth and then back to Rahkki. They reminded him of Tuni Hightower's mother, Kashi. When Kashi served her customers at the trading post, she watched with great anticipation until they took their first bite.

Pushing away all thoughts of what might be in the soup, Rahkki tipped the bowl and drank. As happened each time, contentment washed through his body like a warm river of chocolate, making his belly sing greedily as he lapped the broth. When Rahkki finished, he felt energized and the throbbing pain in his ankle had subsided. "*Good food*," he signed.

The oldest of the siblings, a teen giant with red hair so light that it looked pink, introduced their names. He was Drake. His brothers were Krell and Fallon, and their little giantess sister was named Miah.

Rahkki didn't know the signs for his name, so he shrugged and threw up his hands. To his chagrin, that shrug and hand gesture *became* his Gorlish name. Each sibling used it to say hello to him, and Rahkki couldn't help but laugh.

Howling now, the four Gorlan children charged out of the tent, knocking into one another as they each fought to be the first outside. As they exited, a breeze whooshed through the tent flaps, ruffling Rahkki's hair. It smelled of trees and spring water. Three days of sitting around was driving him crazy. He tried to stand and wobbled on his good leg.

The male healer chuffed and brought him a carved wooden crutch. "*Use this*," he signed. "*I made it small for you.*"

Rahkki accepted the crutch and leaned on it. It fit his

height perfectly. He limped forward a few steps, a grin curving his lips. *"It works."* Then he pointed at the sleeping mare, Rizah. *"Will she live?"*

The healer shrugged and then bent to check on a wounded Gorlan warrior. Feeling dismissed, Rahkki angled toward the tent's exit. No one stopped him and he emerged into the sunlight. All around the Highland Horde camp, Gorlanders ceased what they were doing to watch. Rahkki expected reprimands from the adults—angry snarls, cuffs to the back of the head—but they didn't seem to care that he was loose. Small, wounded, and weaponless, he posed no threat to the Gorlanders. A few adults tracked his movements, but otherwise, the giants went back to what they were doing.

Rahkki took the opportunity to study the encampment. A combination of hard mesa and softer fields spread between four mountain peaks. He knew that Great Cave Horde lived across the pass on the western side of the mountain. There they raised their saber cats. The soot-smudged Fire Horde giants lived north, close to the volcanoes. They trapped and trained burners, the tiny colorful fire-breathing dragons.

This horde raised elephants. They rode them into

battle and used their hides to make tents, their ivory to fashion weapons, and their strength to pull huge wagons. When not in use, the beasts themselves roamed free. Rahkki heard them crashing along the heavily treed slopes, chomping on leaves. Others trumpeted to one another as they lingered in the well-grazed meadowlands.

Surrounding the Highland camp loomed the jungle. It gaped at him like a dark mouth full of tree-shaped teeth. As Rahkki limped about the stone mesa, he noticed that at least one adult giant had eyes on him at all times. A daytime escape would be impossible under their watch, which left the night. But drooling dragons, monstrous insects, panthers, boars, and snakes hunted in the dark. Rahkki doubted he'd make it all the way home alive, not traveling overland anyway, and not with a fractured ankle.

He needed Rizah. If the mare recovered, he could fly her home. He returned to the medical tent to check on her. The Gorlan healers had redressed her wounds while he was gone and she continued to sleep. He crawled to her side and peeked beneath her bandages. Her injured flesh was pink and raw, but not swollen or festering. Impressed with the healers' skills, Rahkki sat and smoothed Rizah's gold-edged pink feathers.

Later that evening, after Rahkki had finished another

bowl of the amazing soup, Prince Daanath entered the tent and lifted the boy off his furs. "Hey," Rahkki protested. "I can walk on my own." He snatched his satchel and crutch before they were out of reach.

The prince rumbled softly and strode outside with Rahkki. There, the boy spotted an envoy of ten elephants and several calves. They stood ready, packed with saddlebags and ridden by Gorlanders. Drake sat on his small-tusked juvenile. Miah, Krell, and Fallon followed aboard their calves; and each young elephant held the tail of the one in front, creating a chain.

The prince placed Rahkki carefully atop his bull elephant's head and then climbed aboard behind him. An adult giantess opened the door of a fireproof blackwood cage and a flight of bat-sized fire-breathing dragons, at least thirty of them, erupted from it and swarmed the sky, trailing smoke and electric white flames. Their glittering red, orange, and yellow scales reflected the moonlight.

With the burners lighting the way and the giants packed and ready to go, Prince Daanath roared and tapped his elephant. The envoy walked forward, and a few minutes later, Rahkki was leaving the Highland Horde camp behind and entering the jungle slopes.

"*Where we going?*" Rahkki signed. He pointed at the

vanishing medical tent. *"I stay with horse."* He made a flying motion to indicate he meant Rizah.

The prince grunted. *"The horde meeting is at the warren."*

The warren? Only Fire Horde lived underground, which meant they were traveling to the volcanoes in the north. *"But my horse?"* Rahkki couldn't leave Tuni's Flier alone.

"She can't travel yet," answered the prince. *"She must stay."*

Rahkki faced forward. He would memorize the path, and as soon as he could walk, he would break free, collect Rizah, and fly home.

Hours passed as the Highland elephants traveled between the peaks of Mount Crim, lumbering toward the volcanoes. Rahkki drifted in and out of sleep, his body swaying in rhythm to the march.

Of the thirty or so tiny dragons that escorted the Highland prince's envoy, one stood out from the rest. His entire body was golden in color except for his spiked tail barbs, the ridges over his eyes, and his webbed frills, which shimmered in mixed tones of aqua, emerald, and scarlet. Rahkki studied him, curious, and the creature soon took notice of the boy.

Without warning, the dragon suddenly swooped down and landed on his shoulder. Rahkki froze. The creature angled his head and stared into Rahkki's eyes. His jaws parted, revealing sharp piranha-like teeth.

"Shoo," Rahkki said, waving him off. The little dragon recoiled and then lifted off to join his flight, but the other dragons hissed at him and chased him away. He returned, landing again on Rahkki's shoulder.

"You don't fit in with the others, do you?" Rahkki whispered.

"Crawk," screeched the rare golden dragon. He lifted his tail and loosed droppings all down Rahkki's neck and chest. They smelled like rotting eggs.

"Ah, gross!" Rahkki cried, and Prince Daanath grunted at both of them to be silent.

The dragon, a creature worth a thousand dramals in Daakur, blinked at the dung that had pooled in Rahkki's lap. Then he issued a soft chortle and blasted the pellets with red-colored flames. They exploded, covering Rahkki in odorless ash.

Wiping his eyes and coughing on dust, Rahkki shook his head, but the dragon grew content. He snuggled against Rahkki's skin, humming softly. Rahkki reached up and cautiously stroked his golden scales. The dragon blinked at him and Rahkki noticed that their eyes were the exact same color.

The creature pressed closer and Rahkki sighed. "All right, I won't drive you off like they do," he whispered, glaring at the dragons swooping overhead. "I'm going to name you Tak." *Tak* meant "sun" in Talu, the language of the Daakuran Empire located on the other side of Cinder Bay.

The Highland caravan traveled north all night. The elephants marched with tireless grace, their trunks swinging. Rahkki dozed, but when awake, he studied the giants' language. The longer he watched their hands, the more bits of Gorlish he remembered.

He stretched and sat up as an arc of light finally appeared on the horizon, warming the cool-gray sky. Below him, the elephant's feet parted the mist as they trudged up the winding jungle path. Around them, the forest creatures inhaled the deep predawn breath that preceded sunrise.

Three active volcanoes steamed and shuddered ahead.

They'd arrived at the blackrock ranges in the north, the home of the Fire Horde giants. Rahkki glanced back to see Drake, Krell, Fallon, and Miah still following on their smaller elephants. Miah waved her clawed fingers at him, grinning her ferocious grin.

The flight of dragons, all except Tak, rushed through the trees, happy to be home. All burners belonged to the Fire Horde giants, but sometimes the reclusive Gorlanders lent their flights to the other hordes. Rahkki guessed that Highland Horde was returning this group.

Prince Daanath grunted and abruptly halted his elephant. A line of Fire Horde giants had gathered to greet the caravan. Shorter than the Highland Horde beasts, they averaged ten lengths. Thick red hair hung in long plaits down their backs and their pale skin was stained gray from mining gemstones deep beneath the volcanoes.

This horde lived in an underground warren. They tolerated sunlight but avoided it, and now they shielded their brows as the blazing sun rose in the east, casting their hunched bodies in a yellow glow. They studied Rahkki as closely as he studied them.

Prince Daanath dismounted to greet the Fire prince, who was wearing a half wreath of luminescent gems around his neck. They spoke rapid Gorlish, and then the Highland prince set Rahkki on the hard ground and handed him his crutch.

"*Thanks,*" Rahkki signed, leaning on it.

The Fire prince inspected Rahkki. "*He's small, even for a Sandwen.*" He gently pressed on Rahkki's teeth, testing their sharpness, and squished Rahkki's wiry muscles. The boy submitted to this inspection with a racing heart.

Then Prince Daanath retreated to his elephant's saddlebags and returned with Rahkki's blowgun and darts. The two leaders examined the weapons, careful not to touch the darts' tips.

"*How did you kill and then unkill our warriors?*" the Fire Horde prince asked.

Rahkki lifted his fingers, trying to answer. The trick was simple enough, if he only knew the Gorlish words to describe it. He'd soaked his darts in poisonous dragon drool after first boiling out all the toxins, leaving only the anesthetic properties intact.

Brim had explained the process to him. After his Flier, Sula, had accidentally kicked Brauk and paralyzed him, Brim had needed a way to keep Rahkki's brother calm and quiet. She'd created a sleeping medicine out of dragon drool and fed it to Brauk while his spine healed. But Rahkki didn't know how to describe the steps in Gorlish.

Finally, he dropped his hands and shrugged.

Annoyed, the Fire prince signed, "*Follow me.*"

Rahkki limped after the prince, sweating. Red-orange lava bubbled down the volcanoes' peaks and hardened before it reached the warren that had been dug into its base. Wildflowers layered the lower slopes in arrays of colors from silken pastels to vibrant shades of blue, red, green, and yellow.

The Highland giants unpacked their elephants and led them toward a steaming river to bathe while Rahkki followed the prince's bare heels. They halted at a large hole in the ground. As Rahkki scanned the area, he noticed dozens of such dark holes. Each housed a carved stone staircase that circled into the bowels of the land.

Torches flickered, maybe fifty lengths below. The king grunted, nudging Rahkki again, and the boy understood he was to descend into the pit. Just then Tak landed on his shoulder. "Crawk!" the dragon shrieked, bobbing his golden-scaled neck.

The Fire prince snorted at Rahkki. "*Keep going.*"

Rahkki lowered his crutch and then himself into the darkness. Behind him, the prince smacked his lips and a line of drool rolled from the corner of his mouth. All of Rahkki's fears resurfaced. Had the Highland prince spared him so the Fire prince could eat him? Fresh sweat burst across his brow and dripped into his eyes. So what if the Gorlanders had splinted his ankle and fed him delicious soup—they were still *giants*, the sworn enemies of his clan.

Rahkki swallowed as he scuttled down the wide stone staircase. Looking up, he caught a glimpse of the mist-shrouded sky. He imagined a Sky Guard patrol, one led by his brother, descending to rescue him. But Rahkki's brother was still paralyzed. He couldn't walk, let alone fly. "By Granak and the Seven Sisters," Rahkki implored his clan's protectors, "watch over me."

Tak shot green-colored fire into the darkness ahead and hummed in Rahkki's ear as the frightened boy shuffled deeper into the warren.

5

BIG RAIN

THE FIRST THING THE FIRE KING DID WAS TO serve Rahkki soup in an enormous underground cavern. This broth tasted even better than the Highland mixture, smoother yet spicier. Miah sat next to Rahkki.

"When is the horde meeting?" he signed.

"When Great Cave Horde arrives." She addressed him using his new Gorlish name, a shrug combined with helpless-looking hands. The silly gesture made many Fire Horde giants smile.

Ignoring them, Rahkki asked about Rizah. *"How is winged horse?"*

Miah shrugged again, and Rahkki sagged against the rock wall.

After soup, the giants assigned Rahkki to a small cavern of his own. Miah followed him and Rahkki's golden dragon perched on his shoulder, breathing hot steam into his ear.

Over the next few days, life in the warren quickly settled into a pattern. During waking hours, the giants allowed Rahkki to explore the caverns and passageways that made up the underground settlement. Embedded glow stones helped brighten the darkest areas of the warren, and a lava river flowed far below the chiseled pathways, sometimes diving deeper underground and then reappearing elsewhere. Miah or one of her brothers always accompanied him, and he was glad for the escort, because the passageways spread in a maze of tentacles beneath the three volcanoes. It would be easy to become lost forever.

Now, he and Miah were wandering the tunnels and chucking rocks into seemingly bottomless pits that dotted the caverns. Rahkki leaned heavily on his crutch, which had begun to chafe the skin under his arm. The warren was hot and loud. Rahkki needed fresh air and new possibilities for escape. *"Can we go up?"* he asked, pointing overhead.

Miah frowned and then acquiesced. *"Okay."*

Rahkki hadn't expected her to say yes. She led him

onto the main thoroughfare, a wide stone pathway worn smooth from years of use. It connected all the warren's caves and the narrower paths that branched off in every direction. Tak rode happily in Rahkki's shirt.

They crossed a bamboo bridge and padded down a stone pathway toward one of the many spiral staircases that led up to the jungle floor. A rain-scented breeze swept toward Rahkki from above as Miah helped him climb the stairs. They emerged at the base of a volcano.

The cropped mountaintop belched a smoky greeting. It was nighttime aboveground, which surprised Rahkki since he'd just eaten breakfast. He wondered if Fire Horde slept during the day so they could venture outside after dark and avoid the sun. Static and moisture filled the air and Rahkki's crutch sank into the soft soil.

Miah paused, breathing in the fresh air. *"It's going to rain,"* she signed. *"We can't stay long."*

Tak climbed onto Rahkki's shoulder and then winged into the sky, chasing insects, singeing them with his blue flame and then swallowing them whole. His golden scales appeared white in the moonlight.

A few raindrops splattered Rahkki's nose as he stretched his arms and inhaled the humid air. On the volcano's western slope, a small group of Fire Horde giants were hunched over, picking herbs and pruning flowers. It seemed delicate work for their large clawed hands, but the giants were gentle and careful. He glanced at the nearby forest and considered running away, but there were too many giants outside—they would catch him in three strides.

Rahkki squinted past the clouds that shaped the gray expanse and thought of Sula. Had she survived Harak's arrow? He hoped so. Fire Horde's flight of burners was out hunting, and when they spotted Tak flying on his own, they veered closer, hissing and shooting cold-purple flames at him.

Tak pinned his wings and dived toward land.

They followed, singeing him with hotter flames and screeching. Tak's scales were fireproof, but his delicate frills were not. He sprang his wings wide and tried to glide away. They chased him.

"Tak! Come here," Rahkki cried.

The dragon's small eyes landed on Rahkki. He emitted a soft, grateful cry and dived straight at him. Rahkki held out his shirt like a net. Tak slammed into it and Rahkki quickly wrapped him up. His little golden body was trembling, and his small heart thumped rapidly.

"Get," Rahkki yelled at the flight of burners. They

hissed at him and then winged away, chirping and flaming the clouds, back on the hunt.

Just then the sky shuddered and dropped rain like a waterfall, instantly dousing Rahkki. The Gorlanders who'd been gardening on the hill stampeded, their eyes wide, their tusks flashing. Tak scuttled beneath Rahkki's arm.

"*Run!*" Miah signed. She sprinted toward the warren.

The Gorlanders poured into the stairwells, and no one was paying any attention to Rahkki. This was his chance to get back to Highland Horde, retrieve Rizah, and fly home. He turned and limped away as fast as he could.

A massive giantess spotted him. With a low growl, she snatched him up and raced to a stairwell. With a mighty push, she leaped off the ground. Rahkki shrieked as they flew straight up, thirty lengths in the air, and then dropped at a dizzying speed into the warren, bypassing the steps altogether. The walls blurred as Rahkki fell with her, screaming all the way down. Tak bit Rahkki's skin to better hold on and Rahkki howled louder.

They landed with a crashing thud, and Rahkki's head snapped forward and then back. His vision blackened, then returned.

The giantess shook the rain out of her hair. Gray soot

ran down her cheeks like war stripes. She gazed up with fearful eyes.

"Bloody rain," Rahkki cried in Sandwen. "It's just a storm."

The adult giantess set him down in front of Miah, who was wringing out her dress and glaring at him. *"Did you try to run away?"* she asked.

Rahkki stared at her, wobbling on his crutch. "Don't you get it, I want to go home. *Home,*" he signed, pointing west.

Miah puffed her lips, a Gorlish pout. *"My da won't be happy if I lose you."*

Rahkki exhaled, reminding himself she was just a child. *"I'm sorry,"* he gestured, and then asked, *"Is rain scary?"* He was wondering why the giants had stampeded.

She glared at the cavern ceiling, as if she could see the sky beyond. *"Big rain is scary,"* she signed, spreading her arms wide.

"Like a monsoon?"

Miah's sire approached and cuffed Rahkki. *"To the soup,"* he signed, scowling.

Rahkki, Miah, and Tak followed him to the main cavern, which soon filled with snarls, growls, and soft rumbles. Miah's brothers, Drake, Krell, and Fallon, joined them.

Prince Daanath squatted, leaning toward Rahkki like a bent tree. *"Do not try to run away again."* He grunted accusingly, his brows hunching. *"You will attend our horde meeting. I told you that,"* he signed.

Rahkki understood more Gorlish words each day he lived with the giants and felt more confident communicating. *"Do you promise I go home after horde meeting?"*

The prince flashed his yellow tusks. *"I'll take you myself."*

Rahkki peered at the prince whose life he'd once saved from an attacking python. Could he trust him? Did he have a choice? Rahkki offered a curt nod and the giant left him, looking satisfied.

Miah brought Rahkki a bowl of soup. They sat and she held his hand. Her blue eyes glowed in the warm light of the cooking fire and her long red tangles fell about her shoulders.

"Thanks," he signed, taking the bowl and shaking his wet hair, flinging water droplets in an arc.

As the giants settled to wait out the storm, a resounding roar filled the chamber and every single giant rose.

Rahkki propped himself against Miah, straining to see between all the bodies. A hulking Gorlander appeared at the entranceway to the cavern, wearing a half wreath of saber-cat tusks. He roared again, sounding like a lion.

The other hordes roared back, shaking the walls and vibrating Rahkki's chest. Tak darted down from the ceiling and shot happy green flames over everyone's heads.

Rahkki smiled. Great Cave Horde had finally arrived.

6

THE PLAN

ECHOFROST OPENED HER EYES, FEELING GROGGY. She spied jade feathers and a long black forelock—Hazelwind. They were lying together beneath a Kapok tree just outside the Sandwen settlement. A basket of grain and a pile of fresh hay waited untouched beside her. Echofrost flared her nostrils. Brim's scent lingered in the area, but the Sandwen healer was not currently present.

Around the Kapok tree, the Storm Herd pegasi grazed, ripping succulent jungle plants out of the soil with their teeth and drinking from a shallow creek. Pegasus warriors formed a perimeter, protecting them. Echofrost let out a huge breath. *This* was home—a pegasus herd.

"Welcome back," Hazelwind nickered, looking relieved.

Echofrost blinked in confusion. "What do you mean?"

"You've been asleep for three days." He slid his wing across her back. "Look what the Landwalker healer did to you."

She glanced down at her injury. "Oh!" Harak's arrow was gone, and in its place was a threaded stripe. She flared her nostrils, scenting soap and sinew. There should be a hole where the shaft had been, but Brim had sewn her hide back together as if it were a Sandwen satchel or piece of clothing. The even stitching created a neat line that ran between two rib bones. "By the Ancestors," Echofrost nickered, "she *repaired* me."

"Yes," he answered. "But first, she inserted an open reed into the wound, allowing your lung to refill. I—I've never seen anything like it. She's returned each night to check on you, and she brought this . . . Kihlari food." His lip curled in distaste at the hay.

Echofrost nickered. "Hay isn't so bad once you get used to it, and the grain is quite good." Starving, she nosed the basket closer and devoured the millet.

"How do you feel?" he asked.

Her side ached where Brim had removed Harak's arrow and she was still unable to draw a deep breath, but the pain had eased. "Better." Hazelwind grew quiet. "What's wrong?" she asked.

He ruffled his jade feathers. "I should have rescued Shysong and gotten us out of here right away."

"We've talked about this. You did what was best for Storm Herd," she said. "Not even Shysong blames you for that."

He shook his heavy black mane. "My sire taught me to protect the *herd* over the individual steeds, but that doesn't make sense anymore." His thoughts stormed across his face and shudders rippled through his jade plumage. "I was so sure of myself, but now . . . I don't know anything. I'm confused and I can't sleep. My stomach is spitting fire. I'm certain of only one thing—that I failed all of us when I abandoned Shysong."

Echofrost lowered her head. "Your sire had the same regrets for how he treated Star in Anok." When the supernatural black foal named Star had been born to Sun Herd—helpless and unable to fly, but destined to inherit potentially destructive powers—Hazelwind's sire had chosen to execute him on his first birthday. But his choice had fueled the herd's fear and caused wars and destruction.

Hazelwind nickered. "I should have learned."

She pressed her forehead to his. "I think that leading a herd is complicated."

His dark gaze swallowed hers and Echofrost's ears grew hot. Hazelwind was so much like his sire, Thundersky—duty bound, practical, and decisive. She'd relied on him in war and in captivity. She'd heaped her grief and anger upon him, and Hazelwind hadn't flinched. But since they'd arrived here, softer feelings for the buckskin slithered through her, as quick and elusive as minnows.

"What are you thinking about?" he asked.

"Nothing," she nickered, still feeling disoriented. "Just . . . we need to figure out how to save Rahkki." She imagined her cub's small face, his bright-yellow eyes, his gentle fingers, and his woody, spiced breath. A painful longing to see him filled her. "We *are* saving him, aren't we?"

"Yes," Hazelwind nickered. "He's the one who freed us, and Storm Herd won't abandon him. Haven't you been listening to anything I've said? When we fail one, we fail all."

"Yes, but I wasn't sure if you counted Rahkki as one of us."

Hazelwind's eyes brightened. "Just barely," he teased.

She lurched to her hooves. "We should leave for Mount Crim now. It could already be too late."

"No, let's not rush this," Hazelwind said, flipping aside his long, tangled forelock. "The giants captured Storm Herd because we weren't prepared. We need trained sky herders to repel the burner dragons and we need more battle steeds. Gorlanders aren't creatures we can easily overpower or spook, and beside all that, you're not ready for battle." He nodded toward the thin line of blood seeping from her closed wound.

"Rahkki can't wait," she grumbled.

"I think he can," Hazelwind argued. "If they stole your cub to . . . to eat him . . . then he's already dead. But if he's alive, then they've taken him for another purpose. Better to prepare and do this right than to fail."

She reluctantly agreed, and Hazelwind called Storm Herd with a crisp clap of his wings.

The steeds drew closer, as silent as shadows. Many approached and pressed their foreheads against Echofrost's. Their folded wings glistened in the striped sunlight and she nodded approval. It appeared they'd spent the last three days preening and smoothing their crumpled feathers, replenishing their bellies, and treating their wounds while she slept. Freedom from the giants had caused the pegasi to bloom like spring flowers, and contentment flowed through Echofrost at the sight of them.

When all were gathered, they discussed saving Rahkki.

"We should send a scout to Mount Crim," Shysong suggested.

"I'll go," Redfire volunteered. "I can ride the jet streams—no one will see me and it's the fastest way to travel."

Echofrost nodded and Graystone, who'd been grazing nearby, interjected. "What about the tame Kihlari?" he asked. "I agree with rescuing the cub—he saved us on Mount Crim—but Dewberry is furious about the Landwalkers selling foals. She won't leave this place without the Ruk steeds."

"Neither will I," Hazelwind nickered. "Those Kihlari descend from the ancient Lake Herd pegasi of Anok. We can't leave any behind who want to join us."

"He's right," Echofrost nickered. Four hundred years earlier, when the ancient black foal named Nightwing had gained his power, he attacked his own kind. The Lake Herd steeds had fled Anok and flown south, landing here.

Sandwens had captured them, tamed them, and turned them into flying warhorses.

When Storm Herd fled Anok for the same reason—fear of Nightwing, who had awakened from hibernation and was menacing the herds again—they'd landed on the same continent. But the Lake Herd pegasi had forgotten their wild roots and most had no desire to leave their safe stalls and regular meals.

Shysong spoke, affirming Echofrost's thoughts. "Most Kihlari don't want to leave, and I'm not sure how to convince them."

"Leave it to Dewberry," Graystone suggested. "That mare is persuasive."

Panic bloomed in Echofrost's chest. "Where is Dewberry?" she nickered. Through the fog of her long sleep and her concern for Rahkki, she hadn't realized the pinto mare wasn't present. She twirled on her back heels, about to utter a shrill whinny for her friend.

"Shh," Hazelwind nickered, eyes glowing. "I hear her coming. She's just moving a little slower these days."

"Why? Is it the twins? Have they come?"

"Why don't you see for yourself?"

A moment later, Dewberry stepped between the trees.

Behind her, twin foals skittered out of the brush on unsteady legs. "You two are always off playing," Dewberry groused, nosing them ahead of her. She spotted Echofrost and brightened. "You're awake!"

Tears filled Echofrost's eyes at the sight of her deceased brother's family. The twins, a filly and a colt, flapped their fluffy wings to keep up with their dam. They were both pintos, just like their mother and their late sire, Bumblewind.

"This is Windheart," Dewberry said, nudging the chestnut pinto filly whose coloring was as wild as an untamed sky. Her wings, which were dark emerald at the mantle, faded all the way to white at the ends.

"And this is Thornblaze," she said, eyeing the colt.

The compact gray pinto had blue-edged white feathers. His short black mane and tail were streaked in shades of gray. The twin foals sported matching white blazes and the blue eyes of their grandmother Crystalfeather.

"Hello," Echofrost nickered to her brother's foals.

They flicked their curved ears and leaned toward their aunt, exchanging breath with her.

As Echofrost inhaled their scents, the huge world she inhabited seemed to rapidly shrink. At the same time her heart expanded, stretching to embrace these two perfect creatures standing before her. "They're beautiful," she breathed.

The tiny foals dived toward their dam to nurse. "They're stubborn too," Dewberry nickered, arching her neck proudly.

Redfire interrupted the moment. "Can you fly?" he asked Echofrost.

"There's only one way to find out." She flared her wings, trotted a few steps, and then lifted off the ground. Hot pain splayed from her stitched wound to her limbs and she felt weak, but she could fly. "I think I'll be able to keep up."

"So how do we save that golden-eyed cub from the giants?" Graystone asked.

Echofrost collected herself. "Like Hazelwind suggested, we need to train a group of sky herders to handle the little dragons, and we could use some help from the Landwalkers."

"The Fifth Clan is not at peace," Hazelwind said. "And they don't know we're hiding here. Who will help us?"

"Rahkki's family," Echofrost nickered. "We'll fly to the rice farm as soon as it's dark."

Shysong sidled close and the mares exchanged breath. "I was wondering," the roan nickered, "will we rescue I'Lenna too?"

Echofrost pricked her ears. How selfish she'd been to think only about Rahkki! "Yes, we can try. Where is she?"

"All I know is that Harak took her."

Echofrost sighed. "I'm not sure how we're going to battle the Gorlanders *and* Harak's armies."

"We need more flying warriors," Dewberry said, rattling her emerald feathers. Beside her, the twins puffed their short feathers in close imitation, making Storm Herd nicker in amusement. "And don't forget the Ruk steeds, we have to free them too," Dewberry whinnied, referring to the retired and breeding Kihlari steeds that the Sandwens kept locked in a special barn. Their colts and fillies were sold to other clans when they reached one year old. "Can you rally that overfed chestnut stallion and his winged army to help us?"

"You mean Kol?" Echofrost nickered. "I don't know, everything's changed now that the Sandwens are fighting one another."

"I can't believe I'm saying this," Redfire began, "but I'd rather fight giants *with* the Landwalkers and their weapons than without them."

"Yeah," Dewberry agreed. "What I wouldn't give to hold a sard."

"You mean a sword," Echofrost corrected.

"Whatever!" Dewberry's eyes tracked her newborn foals. "I thought my hooves were sharp, but those swords are fierce."

"Rahkki's family can help with all of this," Echofrost decided. "Brauk *knows* the giants and the clan. He can get weapons and find Landwalker warriors to ride us."

Graystone reared. "No one is riding me!"

Redfire pranced and Storm Herd buzzed their feathers.

Echofrost spread her wings, catching their attention. "Imagine an armed Landwalker on your back, cutting down one enemy while you strike another. Think of arrows shooting faster than you can fly." Echofrost lost her breath remembering how Rahkki had shot his darts and how the fearsome giants had fallen like rotten trees, clearing a path for her in the battle. "Landwalkers are powerful, ferocious, and fearless—just like us!"

Graystone shrugged, unconvinced, but Dewberry nodded and her emerald feathers gave another soft, excited rattle.

"Look around you," Echofrost said, scanning Storm

Herd with her dark eyes. "We *are* a winged army!"

Hazelwind lowered his head, looking resigned. "But we can't communicate with Rahkki's family, Echofrost. How is this going to work?"

"I don't know," she admitted. "But I'm sure we want the same thing—to get Rahkki back. If we fly to the rice farm, the Stormrunners will put us to use. Landwalkers are not all-powerful. They need our wings as much as we need their swords."

"All right," Hazelwind relented. "To the rice farm then, as soon as it's full dark, but no flying. We can't risk Dusk Patrol spotting us and the foals aren't ready." Hazelwind had studied the Sandwen patrols during Echofrost's captivity and understood their patterns, so Storm Herd stamped their agreement.

"When will you scout for Rahkki?" Echofrost asked Redfire.

"I'll go now. I can catch the eastern jet stream to Mount Crim," Redfire said. "I'll meet you later at the farm."

The herd dispersed to fill their bellies until dark, and Echofrost grazed beside Dewberry. The foals, Windheart and Thornblaze, grew tired and collapsed on top of each other, making a small pile of legs and feathers that twitched as they dreamed. They reminded Echofrost of life with her twin brother, Bumblewind, in Dawn Meadow, and she felt something she hadn't felt since the night Star had received his power in Anok—she felt *hope*.

7

RICE FARM

WHEN FULL DARK ARRIVED IN THE SANDWEN Realm, Echofrost and Shysong led Storm Herd to Darthan Stormrunner's rice field, trotting swiftly between the palms.

The temperature cooled as clouds blew in from the northern coast. Echofrost traveled beside Dewberry and her twins. Windheart blinked sleepily as she pranced beside her mother. Thornblaze yawned and became distracted by every lizard or rodent that skittered past his hooves. The foals were sturdy, but they needed rest.

Dewberry guessed Echofrost's thoughts. "They won't learn to keep up if we coddle them," she nickered.

Echofrost kept silent. She would not tell Dewberry how to raise her twins. Anyway, perhaps the pinto mare was right. Many trials loomed before Storm Herd could leave the Realm, trials that would challenge the young pegasi.

"There it is," Shysong nickered.

The herd paused at the rim of the jungle. Ahead was Darthan's hut. The sky spanned above, full of dark, scudding clouds and winged bats that flew at hyperspeeds. The palms swished in the salt-tinged gusts of wind. "Let's go," Echofrost urged. Her hooves squelched in the mud as she led Storm Herd to Rahkki's family.

When they reached Darthan's porch, the herd halted. Several voices drifted from the small hut and firelight brightened the windows. It was long past dusk and the scent of frying rice and fish swirled in the air around the small cabin.

Peering up, Echofrost glimpsed the high window that led to Rahkki's sleeping loft. She'd spent several days at this farm before the Kihlari auction that had led to her Pairing with Rahkki, and she remembered him taking her for short swims in the river that flowed west of the farm. His scent lingered, though she knew the boy wasn't here.

Graystone flared his nostrils at the rising smoke. "Have you learned how Landwalkers control fire?" he asked.

"Not exactly," Echofrost admitted. Beyond the rough smoke, she scented the animals that lived in the barn: Lutegar the swamp buffalo, several pigs, two goats, and loose fowl. "I'll get Darthan's attention." She stamped her hoof and whinnied.

"Shh," a voice whispered from inside the hut. "You hear that?"

The door burst open and Darthan leaped onto the porch, sword lifted. He squinted, trying to adjust to the darkness outside. Then a chestnut Kihlara charged out of the hut, leaped past Darthan, and rushed Echofrost.

She reared up just as Graystone thrust his large body between her and the charging steed. The chestnut smacked into Graystone's chest and rocked backward, smashing into Hazelwind, who bit the chestnut's neck and tossed him onto his side.

A bit late, Echofrost recognized the shiny stallion. "Kol!" she chided. "It's just me."

Kol rolled to his hooves, chest heaving. Hazelwind and Graystone circled him, flexing their powerful wings.

"Sula?" Kol said, using her Sandwen name. "I thought

you and your herd left the Realm." His yellow-streaked red forelock hung in a tangle, shadowing his white blaze. Several drops of blood oozed from the crest of his neck.

Hazelwind danced closer, his tail striking his sides. "Stand down," he whinnied.

Kol's body was still poised to attack, his front hooves light and ready to strike. The stallion lowered his head and folded his glimmering wings, signaling submission, and Hazelwind relaxed.

"Why did you attack us?" Echofrost asked, baffled by Kol's thoughtless charge. "You're outnumbered. My friends could have killed you."

The glossy stallion nodded understanding. "I—I thought you were the Sky Guard, coming to get Brauk," he neighed. "Since the armies returned from Mount Crim, everything's changed. No one is safe." His eyes rolled, showing the whites.

Hazelwind and Graystone folded their wings.

Darthan, seeing that the stallions would not fight, lowered his sword and cleared his throat. "You're back," he said to Echofrost, stunned. He moved toward her, glancing nervously at the herd.

Echofrost softened her stance and nickered, inviting him closer. Darthan studied the stitched wound on her side and a smile spread across his face. "You've been to Brim."

She stared at Darthan, frustrated because she had no way to talk to him, but surely he knew that Rahkki was with the giants. The Fifth Clan soldiers would have reported that news, wouldn't they? Besides, she was here without Rahkki, her Rider, so clearly the cub was missing. But how could she ask Darthan for help?

She faced east, toward Mount Crim. Then she emitted the loudest whinny a pegasus could make—it was the urgent cry of a mare calling for her foal, and it was a sound Darthan should recognize, because the Ruk mares made the same whinny when their foals were sold and taken away.

He peered at her, curious.

Echofrost whinnied again, adding the same strident pitch to her voice.

A dark head appeared in the window—Brauk Stormrunner. He rested his upper body on the ledge and glared at her. "Is that viper calling for Rahkki?" he asked Darthan.

Echofrost flattened her ears. This was the man she'd kicked so hard he could no longer walk. Brauk's red-headed caretaker, Ossi Finn, squatted next to him, her blue eyes round with awe. "Sula brought her friends," she said.

"Friends?" Brauk grumbled. "She's just an animal."

"Show respect," Darthan warned. "This is your brother's Flier."

Brauk pulled his chest up higher for a better view. "A Flier doesn't leave her Rider," he said, speaking directly to Echofrost. "After everything Rahkki's done for you, you left him alone with those stinkin' giants." He spit out the window and Hazelwind rattled his feathers.

"Shh." Ossi touched Brauk's shoulder and he turned his anguished gaze on her. She spoke softly. "Harak said that the Highland prince took Rahkki. What was Sula supposed to do? Fight the giants by herself? And you heard her just now, she's calling for him."

"I don't know what she's doing," Brauk stated. "For all we know, she's calling for a mate."

The woman laughed. "A mate? All the wild steeds are here." She swept her pale, freckled fingers toward the herd, and a small gasp escaped her lips when she noticed the newly born foals. "Look, they're starting families."

Brauk snorted. "You sound like my brother." But his eyes glistened sadly as he pressed his head against Ossi's belly.

Clucking her tongue, Ossi considered the wild pegasi

and turned to Rahkki's uncle. "Why do you think they're here, Darthan? They could have flown away after Brim fixed Sula up."

He stroked his chin. "I don't know. But maybe they can help us."

Brauk sucked air through his teeth. "Help us? How? I can't walk, fight, or ride."

Darthan sheathed his sword and exhaled, rubbing his eyes. He appeared much older than he had before Echofrost and Rahkki had left for Mount Crim with the Sandwen armies. "I don't know," he said. "But they landed here on purpose. Rahkki helped free them, maybe they want to return the favor?"

"Not you too," Brauk said with a grunt. "If they want anything from us, it's food. They're probably starving."

Ossi laughed. "They're *wild*, Brauk. They know how to feed themselves."

Brauk withdrew his head, still angry and muttering. His grip on the ledge slipped and he hit his chin on the windowsill. "Oof!" he grunted, and then punched the ledge that had offended him.

Cocking her head, Echofrost watched Brauk struggle. He'd cut her flight feathers after first capturing her, and she'd been unable to fly for a full moon. She'd dreamed of disabling him in a similar way, but to her surprise, she felt no pleasure watching him suffer. And while she couldn't understand his words, she understood that Brauk hated her.

"Why did you return?" Kol nickered to Storm Herd. "I thought you wanted to find a new home and live free."

"We do," Shysong replied, "but we want to help Rahkki and I'Lenna first."

Kol turned to Echofrost. "So you weren't just using him to save your friends?"

"I was," she admitted. "But now I want to help him."

Kol folded his wings, looking smug. "Rahkki tamed you," he nickered.

Echofrost gasped. "He did not!"

But Kol ignored her and trotted off, swishing his long tail in a very annoying and very self-satisfied way.

Echofrost folded her wings and blew hotly out her nostrils. Kol did not understand her and probably never would. She dipped her head to graze and pushed the stallion's ridiculous claim out of her mind.

8

THE DRAGON

I'LENNA WHITEHALL HAD BEEN TIED TO THE SUN-stone for two nights without Granak or any dragon showing up. The guards blamed the bright moon for keeping the droolers away, but tonight was different. Clouds had rolled in, masking the silver light.

Earlier this evening, the Borla played the drums again, calling their guardian mascot forth, and the clansfolk had disappeared into their rooms and homes. No one wanted to be caught outside when the hungry drooler appeared.

I'Lenna waited beneath the dim sky, watching the three guards who were not allowed to leave her until the dragon arrived. They'd fed her small meals and freed her for short periods to take care of her needs. Creatures had come and gone—jungle rats and a curious snake. The guards had scared them off by shouting, but they were not permitted to help her against Granak or any drooler that arrived in his place.

Now her tongue filled her mouth like a useless lump of cloth and her belly clamored ferociously. Chewing her lip, I'Lenna vowed to find Rahkki and bring him home. And in spite of how things appeared, the rebellion wasn't over. If she survived the night, she had one final hand to play before she would admit defeat—the Stormrunners.

She'd promised herself to keep the bloodborn family out of the uprising, even though General Tsun had pressured her to recruit them. The family had gone against her mother before and lost everything. And she'd never meant to befriend Rahkki that day in the Kihlari stable, right after the wild mares were captured, but then he'd *smiled* at her, and their awful past had fallen away.

Since that moment, their friendship had risen from the deep like a giant octopus and wrapped its tentacles around them both. And now I'Lenna needed his family's support, since all her followers were in prison.

She studied the sky behind the drifting clouds. A

sprinkling of stars lit the Realm, and the shadowy wings of the Dusk Patrol steeds veered south as they patrolled the clan's boundaries. Tuni Hightower normally led Dusk Patrol, but since she'd also been arrested, Harak had assigned someone new.

As the Sky Guard vanished behind the trees, I'Lenna spoke. "May I have some water?"

The female soldier crossed the cordon, opened her waterskin, and offered I'Lenna a drink. As she sipped, water dribbled down her chin. "Why don't you let me go? You know my mother is bad for the clan."

The woman shook her head. "I'm sworn to protect the *monarch*, Princess I'Lenna. I won't break my vow."

The guard withdrew and I'Lenna scowled, but she understood the woman's devotion. The soldiers and Riders took their oaths seriously, and it would not be easy for the Stormrunners to rally them against a sitting queen—if the family agreed to help her at all. I'Lenna might have to confess the truth about Lilliam stealing from the clan— that might convince them—but it would also endanger I'Lenna's sisters and new brother.

When the darkness was so deep that it swallowed even the shadows, I'Lenna heard a tree crack and topple over.

Fear iced her veins. "What was that?"

"Shh," said one of the guards.

Bracing herself, I'Lenna yanked against the iron manacles at the ends of the ropes, rubbing her flesh raw on the hard metal.

More trees crashed against one another and then I'Lenna heard the terrifying four-beat gait of a spit dragon.

"Time to go," one guard said to the other. With sorrowful glances at I'Lenna, the soldiers retreated.

Suddenly she wanted them to stay. "Don't leave me!" But they had orders to obey.

The dragon drew closer.

I'Lenna tightened her muscles and crunched her belly, trying to pull her hands through the iron manacles. The hard metal rubbed off more of her skin. She yanked even harder and with a sharp pop, her right thumb suddenly dislocated and that hand slipped free. I'Lenna flushed with pain and triumph.

The stomping grew closer. *No, no, no!*

Then it appeared—a drooler—but not Granak. This was a female spit dragon, as evidenced by her round-ridged spine. She stood thirteen lengths at the shoulder at least—and looked hungry. Her forked tongue slid from her mouth, tasting the air. Her drool dripped and puddled around her huge clawed feet.

I'Lenna tugged on her left arm, trying to free it too.

The dragon spotted her. It stood three hundred lengths away, maybe less. Its eyes locked on hers. *Bloody rain!*

The dragon crept forward, tail vibrating.

Four moving figures suddenly caught I'Lenna's eye. They glided toward her from the Kihlari stable. She recognized Rahkki's friends Koko Dale, Mut Finn, Jul Ranger, and Tambor Woodson. "Over here," she rasped.

These teens had protected Rahkki during the march to Mount Crim and scouted the giant hordes with him. They didn't trust I'Lenna because she was a Whitehall, but Rahkki had forced them to accept her. They rushed closer and I'Lenna's breath hitched.

"Need some 'elp?" Koko asked.

I'Lenna exhaled loudly. "I do!" she cried.

Mut drew his hunting knife, the only type of weapon Harak's army had allowed the villagers to keep. He and Koko sprinted forward to bait the dragon away from I'Lenna. Jul and Tambor, who went by Tam, raced to free her. "Land to skies, your hand!" Jul whispered, gaping at her dangling thumb.

"It's nothing, just cut me loose."

Jul's hunting knife sliced easily through the final lashings and I'Lenna staggered free.

The black dragon lunged at Koko. The girl ripped off her bright-yellow cloak and waved it at the beast. Mut sliced his arm, using the scent of his blood as bait. The drooler hissed at them, her tail lashing. Purple, blue, and green hues shimmered across her scales as she lowered her neck and charged Mut and Koko. The pair sprinted off, leading the dragon away.

Jul and Tam steadied I'Lenna. "Are you hurt?"

"No, not really," she said, cradling her injured thumb.

Mut and Koko zipped like rabbits, crossing their paths and confusing the reptile. The dragon swung her head in frustration. Mut's long legs got tangled and he fell. The lizard sprang.

I'Lenna, Jul, and Tam leaped toward him.

But Koko was already there. She snatched Mut's dagger and stabbed the dragon in the leg. The reptile twisted around, teeth flashing.

Mut rolled back onto his feet.

"Over here!" Koko shouted, sprinting toward the trees.

The dragon reared, standing thirty lengths.

I'Lenna gaped at it, her mind racing. "Release one of the pigs!" she shouted to Jul. "Now!" This dragon was not going to leave without eating *something*.

Jul sprang away to the animal pens and threw open a gate. It was goats, not pigs, but what was the difference to a dragon? The confused herd blasted out of their pen and frolicked across the trampled grass. Having been protected by Sandwens their entire lives, their instincts had dulled to danger.

As hoped, the easy prey drew the dragon's bright eyes. She quivered, her tongue flicking. In two mighty steps she reached the goats and bit one, then two more. She lowered herself, waiting for her toxic venom to take effect.

Koko and Mut edged around the chaos, back to I'Lenna.

High on the hill, the smaller gate to Fort Prowl opened and a man appeared, his face lit by a torch—Harak Nightseer. I'Lenna and the teens ducked behind a water trough.

Harak peered into the darkness. The dragon hissed and Harak's grin was noticeable even from a distance.

"Look how happy he is thinking I'm being eaten," I'Lenna huffed.

"It's good though," Mut replied, his chest heaving as he caught his breath. "In the morning, when he sees that you're gone, he'll assume the dragon ate you. He won't go looking for you."

"True," she answered.

"Wha' now?" Koko asked, swiping her sweaty blond hair off her face.

"Follow me," I'Lenna urged, and she angled toward Leshi Creek. The huge dragon had lost interest in them as she swallowed the first goat. Clouds rolled in, covering the few glittering stars. I'Lenna glanced gratefully at Mut and his pals. "Why did you guys save me?"

"We didn't plan to," Mut said. "We were on our way to Mount Crim to rescue Rahkki when we spotted the drooler. We . . . we couldn't let you get eaten."

I'Lenna straightened, offering a wry smile. "I appreciate that."

Mut grinned at her. "Turns out we're on the same side, right?"

I'Lenna nodded, glad she wasn't alone. "So you four are on your way to save Rahkki? Just you?"

"Yeah," said Jul. "But we're going to the trading post first to buy weapons, since Harak stole most of ours." Jul's family was wealthy; he could afford enough weapons for all of them.

Mut glanced at I'Lenna. "Maybe you know something about this," he said. "I was at the trading post yesterday and I overhead a Daakuran man asking a lot of questions about Rahkki. Why do you think that is?"

She stiffened. "I don't know. Why would *anyone* from Daakur be asking about Rahkki? What did the man look like? Who was he questioning?"

Mut shrugged. "He was young, had blond hair and a beard. He was at the import-and-export tent, talking to Willa Green."

A tingle ran up I'Lenna's spine as she considered this. "Rahkki sold a very special Kihlara blanket to that woman for resale in Daakur. It had belonged to his mother's mount, Drael. Did Willa mention the blanket?"

Mut squinted, thinking. "I don't remember exactly. But the man asked about Rahkki's uncle and brother too."

"Wha' does it mean?" Koko asked.

"I'm not sure," I'Lenna said. Her injured thumb had begun to throb. "He's probably just looking for more Kihlara blankets to buy. So how do you four plan to free Rahkki from the giants?" she asked, not meaning to sound skeptical.

Tam sheathed his hunting knife. "We'll figure it out when we get there. Anyway, there's no one else to do it."

"Not true," I'Lenna said. "His family will help once they hear my idea."

Koko shook her head. "Brauk 'ates the White'alls. I don' think 'e'll listen to yuh. Beside, he can't walk."

"I know that," I'Lenna said. "But I have a plan. Don't go to Mount Crim by yourselves, okay? Stay with me. I just have to get to the southern drainage ditch that leads into Fort Prowl. There's something inside the fortress I need to steal, and the clan is on vigil until morning. No one will see us. And then we'll go straight to Darthan's rice farm."

The four teens glanced at one another, debating with their eyes. Then Mut nodded and the decision was made. "We'll stay with you."

Jul nudged Koko. "If we're not going to Mount Crim right now, you and I should return to our posts before we're missed."

"Yur righ'," Koko agreed. She eyed I'Lenna. "When yur ready ta save 'im, let us know."

I'Lenna nodded. "I'll get word to you as soon as I can," she said. Koko and Jul turned and vanished into the darkness.

"So, what are we stealing?" Mut asked, smiling down at the princess.

She grinned. "Medicine. Now hurry, let's go!" After a suspicious glance from Tam, the group jogged toward the drainage ditch at the south end of Fort Prowl.

9

GUILT

RETRIEVING THE SPECIAL MEDICINE FROM FORT
Prowl was easy for I'Lenna because most folks had
retreated to their rooms, and the dining hour had passed.
The mood in the fortress was grim. No one liked knowing their crown princess was tied up outside and that half
the clan's militia was imprisoned in the Eighth Tower.
I'Lenna used the secret tunnels she was so familiar with
to break into the Borla's medicinal supplies and take what
she needed.

Now she, Mut, and Tam were sneaking through the
jungle toward Darthan's hut. They stopped cold when they
arrived. Over a hundred wild Kihlari had gathered on
Darthan's front lawn.

"Land to skies," Tam whispered.

Some of the Kihlari were grazing, others dozing, but when the first one spotted them, they all threw up their heads. Firo whinnied a greeting and glided toward I'Lenna.

The princess rushed to greet her. When Firo touched down, she nuzzled I'Lenna's hair, and the girl wrapped her arms around the roan's neck. "I was so worried about you," I'Lenna whispered to her pet.

Darthan opened his door and stepped out of the shadows, looking as stunned as I'Lenna felt. "You escaped the Sunstone?"

I'Lenna nodded toward Mut and Tam. "With a little help," she answered, feeling giddy with exhaustion and relief.

A flame-haired woman poked her head out the window. "Ay, Mut!" she called. I'Lenna recognized her from the clan. It was Mut's sister, Ossi Finn. "What in Granak's name are you doing here?" Ossi asked her brother.

Mut spread his arms. "Rescuing a princess, what else?"

"Well, hurry inside," she urged. "It's a night for dragons."

"You think?" Mut quipped, and I'Lenna and her new

friends sputtered into laughter as they walked toward the hut.

I'Lenna spotted Rahkki's Flier, Sula, and her heart surged. "Is Rahkki here?" she asked Darthan.

With a small shake of his head, he motioned them inside.

I'Lenna, Tam, and Mut had to pass through the herd of untamed Kihlari first. Even with Firo beside her, I'Lenna's heart hammered with fear. These wild steeds smelled of soil and sweat. Their hair was tangled with burrs and crawling with insects, and they were thin and wiry. But I'Lenna was not fooled by their sorry appearance. Savage power lurked within those flared wings and tight muscles. Proud spirit sparked from their eyes.

She slid a nervous glance toward Firo. I'Lenna had fallen for the roan's beautiful ice-blue eyes and shiny feathers. She'd slept beside her and braided her tail countless times, never truly grasping—until this moment—that the mare was *wild*.

"Land to skies," I'Lenna whispered, suddenly seeing Firo's sharpened hooves, muscular jaws, battle scars, and the fierce intelligence that burned inside her striking glance. In that moment, she realized she'd never *owned*

89

Firo; the braya had tolerated her by choice. "You're not a pet, are you?"

"What did you say?" Mut asked.

"Nothing. I'm just—look at these steeds! They're so . . ."

"Wild?" Mut finished. "Yeah, I noticed."

Brauk's Flier, Kol, stood among the wild herd, looking overfed and underworked in comparison, but his lax appearance didn't fool I'Lenna either. A Kihlara steed needed a Rider to activate its power. One command from Brauk and Kol would transform from docile pet to dangerous warrior in the span of a blink.

As they made their way to Darthan's porch, moving carefully through the herd, I'Lenna spotted a gaunt pinto mare with two newborn foals and her heart squeezed. She could not imagine this poor mare suffering captivity with giants while pregnant!

But the proud pinto met I'Lenna's gaze. She sported knife-sharp hooves and battle scars like the others. Her eyes, bright and undaunted, showed no fear. She whinnied to her foals and they drew closer, tucking safely beneath her wings. I'Lenna swallowed as her throat tightened. Unlike a Kihlara dam, this braya was a mother *and a warrior.* What had the clan been thinking to pluck these creatures out of the sky as if they were pretty flowers?

"Why is the wild herd here?" she asked Darthan when her group reached his front porch. "They're not tethered. They're free to go."

"We're not sure," he said. "Come inside." The old wooden stair boards creaked as they ascended and Darthan allowed them into his hut. Dark smoke lingered in the air. "I burned dinner," he explained.

I'Lenna's belly grumbled at the word *dinner.*

"Sit," Darthan invited, indicating a bench and two chairs by the fire. I'Lenna's eyes flitted about the room. Ossi had taken a seat at the small dining table and Brauk reclined in a raised makeshift cot.

His lip curled when he caught her staring at his useless legs, and I'Lenna felt her cheeks grow hot. She fingered the medicine she'd stolen from the fortress on the way here and then dropped the vial back into her pocket. She'd taken it for Brauk, but his hot stare warned her off. *Not yet*, she thought.

"Sit," Darthan repeated. "I'll find something for you all to eat, and then I want to look at your thumb, I'Lenna."

I'Lenna lowered herself into a hard chair while

Rahkki's uncle poked through his larder and returned with spiced rice, cut pineapple, chickpeas, and three shards of honeycomb. He portioned the food onto three plates and then handed them to I'Lenna, Mut, and Tam.

Mut dived onto his plate like a hawk, arms mantling around his face. Tam happily bit into the rice and I'Lenna crunched into her honeycomb first, her belly singing with pleasure.

While they ate their dinners, Mut spoke freely, telling Darthan, Brauk, and Ossi how I'Lenna had freed one hand from the Sunstone when a huge drooler stomped out of the woods. He and Tam paused eating to act out what had happened next, baiting the dragon, loosing the goats, and hiding from Harak behind a water trough.

"Come morning, the clan will think the dragon ate I'Lenna. No one will look for her," Mut finished, licking juice from his lips.

While the boys were telling the story, Darthan had wrenched I'Lenna's right thumb back in place and splinted it because the thumb ached whenever she moved it. I'Lenna sighed with relief and addressed the group. "That's enough about me," she said. Darthan's meal and the sugar from the honeycomb had begun to revive her. "Let's talk about Rahkki."

The room quieted and Brauk turned the full force of his black-lashed golden eyes on I'Lenna. She lost her breath—he looked so much like his little brother!

"What about Rahkki?" he asked.

"We need to get him back from the giants."

Brauk spit in Darthan's fire, making it sizzle. "You think we don't know that, I'Lenna?"

She dropped her eyes. "Rahkki saved my life."

Brauk grimaced. "Yeah, he took a Gorlan punishment that was meant for you; I heard about that." His voice tightened, his fists hardened. "What I don't understand is why you lied to my brother. You told him you didn't want the throne."

Darthan, who was filling his pipe, grunted softly at his nephew.

Heat rose in I'Lenna's cheeks. "I don't *want* it, but I can't let my mother keep it. There's a difference."

Brauk's eyes flashed. "Not to me."

Darthan took a long draw on his pipe, releasing sweet clover into the room. "I don't think I'Lenna came here to argue," he said.

"I didn't," she agreed. "I came to finish what I started. The rebellion isn't over."

"Isn't over?" Brauk huffed. "Everyone loyal to you is

either dead, captured, or locked in the Eighth Tower. It's over, I'Lenna."

She shook her head. "No, we can't give up. My timing was terrible; I'll give you that. I should have held the throne until Harak returned and then arrested him, but I was more concerned about stopping the war with the giants."

Brauk crumpled his fists around his trousers. "You think your *timing* was your mistake?" He made a disgusted noise. "Every Sandwen knows that the safest way to kill a snake is to cut off its head. You left your mother alive, *that's* where you failed."

"Ease off her, Brauk," Ossi chided. "She's just a girl."

In the soft light of Darthan's fire, I'Lenna's guilt exploded. "I know I made things worse," she cried, startling everyone. "Rahkki might be dead, *because of me.*" Tears streamed down her cheeks. "I lied to him, it's true. I befriended him when I shouldn't have, I know. I brought civil war to my clan and got my general assassinated. It's all bloody true! People are dead! I know what I've done." She choked and turned to Brauk. "I know that the best way to kill a snake is to cut off its head, but I *can't.* I love my mom, don't you see? But I have to *stop* her. I don't know how, but this time I can't fail."

"First things first," Darthan interrupted. "What do you want from us, princess? How can we help you?"

She took a deep breath. "I'm here because I need an army. I need to rally the villagers, but no one will fight for me, not again." She wiped her nose with her sleeve and looked from Darthan to Brauk. "But they will fight for the Stormrunners."

Brauk laughed, his voice bitter and hollow. "Look at me," he rasped, pointing at his paralyzed legs. "I can't *walk*, I'Lenna, or fly my stallion. I can't lead an army."

She ignored that and pushed on. "Once we overthrow Harak and Lilliam, we can take over both the Fifth Clan armies, fly to Mount Crim, and rescue Rahkki."

Just then thunder boomed and pent-up rain began to fall in heaps, pounding Darthan's thatched roof.

"By Granak," Tam groused. "The clouds are angry."

Darthan drew on his pipe. "It's an early monsoon."

Mut groaned. "Another bad omen. Nothing has gone right since Granak rejected the sow after the winged horse auction."

"Not true. Our bad luck stems directly from my mother." I'Lenna peered at the Stormrunners. "For you two, it started eight years ago."

Brauk whipped his head toward her. "Don't talk about that night."

"Do you want Lilliam off Reyella's throne, or not?"

"Yes," he snarled, "but not so I can see *you* on it! Trade one Whitehall for another? Why?"

"Then who will take it?" I'Lenna leaned forward, imploring him. "It has to be a Sandwen princess, Brauk. I'm here and I'm the heir."

Brauk slammed his fist onto the table, making Ossi jump. "Even if I wanted to, how could I be of *any* use?" He scowled at his limp legs.

"This is how." I'Lenna produced the crimson vial she'd stolen from the Borla. She swirled the elixir and the dark liquid shimmered within the red glass.

Everyone leaned closer and Darthan sucked a breath. "Is that what I think it is?"

"Yes," I'Lenna answered. "It's the Queen's Elixir, the one and only dose." She glanced at Brauk.

His back had gone rigid. His golden eyes latched onto the vial, blazing with hunger for it. Ossi wrung her hands.

"Where did you get that?" Darthan asked.

"I stole it for Brauk," she answered. Brauk flicked his eyes to hers and I'Lenna met his gaze. "Whether or not you decide to help me," she said, her voice husky, "you will walk again."

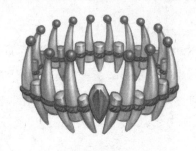

⟳ 10 ⟲

THE QUEEN'S ELIXIR

"PRAISE THE WIND!" OSSI CRIED, HER TEARS SPLAT-tering the dusty floor.

I'Lenna uncorked the vial of elixir. Each Sandwen Clan kept a dose of black magna spider venom on hand for its queen. Unlike most poisonous creatures, this spider's venom didn't injure or kill—it *healed* its prey, rapidly curing diseases, knitting broken bones, and restoring damaged tissue and organs. Black magna spiderlings were sensitive, picky eaters and, in this way, the adults ensured healthy, disease-free meals for their young.

The Sandwen clans could only collect the healing elixir from live spiders, and since it was almost impossible to capture a black magna alive, most clans owned only a single dose, which was reserved for their queen. Were she to become terminally ill or mortally wounded, the potent elixir would restore the monarch's health. "It's yours," I'Lenna said, reaching the vial toward Brauk.

He recoiled from it.

I'Lenna frowned, her hand wavering. "What's wrong?"

Trembles racked his body as hope and then disbelief slid across his features. "Gah, I'Lenna, does this mean I'll *owe* you?"

"Brauk!" Ossi scolded.

He lifted his chin. "What I mean—" He struggled for words. "What I'm saying is that she's a Whitehall and I'm still a Stormrunner. We're enemies."

I'Lenna understood—healing Brauk didn't fix the wrong her mother had done to his. "You won't owe me anything," she promised.

"Good then," he grumbled.

Ossi and Darthan exchanged a glance.

I'Lenna moved to Brauk's side and handed him the vial. "Drink."

Taking the crimson glass, Brauk stared at the liquid inside, swirling it. Doubt etched his features. "You must want *something* in return."

Ossi groaned and threw her hands over her face. "Just drink it!"

Frustrated, I'Lenna pursed her lips. She and Brauk locked eyes, the past swirling between them. The others quieted, as if Brauk and I'Lenna were deciding the fate of the Realm.

I'Lenna blinked first and dropped her eyes. "Maybe I am hoping for something in return," she admitted. "Maybe if I heal you, you'll stop running from what happened eight years ago and help your clan and your brother."

Brauk's torso lunged at her and Darthan leaped to his feet. "Don't talk to me like that," Brauk spit at her. "You've *no* right."

I'Lenna leaned toward him, their faces a handspan apart. "This is the truth, Brauk. You and Darthan wanted no part in the uprising. I know General Tsun approached you to help us. I asked him not to, but he believed the *entire clan* would fight for the Stormrunners. All you had to do was ask them." Her voice rose and she ignored the warning glance from Ossi.

"But you both refused him. Why?" I'Lenna wiped her eyes. "Why do you hide on your farm?" she asked Darthan. "And why do you battle every living creature *except* my mother?" she asked Brauk. She stood, feeling angry, dizzy, and weak all at once. "The rebellion failed because only *half* the clan would fight for me. I don't know if you Stormrunners are afraid or if you just don't care, but at least I'm *trying* to put things right."

"Afraid?" Brauk's eyes bored into hers. "*This* is the truth: I stayed out of the rebellion for Rahkki's sake. I did a poor job of raising him, I'Lenna. Always fighting, never home . . . ah, bloody rain, just being a rotten brother."

I'Lenna remembered Brauk's dark days. He'd frightened her then, always strutting through the fortress on the balls of his feet, scrapping with soldiers and laughing like a madman whether he lost or won. Back then he was always yelling at young Rahkki for crying, or spilling his juice, or running from Mut and his gang. Brauk was rough, trying to teach his little brother to fight and forcing him to eat second helpings so he'd grow bigger. Brauk blasted through their inheritance, spending their last dramals on the stallion Kol. I'Lenna could smell his regret. It fluttered around him like a cape.

Brauk's voice softened as he continued. "I came around after a while, tried to do right by him. But if your mom had gotten wind that Darthan and I were helping to oust her—she'd have ordered Harak to slit our throats and toss us to the pigs. Then where would Rahkki be?"

I'Lenna sagged into her chair. It had never occurred to her that Brauk and Darthan had been protecting Rahkki. "You did the right thing then," she said.

Brauk cut his eyes away as tension eased from the hut. "I don't need your pardon, I'Lenna, or anyone's."

She bit the inside of her cheek. Convincing Brauk to help her was going to be more difficult than she'd imagined—unless she revealed the fact that Lilliam was stealing clan tithes. She'd told General Tsun, and that's why he'd broken his oath to his monarch. Now she'd have to tell the Stormrunners—but if they knew the truth, would they be content to banish her mother, or would they seek to destroy her? She sighed. She wasn't ready to tell them, not yet.

Brauk continued. "Nothing we do will bring my mother back," he said.

"Then consider the elixir a gift," I'Lenna offered. "If you decide to help me, I'll be grateful. If you don't, at least you'll be healthy again. But either way, you won't *owe* me. I'll never ask you for a favor. I promise."

Brauk studied the princess, then nodded. "Okay, I'll drink it." He pulled the stopper out of the vial and tossed back the venom in one greedy gulp.

A long moment passed. "I don't feel anything," he said. Ossi crossed the room to hold his hand.

"Don't," I'Lenna warned. "Once it starts, I'm not sure how he'll react."

Ossi paused, studying Brauk and feeling his forehead. She peered back at I'Lenna, confused. "I thought the elixir worked fast."

Just then Brauk's torso flattened out and he began to shake. His arm flailed, striking Ossi, and Mut snatched his sister away.

"Oh, I think it's working now," Ossi cried.

As quickly as they had started, Brauk's convulsions ceased. His body suddenly stilled. His eyelids closed and he relaxed, looking asleep.

"What happened?" Mut asked as Ossi struggled in his arms.

"He's fainted," I'Lenna said, stifling a deep yawn. "The venom is healing him, but it's not immediate. Now we wait."

Darthan stoked the fire and replaced Brauk's blanket across his body. "You need to sleep," he said to I'Lenna. "We should all get some rest."

Ossi pulled a chair up to Brauk's cot. "I'm staying awake."

Darthan retreated to his room and returned with an armload of furs and blankets. "We'll take turns watching him. Here." He handed out the coverings and each person made up a bed on a chair or on the floor. I'Lenna spread a wool blanket by the window. Peering outside, she saw the wild herd huddled beneath a cluster of gigantic palms in Darthan's field. Kol stood off by himself.

As she collapsed onto the blanket, she remembered what Mut had told her about the trading post. "Darthan?" she asked. "Do you know why a Daakuran trader or merchant would be looking for Rahkki? Mut said a man was asking questions at the trading post."

"That's right," Mut said. "He was in Willa Green's tent, talking to her, and I thought it was strange. It's not like Rahkki is known outside of the Fifth Clan. He's just a kid."

I'Lenna smirked because Mut was also "just a kid."

Darthan drew on his pipe and when he spoke, soft sweet smoke rolled out with his words. "Maybe this man has news of his mother," he offered. "I was in Daakur recently, walking the docks and asking questions about Reyella."

Mut frowned. "Maybe, but I didn't hear her name and

the man didn't leave any kind of message. Just wanted to know where to find Rahkki."

I'Lenna interrupted. "I think he's a collector and wants another Kihlara ceremonial blanket, like the one Rahkki sold Willa."

Darthan tapped his pipe. "That makes sense. Ceremonial blankets of that quality are rare on either shore." His creased face looked sad in the firelight. "It's strange, but probably nothing to worry about."

I'Lenna nodded, but unease soured her gut. Something about this man searching for Rahkki bothered her. And she worried that even if she saved Rahkki from the giants, more trouble could be lurking.

∽ 11 ∾

A WAY HOME

"*WATCH ME,*" MIAH SIGNED AFTER CATCHING Rahkki's attention with a gentle roar.

He waved at her from his position on the bamboo bridge. Four days had passed since the rains began and the Great Cave Horde envoy had arrived. Rahkki had expected the horde meeting to take place immediately, but the giants had a long agenda of ceremonial activities planned first.

The heavy rains had continued and kept the hordes corralled underground and, all over the warren, tempers flared among the giants. Rahkki's skin crawled with impatience. He had no way of knowing if Tuni's Flier was still healing or had succumbed to her wounds, and he was worried about I'Lenna. Who had control of the Fifth—his best friend or her mother?

With his frustration mounting, Rahkki watched the Gorlish children play a game called Blast, a favorite of the giants. It involved charging through the warren and kicking a ball that was really a white mass of dried rubberwood sap. The object of Blast was to count the number of ricochets before the ball hit the floor or sank into a rivulet of lava. The giants played in teams and the team with the most ricochets after three rounds was the winner. Rahkki leaned against the bamboo bridge and tried to stay out of the way.

"*Play with us,*" Drake signed.

Rahkki gaped up at the teen. "*Me?*"

Drake grabbed Rahkki's arm and dragged him across the bridge. Rahkki had abandoned his cast and crutch the day before. He attributed his rapid recovery to the soup. He felt stronger, healthier, and even taller since he'd begun eating it. His ankle still felt a bit weak, but it carried his weight.

"*You're on my team,*" Drake gestured, using Rahkki's Gorlish name, a shrug and helpless hands.

A player on the other team ratcheted back his leg and drove it into the sticky spiral. The ball winged across the cavern, slammed into the stone, bounced off, and careened into three more walls before it landed.

Everyone raced toward it, roaring and shoving, including Miah. She never reached the ball first, every single player could outrun her, but that never stopped her from trying.

Drake reached the ball, kicked, and it zoomed toward Rahkki.

The opposing team galloped to intercept it. Rahkki dodged between their thick legs like a rabbit. "Don't step on me!" he shouted in Sandwen, but the cavern was so full of growls and snarls that no one heard him.

The ball spiraled over the river of lava and struck the opposite wall, hitting at a crazy angle. There was no predicting where it would land.

But it never hit the ground. A very bored saber cat that had traveled to the warren with the Great Cave envoy had been watching them. Now it leaped off its rock ledge, caught the ball in its jaws, and landed facing the charging giants.

They skidded to a halt.

With a threatening growl, it walked away with its prize and the game was over.

The teams sat to collect their breath and Miah

inspected Rahkki's ankle.

"*I'm okay,*" he signed. Then Tak, who'd been perched on a stalagmite watching the game, swooped down and landed on Rahkki's shoulder.

As they all wiped their sweating faces, Rahkki thought of home. His friends and family probably believed he was dead, drowned in the soup. They would never guess he was living underground and playing Blast with kids the size of trees.

As Rahkki drank goat milk from Miah's waterskin, the sharp whistling of reed pipes breezed through the warren.

"*It's time for the horde meeting,*" Drake signed, standing up.

"*Finally,*" Rahkki gestured.

As the group made their way back toward the main cavern, Rahkki studied the walkways, trying to map the warren in his head. He didn't recognize this path that Drake had chosen. Bright blue and red veins ran through the rocks and sparkling crystals had sprouted from fissures in the stone. Tak soared overhead, shooting white flames at insects, sizzling them in midair and swallowing them.

They rounded a bend and Rahkki gasped. Before him

was a vast, sunlit cavern. The sunlight filtered through a gash in the crust high above their heads and was dimmed by the clouds. From this gash, a waterfall also poured into the cavern and splashed into a wide blue river that flowed below.

Rahkki couldn't remember the last time he'd bathed. His body was sticky and sweat matted his hair, making his scalp itch something awful. If Prince Daanath kept his promise and took Rahkki home after the meeting, he wanted to be clean.

"*I wash up,*" he signed, pointing at the water. "*I'll be quick.*"

The four young giants stared at him as if they hadn't understood.

Rahkki ripped off his tunic and dived in. His head cut the water first, then the rest of him sliced through like an arrow. He dived deep and swam somersaults. The cold water soothed the aches and bruises he'd acquired from living with giants. Dirt lifted from his hair.

He kicked to the surface, laughing, ready to invite the giants to join him, but they were screaming in alarm. Miah was bawling.

"What's wrong?" he forgot himself and spoke in Sandwen.

Krell snarled at him, his blue eyes squinting hard. *"Get out of the water,"* he signed.

"Get out," Miah gestured, her eyes round with terror.

Panic bloomed. What was in the water? Rahkki kicked hard toward the channel's ledge.

Krell reached down and Rahkki lunged for his hand. Something slithered past, touching his belly. He yelped and Miah cried harder. Krell about ripped Rahkki's arm off as he dragged the boy out of the water and tossed him onto the rocks.

Rahkki inspected his skin for bites or leeches. *"What's in there?"* he asked. *"Why did you pull me out?"* He slid on his tunic, his body shaking.

"It's deep," Miah gestured, squeezing Rahkki to her chest. *"You could have drowned."*

Rahkki chuckled, relieved. *"No,"* he assured. *"I can swim."*

Miah peered at him doubtfully. *"It's very deep,"* she insisted.

"Doesn't matter," Rahkki gestured. *"I can swim in the ocean if I want."*

Miah's eyes popped, and she shook her head. She didn't believe him.

Drake shook his head too, glancing fearfully at the

river, and Rahkki remembered something his brother had once told him: Gorlanders were terrible swimmers. But he hadn't realized they couldn't swim *at all*.

Rahkki's mind seized on that: *giants can't swim—but I can!* When he was in the river, he'd spied more natural daylight downstream. It was possibly an exit, a way out. A way home!

Rahkki grinned. If the giants had lied about escorting him safely home after the meeting, he now knew how to escape the warren—and no giant could follow him or stop him. He'd swim out.

Drake led Rahkki and his siblings into the largest of the underground caverns. It housed their soup cauldron and served as their communal gathering place. The three princes from each horde sat cross-legged on the grimy stone floor, waiting for the Fire king. The Highland envoy and the Great Cave envoy squatted behind their respective princes, and most of Fire Horde's giants filled the empty spaces. The cavern had grown steamy with hot breath and bubbling soup.

Rahkki followed Miah toward the back of the chamber. She chuffed and gently shoved him toward her sire. *"You sit with the princes."*

Rahkki's heart sped as he approached the thick-bodied leaders. They filled the room like planets and their horde-mates orbited them like moons. Daanath, the Highland prince, slapped the rock floor, indicating that Rahkki should sit beside him. His half wreath of elephant tusks rattled around his neck. The python's arched bite still showed as divots in his flesh.

Rahkki folded onto the stone and stared up at the three Gorlan leaders. Their faces had pulled into dark scowls; their eyes had narrowed with focus. This meeting was about his clan, and Rahkki was the sole representative of his people. He sat taller and stilled his breathing. *Don't mess this up*, he thought.

The Fire king arrived to observe the meeting, but the Gorlan princes would conduct it. When the room had settled, the Great Cave prince gestured to Rahkki. "*We want our land back.*" This prince was the largest of the three. A thick, jagged scar ran from his temple, across one eye, and ended at his lower jaw. He curled his lip, fully revealing chipped, yellowed tusks. The Great Cave giants were aloof and were believed to be the most aggressive of the three hordes.

"*I know,*" Rahkki signed, not sure what else to say.

The giant snorted and shifted his eyes to the Highland prince. *"How is this boy supposed to help us?"* he signed with a snarl.

Prince Daanath turned to Rahkki. *"Your queen refused our soup at the parlay. Why?"*

Rahkki's mouth opened and closed. How could he speak for Lilliam? He wasn't one of her advisers. But with all three hordes staring at him, he had to say something. He signed the truth, as best he could. *"Our queen—she can't speak Gorlish. She's uneducated."*

The princes grunted, becoming angry. They gestured to one another.

"My people want peace," Rahkki assured them quickly.

Prince Daanath nodded. *"What does your clan want in exchange for the land?"*

What did Lilliam want most? Rahkki wondered and the answer came easily; Lilliam loved wealth. *"Our queen will sell the land for gems and furs, maybe a few elephants."* Rahkki had no authority to bargain—but he believed Lilliam would sell her children for the right price.

The Fire Horde prince shook his head at Daanath, signing angrily. *"Why should we have to pay for our own land? Why should we trade anything?"*

Around the cavern, giants snarled agreement.

The Great Cave prince added his opinion. *"I agree. Why bargain when we can take our land back by force? We're wasting time talking to this small one. It is time for the hordes to unite."*

Daanath fingered the healing python wound on his neck and then gestured, *"This boy is powerful. He saved my life and saved many giants on the battlefield. His people fear him."* He turned to Rahkki. *"You can make peace for us?"*

Rahkki's gut puddled toward the stone floor. *"I—I don't know."* His heart raced faster. The queen might accept riches, but what if she didn't? *"What if I can't?"*

"Then we'll destroy you," the Fire prince signed, plunging his fist to the floor.

Rahkki stood. *"That's not a negotiation, that's a threat."*

The entire cavern of giants growled at Rahkki, pointing at his legs.

He glanced at Miah.

"Sit," she signed to him, her face aghast. *"No one stands up at a meeting."*

Rahkki plopped back down and the chamber calmed.

He implored the princes. *"If we fight, many will die,"* he signed, his expression flat with truth. *"And I won't help you. I won't wake your dead this time."*

Eerie quiet fell upon the giants. Rahkki wiped his wet hair off his forehead, noticing how long it had grown since his capture. His legs had outgrown his trousers too, leaving his ankles exposed; and more often when he spoke, his voice cracked. It was the soup; it was making him grow up faster.

Focus, he thought.

The Great Cave prince tugged on his fanged wreath necklace. *"The small one can't help us."*

The Fire prince agreed. *"His queen refused our soup. She can't be trusted even if he can."* He turned his cold eyes on Rahkki, but gestured to the others. *"With the hordes working together, we can end the thousand-year war and destroy his people. That land is ours."*

Panic flooded Rahkki's thoughts. What would his mother do? She would not accept this. She would find a way to strike a bargain.

He dug into his thoughts, grasping at ideas. Queen Lilliam would not give up the land for anything less than a fortune, but the giants were unwilling to give it; nor did

they trust her. But what if the giants didn't have to negotiate with *Lilliam*? What did Rahkki's clan need more
than riches? A new queen! An excited chill rolled through
him. He smiled a Gorlish smile, flashing his tiny canines.
"Fight my queen, not my people."

The three princes frowned, but watched Rahkki's
hands with interest as he spoke. The cavern erupted with
hoots and snarls.

When the hordes had quieted, Rahkki continued. *"Half
my clan is against her and they'll help you, the rest will
surrender. I will choose a new queen and she will give your
land back in return."* The new queen would be I'Lenna,
and Rahkki knew she'd happily consign the fallows to the
giants.

The three Gorlan princes conferred, huddling in a circle. Then the Highland prince loomed toward him, blowing
his hot breath on Rahkki's face. *"This plan is good,"* he
signed.

Rahkki swallowed, his scalp tingled. He was making
a pact—with giants!

The Highland prince summarized. *"Our three Gorlan
armies will uproot your queen and you'll give us our lowland fields."*

"*Yes. A new queen for your farmland. It is good.*" Excitement coursed through him—three Gorlan armies at his disposal! He could finish what I'Lenna had started and free the Fifth Clan from Harak Nightseer and Lilliam Whitehall.

But the Gorlanders growled at him. "*It is not farmland,*" the Highland Prince gestured.

"Oh," Rahkki replied in Sandwen. For a thousand years his clan had been battling the giants for the lowland valley, but if it wasn't farmland, then what was it? "*Not farmland?*" he asked.

The massive Fire Horde king, who had hung back to let the princes conduct the meeting, now stood. His gray-streaked red hair and beard hung past his shoulders, his muscles striped his chest and arms, and his face had sunk into a permanent scowl. He stamped toward Rahkki, shaking the floor, and planted his wide bare feet on either side of the boy. *Apparently the king can stand at a meeting,* Rahkki thought churlishly.

"*It is sacred land,*" the king explained. "*It's where the father of all giants—King Lazrah—made the first soup. It is where his three sons took their portions and formed the three hordes.*"

Chills rushed down Rahkki's spine. "*Sacred land?*" he

signed, surprised he'd never heard this story.

"*Ancient, sacred land,*" affirmed the Highland prince.

"By Granak," Rahkki whispered, paling. No wonder the giants had fought so long and so hard for that land. "*We didn't know,*" he signed.

"*You didn't ask,*" the king gestured. "*You took.*"

Rahkki dipped his head to the king and the three princes. "*I'm sorry.*" The words felt small. He wondered how the giants had felt all these years when they raided the Fifth and saw Sandwens trampling over their special place?

The Gorlan princes nodded approval. "*We'll seal this bargain over soup tonight, and gather the three armies tomorrow. When the rains cease, we'll go.*"

The giants within the underground cavern burst into delighted chuffs and happy fist slamming. As the noise filled his ears, Rahkki relaxed. He'd accomplished his mother's dream. He'd struck a deal with the hordes, proving they could be reasonable. And with three Gorlan armies at his command, he could banish Lilliam, free I'Lenna, and finish the rebellion his best friend had started.

All he had to do was eat the soup, and there was no chance of him blowing that honor.

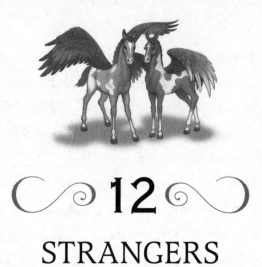

12

STRANGERS

ECHOFROST PACED OUTSIDE DARTHAN'S HUT, churning up mud with her hooves. Storm Herd surrounded her, huddling beneath their sopping feathers. It had rained hard all night, and now, as the rising sun pressed out the darkness, a heavy drizzle soaked the pegasi.

"We're here to help them," Graystone nickered. "So what are the Landwalkers waiting for?"

She flung the water droplets off her forelock. "They're plotting something," Echofrost said, hoping this was true. Rahkki's friends and family would rescue him; it was just a matter of when.

Windheart and Thornblaze cantered past, playing chase. Their long, clumsy legs stabbed the grass like sticks. "The night's rest did them good," Hazelwind said to Dewberry.

The pinto's eyes rarely left her foals. "It's odd that this is their homeland," she nickered. "My twins will never know Anok."

Fear bloomed in Echofrost's heart at her words. Storm Herd could not let their descendants forget Anok like the Kihlari had. "We'll teach them our legends and stories," she said, and wished that her friend Morningleaf had crossed the Dark Water with them. The chestnut mare had memorized every legend ever told. "Thornblaze and Windheart will remember Anok through us."

Dewberry blinked at her, her thoughts storming across her face. "But Anok will always be just a legend to them—a story told by elders. They won't graze in Dawn Meadow or sleep beneath the grandmother tree. They'll never swim in Feather Lake like their sire did. They won't meet Star or understand what he's done to try and save us."

Echofrost drew her wing across Dewberry's back. "It's okay, we'll make new legends here. Look, your foals are happy. They don't know anything else."

The mares locked eyes, each struck by the enormity and ramifications of their mission.

"You'll feel better once we locate a territory of our

own," Echofrost nickered. She tossed a meaningful look at Hazelwind and he nodded his understanding. The sooner they settled the new mother, the better. For all her ferocious bluster, protecting her twins had made Dewberry anxious.

A moaning sound emerged from Darthan's open window. "What's going on in there?" Hazelwind wondered.

Kol, who had spent the night by himself, glided across the grass and landed near the hut. "That's Brauk's voice," he nickered, swishing his tangled tail. "Something's wrong." He trotted onto the porch and peered through the window.

Brauk's moaning woke I'Lenna from a nightmare, and she sat up, panting. Ossi met her gaze. "Brauk's in pain," she said, her face haggard. "I thought the elixir would heal him."

"It will," I'Lenna assured her. "I mean, it is." She threw off her blankets and went to Brauk's cot. He was twisting, rolling from side to side. Ossi and Mut tried to hold him still.

"Let him move around," I'Lenna said.

They ignored her. I'Lenna glanced at Darthan. He sat

near, holding a wet rag in his hand. Tam fed the hearth fire, trying to keep busy.

"Brauk was feverish last night," Darthan said.

"That's good," I'Lenna replied, but in truth, she had no idea how the medicine worked, or if it was working. Had the potency worn off? How old was the dose? I'Lenna thought back, remembering that Lilliam had bought it from the Fourth Clan six years ago after a rare, success- ful black magna hunt.

Before that, the Fifth was without the Queen's Elixir. Reyella had given her dose to a wounded Rider, against everyone's advice, but that was Reyella—the unselfish queen. I'Lenna had never heard of the medicine going bad, but what if it had? If Brauk died— She shut her eyes. If Brauk died, the Stormrunners would blame *her*.

Brauk slid off the cot and thudded onto the wood floor. He began to shout, "I'm on fire!" His hands flew to his injured spine and rubbed it furiously. "Put me out! Fetch water!"

"You're not on fire," Ossi promised, squeezing his hand.

Brauk calmed and a few minutes later began to shiver. Darthan fetched a wool blanket and covered him up to his neck.

"I don't like this," Ossi said, her lips tight.

"Don't worry," Darthan assured. "Brauk's going to be fine, better than fine." But Darthan appeared as nervous as she. To settle himself, he made tea and served them, handing I'Lenna a special concoction. "Ginger tea for the pain." He nodded toward her splinted thumb.

They all sat and waited as the sun rose behind the clouds, lightening the sky from black to gray.

By the time Darthan's morning fire had burned low, Brauk's eyelids fluttered open.

"He's awake," Mut cried.

Brauk blinked and glanced around. He noticed Ossi's tear-stained face. "Hey," he croaked.

"Hey," she whispered, smoothing his long dark hair. "How are you feeling?"

"Alive."

"Can you stand?" Mut asked.

I'Lenna held her breath as Rahkki's brother tugged the wool blanket off his legs, rolled onto his hands, and pushed. His legs bent and then straightened. Soon he was standing, wobbling on two legs. Brauk's eyes grew wide and full of wonder, reminding her again of Rahkki. He took a few steps and then broke into a silent sob. "I can walk," he whispered.

Everyone in the room wept with him, except I'Lenna. It was relief that rushed through her, then desolation. She'd done it; she'd healed Brauk, but now what? He hadn't agreed to help her take over the clan, and without support, she couldn't stay with the Fifth any longer. Harak thought she was dead and the rebels who'd once supported her were locked in the Eighth Tower. There was no one left to hide or protect her from her mother.

I'Lenna would have to leave the clan, today. But with no coin, no friends, and no family, she didn't know what to do next, or where to go, or who would save Rahkki. She'd even lost Firo. Her precious winged braya had rejoined her wild herd. I'Lenna clenched her fists in frustration.

Meanwhile, Brauk tottered around the hut. He tried to swoop Ossi into his arms and almost fell.

"You're not ready for that," she teased, thwacking him on the shoulder.

"I'm weak, but I'm walking," Brauk chirped. He stumbled outside and called for his Flier. "Kol, look at me!"

A smile tugged at I'Lenna's lips. By healing Brauk, she'd done at least one thing right.

Brauk exited the hut and they all followed him outside. Kol pranced with pleasure at the sight of his Rider back on his feet. Firo and the wild steeds flicked their ears in surprise. The morning drizzle soaked Brauk, but he didn't care. He stumbled into a weak jig. "There's no pain, my back is fine! I'Lenna, I could kiss you!"

I'Lenna grinned, but her response was cut short when a stranger emerged from the jungle, startling everyone. Darthan quickly grabbed his sword from the porch and pointed it at the blond man who was dressed in Daakuran clothing. The wild Kihlari surged toward the stranger who had snuck up on all of them.

"Come no closer," Darthan warned.

"Ay," the stranger called, showing his empty hands. "I come in peace. Is this the Stormrunner farm?"

Darthan kept his sword raised. "Who's asking?"

"Name's Tully." He paused. "I've come a long way. I'm looking for Rahkki Stormrunner."

"That's the man I saw at the trading post," Mut whispered.

Darthan exhaled, annoyed, and lowered his sword a hand's breadth. "You've wasted your time, Tully. I've got no Kihlara blankets to sell you."

Tully? I'Lenna had heard that name before. Her mind searched for when.

"I'm not here to buy," the man replied. He reached into his satchel.

In a flash, Darthan was off the porch and beside him, his sword aimed at the man's throat. "Slow down, stranger."

"Is Rahkki here?" the man asked.

Darthan studied him. "What do you want with Rahkki?"

"I have something that belongs to him." The Daakuran man reached into his bag again, more slowly this time, and Darthan allowed it. He drew out a dusk-blue Kihlara blanket. It was one of a kind, trimmed with rabbit fur and tiny bells, and encrusted with gems. With it, Tully displayed a receipt. "I saw this for sale in Daakur and recognized the seller's name." He read the signature on the certificate of authentication. "Rahkki Stormrunner, son of Reyella Stormrunner, bloodborn prince of the Fifth Clan."

Brauk's jaw dropped. "That's the blanket Rahkki sold at the trading post for export to Daakur. It belonged to our mother's stallion, Drael. I never thought we'd see it in the Realm again."

I'Lenna also recognized the beautiful artifact. She'd helped Rahkki negotiate its sale, and she knew how painful it had been for him to give up one of his mother's last possessions.

Darthan worked his jaw, confused and suspicious. "You didn't buy that blanket and then travel all this way to return it, did you? What's your business with my nephew?"

Tully smiled. "It's not my business. It's hers."

Two more figures stepped out of the jungle's shadows—a small girl aboard a winged stallion and another man, each dressed in Daakuran clothing. Brauk, Mut, Tam, and Ossi drew their daggers. Darthan dropped into a fighting stance.

The female removed her helmet. Raven-black hair tumbled around her small face, but it was her dark-lashed golden eyes that arrested everyone. "I'm Feylah Storm-runner," she said. "I'm Rahkki's sister."

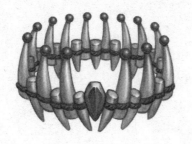

13

QUEEN OF THE FIFTH

SILENCE WASHED OVER THE GROUP AS THEY gaped, slackjawed, at Rahkki's sister and her winged mount.

The golden-eyed child peered at Darthan. "Are you Darthan Stormrunner?" Her eyes slid toward the wild herd that stood behind him and a flicker of appreciation zipped across her otherwise guarded expression. "Are you my uncle?"

Darthan nodded. His sword tipped toward the ground.

Brauk stared at the girl and her steed, blinking in disbelief. His body swayed unsteadily and he leaned against the porch rail to take the weight off his weak legs and newly healed spine.

Ossi, Mut, and Tam sank to their knees. "My queen," they each intoned.

I'Lenna's heart thumped painfully. The existence of Feylah Stormrunner changed *everything*. I'Lenna wanted to laugh and cry and scream. Her mother had lied!

Pregnant Reyella *had* escaped the Realm and birthed an heir. The presence of this girl on Sandwen soil dissolved Lilliam's authority like water on a fire, turning it to smoke. The status of the entire Whitehall family had just evaporated. I'Lenna wasn't a princess—had *never* been a princess! She was a fraud. Her luxurious clothing, the costly gifts she'd received, her expensive education, and her trips to Daakur—none of it belonged to her! All of it belonged to Feylah.

I'Lenna knelt before the girl and her winged stallion, clenching her fists. Her knuckles turned white. "My queen," she said.

Feylah regarded her, and all of them, with silent curiosity. She wore thick boots and creased leather breeches, and she twirled her sword like a soldier. A second man, also blond haired and bearded, rode beside her. He was mounted on a white land horse and he held the reins of a matching steed, which had to be Tully's mount.

"This is Thaan," Feylah said, introducing him. "And you've met Tully. They're brothers and my guardians."

So many questions filled the space between Feylah and her family—too many. Darthan's eyes moved to the obvious first, the winged bay stallion Feylah rode. The Kihlara's dark-amber feathers shimmered even on this foggy morning. "That's Drael," he said.

"Yes," Feylah answered. "This is my mother's stallion."

Drael had been presumed dead all these years and tears streamed down Darthan's cheeks at the sight of him. He had once owned Drael's twin brother, a stallion named Tor, but Tor had died of a heart attack. And Brauk had insisted that black magna spiders had killed Drael the night Lilliam stole the Fifth Clan throne. The sight of Reyella's unborn child and precious stallion now, still alive, took everyone's breath away. I'Lenna wondered if Reyella had also survived, but this was a question no one seemed in a hurry to ask.

Darthan collected himself and clapped his hand on Brauk's shoulder. "This is your brother," he said to Feylah. "This is Brauk."

Brauk, who had been rendered speechless, darted his eyes repeatedly across Feylah's face.

His sister slid off her stallion and dropped her reins. She and Brauk walked slowly toward each other. Feylah's long dark hair, golden eyes, and athletic build matched Brauk like she was his smaller shadow.

The drizzle and fog had lifted somewhat, leaving mottled clouds gathering overhead. Farther north, the sky crackled and white light streaked toward the Dark Water ocean. Brauk spoke. "Our mother's Borla predicted she would not birth a daughter while she was the sitting queen. I didn't know you existed."

Feylah nodded her understanding. "Reyella was *not* the sitting queen when I was born."

Brauk clutched her arm. "Feylah," he rasped. "If I *had* known you existed, I would have torn apart the planet to find you."

The girl's collected expression began to crack.

Brauk swept her into his arms and squeezed her tight. "My sister," he whispered, and he held her until she melted into him. "Sun and stars, you're our mother through and through."

Feylah hid her face in the crook of his arm and they held each other for a long while. Darthan wiped tears off his face, and Ossi grinned, looking as pleased as a hen. Mut and Tam whispered to each other, smiling and gawking. I'Lenna wished Rahkki were here to see that the sacrifice he'd made when he sold his mother's Kihlara blanket had purchased something far more precious than battle armor—it had produced a sister!

Brauk loosed Feylah. The girl's lips had softened and her golden eyes shone raw. She drew a breath and exhaled. "I'm here now."

"Where is our mother?" Brauk finally asked, and everyone braced for the answer.

Feylah's eyes darkened with grief. "She died in Daakur, soon after I was born."

Brauk's weak legs threatened to buckle. Darthan moved closer and circled one arm around his nephew. Mut, Tam, and Ossi murmured to one another.

Feylah blinked hard, ferociously gathering her emotions, and I'Lenna's guilt gutted her. Because of her grandmother's greed and Lilliam's treachery, the Stormrunner children had been separated and raised without their mother.

Darthan wiped his face and replaced his sword. "Let's talk inside where it's dry and warm," he said. "I imagine you're hungry. You can put the horses in the barn."

While Thaan and Tully led the white horses to the barn, Feylah unsaddled Drael and turned him loose. "You have quite a herd of Kihlari," she commented, eyeing the wild herd's wiry bodies and fierce expressions. "They won't hurt Drael, will they?"

Brauk shrugged. "I don't think so, but they don't belong to us. They're wild. Come in and we'll exchange stories."

Inside the hut, everyone settled onto chairs or sat on furs while Darthan stoked his hearth fire and threw sliced bacon into a pan.

Thaan and Tully returned from the barn and I'Lenna suddenly remembered how she knew their names. Her mother had spoken of these two men over the years; they were guards who'd betrayed her. "You're Second Clan soldiers," she said. "You worked for my mother."

"What!" Brauk lunged for his dagger.

Feylah lifted one small hand. "Stand down," she said calmly. "Thaan and Tully turned against Lilliam long ago."

I'Lenna and Ossi exchanged a glance, and I'Lenna wondered what sort of upbringing had produced such a collected and authoritative child—or had Feylah simply inherited her mother's personality? It was said that

Reyella the Pantheress—who'd become queen at age thirteen—had worn her authority like a second skin. Feylah, who was almost nine, already carried herself like a monarch.

Feylah then came to a realization of her own. "You said my guardians worked for your mother. Are you a Whitehall?" she asked, looking directly at I'Lenna.

Darthan moved protectively closer. "I'Lenna is on our side," he assured.

Before he could say more, Brauk interjected. "What happened the night our mom escaped? Can you tell us?"

As Feylah accepted a cup of tea from Darthan, she exhaled. "I'Lenna is correct. Thaan and Tully were once Lilliam's private guards," she began. "On that . . . that awful night Lilliam tried to assassinate our mother, she assigned them to hunt Reyella down after she escaped the fortress. Thaan and Tully were brand-new soldiers at that time and very young, sixteen and seventeen years old. They caught Reyella." Feylah's voice tightened. Thaan dropped his eyes and Brauk gritted his teeth.

"I'll tell the story," Tully murmured. "We got into the woods, and yeah, we caught Reyella but only because she was wounded. Lilliam had stabbed her."

I'Lenna gasped and dared not look at anyone.

Tully continued. "But we couldn't, you know, finish her off." His eyes flicked to Brauk's. "Your mum was heavily pregnant and as angry as a tiger, and she was—I don't know how to describe it—she was convincing. She commanded us to help her." Tully and Thaan exchanged a smile. "There was no way to say no to her."

Darthan nodded and fresh tears washed his face. "That's right, that's Reyella."

"So we changed course and helped her look for her sons and her stallion. We never found you boys, but we found Drael. The spiders had wrapped him up and injected their venom, which healed his injuries. I slipped in and—whack—cut him free." Tully made a slicing motion with his hand.

"By then, Reyella was drifting in and out of wakefulness and she'd lost some blood. We were losing her," Thaan interjected. "We put her on Drael's back and the stallion swam all of us across Cinder Bay. I was going to stay back so he could fly just the two of them, but Reyella wouldn't allow it. Said Lilliam would kill me for failing. And she would have."

I'Lenna's cheeks blazed hotter. By Granak, her mother had done terrible things.

Tully finished the story. "We reached the docks, bought two horses, and rode to our grandparents' farm in Northern Aryndale. Feylah was born there but we couldn't save her mother. We raised Feylah in the Sandwen ways and taught her to fight." Tully's fatherly pride looked almost comical on his youthful face. "We did the best we could with the little mite."

Feylah grinned, her affection for her guardians obvious, and I'Lenna gained new understanding of Rahkki's sister. She'd been raised alone by two young soldiers and trained to fight; no wonder she seemed so much older than her years.

Brauk addressed the brothers, his jaw muscles fluttering. "We owe you our thanks."

"You owe us nothing," Tully replied, leaning back. "We did what we thought was right."

Feylah fingered the precious Kihlara blanket they'd brought with them and continued. "When Tully saw the receipt attached to this blanket at a shop in Daakur, he stole it and brought it home to me. That's how I learned that at least one of my brothers had survived. I knew it was time to come home."

Her words seemed to pierce Brauk, and he groaned. For the past eight years, he'd denied the possibility that

Reyella had survived. Now his voice cracked. "I'm sorry I didn't look for you," he said, and his breaths quickened. "I watched Lilliam stab our mother in the back, and then I watched Drael die, at least I thought I did. And Darthan saw Lilliam burn a body on Reyella's funeral pyre. Even my mother's crown was destroyed. I've been trying to forget *all of it*."

Feylah touched his arm. "We're together now," she said. "And look." She opened another carrying bag and lifted out an ancient crown.

Darthan rose from his chair, excitement shining on his weathered face. "That's Reyella's, that's the original. Lilliam claimed she burned it with the body."

The girl smiled, looking suddenly shy. "Lilliam probably said that to hide the fact she didn't have it. Reyella took it with her that night and now it's mine. I'm the Queen of the Fifth and I'm home."

The sad mood in the tent shifted to one of joy. Everyone gathered around Feylah, hugging her and inspecting the dragon-tooth crown. I'Lenna held back. How did she fit into this group now? Truth was, she didn't.

She slipped outside, feeling miserable and alone. Firo nickered to her. She rushed to her winged horse and buried her face in Firo's mane. She began to cry.

A moment later, Brauk stepped onto the porch. "I'Lenna?" he called. "You should come inside and listen to our plans."

"*Our* plans?"

Brauk smiled at her, looking exhausted and awe-struck. "Yes, our plans to save Rahkki. You're going to help us, aren't you?"

She understood he was offering a truce. "But—"

He gave a small shake of his head. "I know I've been hard on you, and I've been hard on Rahkki," he admitted. "I didn't believe anything he told me—not about the wild steeds, not about our mom, and not about you." He inhaled through his nose. "I think it's time I started believing my brother, and he told me to trust you. So come inside, please, and let's figure out how to get him back."

Warmth swept through I'Lenna at the invitation. She walked through Darthan's doorway, crossing not only the grass but also the great divide that had split their two families. Inside the hut, the scent of sizzling bacon and the group's excited conversation blanketed I'Lenna like a warm fur.

Feylah moved aside, allowing I'Lenna room to join the

group. Brauk, who'd sat down to rest his legs, handed her a slice of pineapple, and Mut brought her a chair.

Darthan served a late breakfast and everyone grew silent as they filled their bellies.

Between the friendly conversation, the delicious meal, and the wild Kihlari grazing loose outside, I'Lenna felt like a wanderer who, after a long and arduous journey, had finally arrived home.

14

GUEST

THE HORDE MEETING HAD DISBANDED AND THE bargain Rahkki had struck with the Gorlanders would be sealed over soup that evening. The rains paused for breath and Rahkki's mood soared higher. He tugged on Miah's arm. *"Let's go outside!"*

The entire warren seemed to have the same idea and the pathways filled with thumping feet, padding paws, and tiny hoofbeats as giants, saber cats, and milk goats swarmed toward the stairs. Tak followed and green smoke drifted from his nostrils, leaving hazy tendrils in his wake.

Outside, the horde was in jubilant spirits. Sunrays slid between the branches and speared the muddy soil. The volcanoes belched, spitting steam and rocks, and the jungle canopy overhead screeched to life. Three giants played music on their reed pipes. Some Sandwens believed giants were deaf, but Rahkki could add that to the many myths about giants that were turning out not to be true.

The adults brought up their hands, gesturing in sweeping, graceful motions, and Rahkki realized they were singing. He studied their gestures as the song repeated over and over, memorizing the lyrics:

Neither friend nor foe
Where giants go.
Deep, deep in the jungle keep.
Neither man nor beast
Where giants feast.
Deep, deep in the jungle keep.
Only flowers and sun
Where giants run.
Only soup and play
Where giants slay.
Only sleep and dawn
Where giants yawn.
Deep, deep in the jungle keep.

He sensed the horde pride nestled within the lyrics, and affection for the giants bloomed in Rahkki's heart. He decided to show them his gratitude for healing his ankle. *"Will you take me to the creek?"* he asked Miah.

Drake overheard them. *"I'll go with you."* They struck out upon an animal path that led to a small swatch of water Rahkki had spotted when he first rode into Fire Horde's camp eight days ago. Miah's brothers, Krell and Fallon, also joined them.

On the shoreline, Rahkki found a stiff branch. He borrowed Miah's knife and whittled it into a spear while she played in the mud with Tak. When the stick was sharp enough, Rahkki waded into the flowing creek and waited. Long minutes passed before a silver shape caught his eye. He drove his spear into the back of the fish and hauled it out. The catfish fluttered on the spearhead until it went limp. Triumphant, Rahkki lifted his prize, but suddenly, it burst into flames.

Tak swooped past Rahkki's head and fired the fish twice more, charring it black; then he ripped it off the sharpened stick and glided back to shore, shredding the fish and swallowing the pieces.

"That was mine!" Rahkki muttered.

"Brrur, brrur," the dragon chirped.

Setting his jaw, Rahkki speared another fish. This time he was quick to wrap it in leaves and slide it into his satchel. To flavor his catch, he dug up a few mushrooms. Rahkki returned to the creek's bank, curled next to Miah, who had fallen asleep in a pool of sunshine, and soon drifted off. Tak squeezed between them, humming with contentment.

That evening the giants returned to the warren and gathered in the largest chamber to seal Rahkki's bargain over soup. Messengers had been sent to Highland and Great Cave Horde to assemble their armies and meet at the warren. They would arrive within a few days. Rahkki tried not to resent the delay. He was ready to go home now.

A line formed that led to the cauldron. As was the custom, all the giants who'd collected ingredients during the day marched down the line and tossed whatever they'd gathered into the soup. Everyone contributed, even Miah. And today, as a thank-you to his hosts, so would Rahkki.

He jogged to the end of the line.

One by one, the Gorlanders noticed him standing there.

The boy flashed his little teeth in imitation of them.

After a surprised silence, the giants slammed their fists to the floor. This gesture could demonstrate anger or appreciation, but when coupled with rumbling sounds, it meant the giants were pleased, and Rahkki's heart warmed again. He'd befriended three Gorlan hordes! And with their combined armies and his insider knowledge of the clan, he'd easily defeat Lilliam. Once I'Lenna was settled as queen, he'd sail to Daakur and search for his missing mother.

The line ambled along as each giant tossed in his or her goods. Rahkki's veins pulsed with excitement. His clan appreciated guests who contributed, and so would the Gorlanders.

After the giant in front of him tossed in some green herbs, it was Rahkki's turn. The Gorlanders stilled, watching the boy with wary indulgence. He reached into his bag and pulled out the wild mushrooms.

The giants smacked their lips, looking pleased, and he tossed his offering into the pot. Next he withdrew the wrapped fish.

The giants cocked their heads, trying to see what was tucked between the leaves.

Deciding to show them what a nice fat catfish he'd

speared, Rahkki gripped it by its open jaws and lifted it high over his head.

The Gorlanders' eyes widened. A mother dropped her empty bowl and it clattered to the stone floor. Miah gasped.

It is a nice fish, Rahkki thought. And then he tossed it into the pot.

Chaos erupted. Giants bolted toward Rahkki. Miah covered her ears and began to cry. Drake roared like a Gorlan king, and the rest clutched one another, shrieking as if they were being slaughtered.

Rahkki curled into a ball. *Land to skies, what have I done?*

Three giants grabbed him and began to pull his limbs in opposite directions. Rahkki howled as pain shot through his body.

The Fire Horde king stomped his foot so hard everyone froze. The giants dropped Rahkki and backed away, flashing their tusks.

The king reached his arm into the soup, grimacing at the temperature, and tried to scoop out the fish, but he couldn't reach it. He sat hard on his rear and sobbed.

Wails burst forth from the Fire Horde giants. Tak flew

down from the stalagmites and crawled inside Rahkki's shirt.

"*What happened?*" Rahkki signed. "*What did I do?*"

"*You put an animal in the soup!*" the Fire king answered, tugging at his red hair. "*Thirty-two years at simmer and now our soup is ruined.*" He glared at Rahkki.

"I—I'm sorry," Rahkki sputtered. Then in Gorlish he asked, "*You don't eat fish?*"

"*No.*" The king's face crumpled. "*We don't eat meat.*"

Rahkki gaped at the king. "*But—but, I don't under-stand. You're giants.*" It was a stupid thing to say. He knew it as soon as he signed the words.

"*And giants are beasts, right?*" The king finished. He punctuated his gestures with snarls. "*We know you Sandwens believe we eat your children. We've let you fear us these long years, but it's over. It's time for the giants to show you who we really are.*" The king leaned over Rahkki, his breath whirling Rahkki's hair like the wind. "*We're not dumb, angry beasts, and we're not friends. We were here before you and we'll be here long after you. We are the children of King Lazrah, and we will reclaim our father's land.*" The king turned to command his horde.

Breathing hard, Rahkki scooted out of the way as

ten of the larger giants lifted the Fire Horde cauldron off its base and carried it out of the cavern. Quiet sobs followed and hundreds of clawed fingers reached to touch the beloved pot. When the ten giants returned, the cauldron was empty. The Gorlanders stacked their empty bowls, desolate, deflated, and grief stricken.

Dread oozed through Rahkki's veins and he began to shiver. Everything he'd thought he knew about the giants had turned out to be false. He grunted to Drake. *"But you hunt animals,"* he signed, making a weak attempt to argue.

"For sinews, bones, hides, and to trade," answered Drake. *"Not for eating."*

Rahkki hunched, backing away. *"I didn't know."*

"Again—you didn't ask." Anguish squished the king's face. *"Get up."*

Rahkki stood.

"Take him away." He pointed to the passageway that led to Rahkki's chamber.

Tears sprang to Rahkki's eyes. All the giants had turned their backs to him except Miah and the Fire Horde king. The Gorlan male flashed his tusks. *"Our deal is canceled. You have brought war on your people."* He turned and strode off to console his horde.

Rahkki wilted. How had he made such a mess of things? The song lyrics bubbled in his mind:

Neither man nor beast
Where giants feast.
Deep, deep in the jungle keep.

Was the song a rebuttal against the Realm's image of flesh-eating giants? Neither people nor animals attended a giant feast—*as the main course!* Had he missed such an obvious clue about their culture? Shoulders drooping, he trod down the passageway, trailed by Miah and escorted by two adult Gorlanders. Tak was still inside his shirt, trembling against his skin. The growling had frightened him and Rahkki stroked his smooth golden scales.

Miah's white face had turned pink and her blue eyes shone with unshed tears. She wrung her dress. "*You're in big trouble*," she signed.

When the hordes warred, they attacked one another's cauldrons, tipping them over or spoiling the broth with wood ashes. There was nothing worse to the giants than losing an old soup. "*I'm sorry*," he signed blindly. "*I—I stupid.*"

They passed a stairwell and Rahkki glanced up the

stone stairs to the sky above. Fresh storm clouds had rolled over the jungle, moist and full of static. A deep rumble reverberated through the clouds, followed by a shock of white light. Rain dropped in sheets, like a thousand giants crying. Rahkki wished Sula were there—that she'd swoop down and rescue him.

One of the adult Gorlanders pushed Rahkki to walk faster, and when they reached his chamber, he shoved him inside. "*Stay here,*" the giant signed, and left. Miah retreated to her furs, ignoring him. Rahkki was a real prisoner this time, not a captured guest. He knew from his days in the warren that the giants tracked him by his scent, and their senses were so strong, they always knew where he was. Escape up the stairwells was impossible.

He wiped his face, appalled. He needed to warn his people that the giants were coming so they had time to prepare. He had to go immediately. *I'm as bad as Lilliam,* he thought. *I ruined a chance at peace because I assumed I knew all about the giants, when in fact I knew nothing. I'm not smart like my mother or brave like my brother.*

The blood of the Pantheress runs through you, Uncle Darthan had once said.

Tak flew out of Rahkki's shirt as the boy paced his small cavern. He'd made a mistake, a horrible mistake, but he wasn't giving up on his people, the giants, or himself. He knew how to get out of here; he just needed to find the underground river, but the horde would know the moment he left his chamber. Could he outrun them? No.

Rahkki glanced at Tak. Maybe he could outsmart them.

15

THE CHUTE

GORLANDERS FALL ASLEEP LIKE STONES FALLING off cliffs; they crash onto their fur mattresses from upright positions and are instantly snoring. Rahkki had been fooled his first night in the warren, thinking that giants slept deeply, but in truth they roused faster than fleas. It wasn't noises that drew them out of their dreams—it was smells. Their noses twitched manically all night. If rats infiltrated the warren, the giants knew immediately. If a toddler wandered away, they knew. If Rahkki exited his sleeping quarters, they knew.

But tonight would be different. Rahkki had a plan and an escape route—the underground river. He just had to get there.

Some hours had passed since he'd ruined Fire Horde's soup, and the warren was still awake. Quiet crying and muffled footsteps echoed throughout the passageways. Miah sat silently beside him, hugging a Gorlish doll. When Prince Daanath passed by, holding a lantern full of glow stones, he paused at Rahkki's chamber and grunted for his daughter.

Miah leaped off her bed. *"Da!"*

The prince bent to one knee and she climbed into his arms. They brushed noses and their contented rumbling filled the passageway. *"Sleep safe,"* the prince signed. He pushed her gently off his lap, flashed his tusks at Rahkki, and continued on his way.

Miah shuffled back to her bed and dropped face first onto her furs. Soon after, her loud snores filled the cavern.

While Rahkki waited for the rest of the warren to settle, he played with Tak, wiggling his fingers and enticing the little burner to chase his digits. Tak fluttered and dived, shooting his green, heatless flames at Rahkki's hands. He needed Tak to fall asleep too, so he stood up and circled his arms, causing Tak to zip and zag in crazy loops. As he hoped, the young dragon tired fast. He plowed onto Rahkki's furs and closed his golden eyes. Steam puffed evenly out his nostrils.

Rahkki quickly scanned the cavern, glancing from the burner to the giantess, and was surprised to feel sadness. He would miss them both, but he was also excited. Soon he'd be home!

During his short time with Tak, Rahkki had taught the dragon to deposit his smelly droppings in one pile. Now, he slipped out of bed and lifted a fistful of the dragon dung off the floor. It stank like rotten eggs. *Here goes nothing*, Rahkki thought. He removed his outer tunic and then smeared the dung onto his undershirt, his skin, and his hair. Gagging, he painted it onto his face last.

Next he tucked the outer tunic that still smelled like him beside Miah so that his scent would remain in the chamber. He spotted her wood-handled dagger. He would need it in the jungle. With remorse tugging at his heels, Rahkki stole the dagger and tiptoed out of the chamber.

Miah did not rouse. Tak rolled over and began to hum in his sleep, but neither woke. Rahkki had done it, he'd fooled them, but would his trick work as well on the adult giants?

Letting out his breath, he scampered along the curve of the rocky trail that wound through the underground caverns, trying to remember exactly where he'd spotted the underground river. He passed more sleeping chambers, but the giants didn't stir. He'd masked his Sandwen scent so well in dragon dung that he was invisible.

With glow stones lighting his way, Rahkki reached a stone pathway that was worn smooth from years of use. It split off in three directions. Which way was the river? Rahkki closed his eyes, listening as Uncle had taught him, sending his ears out into the darkness. There it was—the faint trickle of moving water. The middle path was the one he wanted.

Picking up speed, Rahkki followed the walkway that curved up and down like a hunched spine. Long, bat-infested stalagmites hung overhead and shining crystals littered the trail, reflecting a gentle, pink-hued light. Soon, the steady cadence of falling water filled Rahkki's ears.

He reached the edge of the sparkling blue river and enjoyed a huge burst of relief. Pitching forward, he dived into the cool water and kicked hard, swimming with the current. The water had etched away rocky protrusions and stalagmites in the channel, leaving Rahkki a swift smooth aqueduct. He traveled rapidly downriver.

Rounding a bend, the river widened, forming a dark pool. Disoriented, Rahkki surfaced to see bright shapes darting and shooting flames overhead. He'd drifted into the burners' home den. Rahkki watched the tiny dragons dive and spin. Their noisy chortles and squeaks bounced off the wet cavern walls. A larger red-scaled female slept at the mouth of a cave, oblivious to the energetic males— their queen.

Very few Sandwens ever glimpsed a living burner queen. Sharp angles defined her triangular face, yellow spots faded down her back, and four poisonous white barbs spiked the end of her tail. Turquoise frills fanned her head and purple webbing lined her wings. She hissed a breath and her scales shimmered as her ribs expanded. A year of rest, followed by five days of mating, marked her life—the cycle repeating annually until she died.

Rahkki ducked silently beneath the water, afraid of what the males would do if they noticed a stranger in their den. Swiftly, he swam back into the main channel.

Coasting faster now, he paddled to align his body with the speeding current, scrambling to grab hold of some- thing, anything, to slow himself. But the rock walls were too smooth.

The channel abruptly dipped and Rahkki was sucked into a narrow chute. His body slid across hard, smooth stone, pushed by the water. The chute curved and bent, bumping Rahkki as he shot through it. The water was shallow, leaving his head and chest in open air. A warm breeze struck him and he smelled the tart mulch of the jungle. He braced, sensing the end.

Then he was airborne.

Rahkki's body shot out of a hole in a cliff wall and he dropped through sheeting rain. Legs churning, arms pinwheeling, mouth screaming—he fell through dark space. One thought pulsed in his brain: *This is going to hurt!*

He dropped into a warm lake. The surface smacked his chest, knocking the wind out of him. He sank fast, his wet clothing dragging him toward the bottom. Since he'd screamed out most of his breath, his lungs burned and a few bubbles burst from his lips. He kicked hard off the bottom of the lake and swam toward the surface.

Almost to the top, his fingers scraped against a massive tree root. Grabbing it, Rahkki heaved and his head broke the surface. He inhaled and fresh air drove down his throat, tasting sweeter than candy. He spluttered onto the beach, sucking greedily.

"Crawwk!"

Rahkki peered up in time to see Tak waft out of the same cliff waterfall that had ejected him. The dragon cartwheeled across the sky, shooting white, blue, then purple flames in terrified jets until his instincts took over. His wings snapped from his sides, gripped the wind, and the agile little dragon righted himself. "Brrur, brrur," he trilled.

"Quiet," Rahkki hushed. To his surprise, it was not evening outside but late morning. He'd forgotten that Fire Horde slept during the day.

The golden dragon homed in on the boy's voice, pinned his wings, and dropped into a swirling dive. Rahkki expected a scolding, but instead Tak landed on his shoulder and threw his wings around Rahkki's neck.

"You thought I left you?" Rahkki hugged him, thinking, *Actually, I did leave you.* "I'm sorry, boy."

Tak's claws curled into Rahkki's skin as he broke into a rumbling purr. Rahkki peered skyward to orient himself. He needed to get moving, but the storm clouds created a thick gray ceiling that obscured the sun. This was monsoon weather, come early to the Realm, and it was not good for Sandwen crops. *Big rain*, the giants had called it.

Using the volcanoes as landmarks, Rahkki determined the path home. If he had more time, he'd travel to Highland Horde and try to free Rizah, but with three Gorlan armies about to march on the Fifth Clan, he couldn't risk failure. He had to warn his people, and now that he knew giants didn't eat meat, he believed Rizah was safe with them. Besides, his ankle felt strong. The Gorlan soup had sped his healing, he was sure of it.

Rahkki felt for the dagger he'd stolen from Miah and found it still in his pocket. He sprinted west. Animals scurried out of his way and deep mud squelched between his toes.

Tak lifted off his shoulder and glided, snatching bugs out of the sky and swallowing them whole. "I guess you're coming with me," Rahkki said, and Tak hovered closer.

As Rahkki jogged through the brush, drawing farther away from the warren, his anxiety eased. It didn't appear any giants were following him. He turned his attention to the jungle. Mindful of boy-eating plants, hiding jaguars, and ambushing serpents, he avoided the shadows and thick foliage.

Rain fell in frantic torrents, keeping Rahkki soaked from head to toe, but he was glad for it. Most of the predators would seek shelter, their senses dimmed by the falling water. Also, it washed the rest of the sticky dragon dung off his body. When a thunderous boom announced a heightened storm, Tak swooped to Rahkki's shoulder and bobbed there, mantling his wings like a raptor.

The pair traveled like this for the rest of the day, and by afternoon, hunger bit at Rahkki's belly and he wondered if he were lost. Every ridge, tree, and animal path looked the same. Why couldn't he find the main trail home?

He paused to stretch and peer at the churning clouds. He belonged up there, on the back of a winged steed, but he'd lost everything: The boy's Flier, his princess, and now his mighty allies—the giants.

Squirming, Tak peeked at Rahkki through the open neck of his shirt. He'd crawled inside for a nap, but now he was hungry too. "Crawk," he screeched, and then he lunged upward and nipped Rahkki's ear.

"Stop biting me."

"Brrur, brrrur!" Tak answered.

"I know you're hungry, so am I." Rahkki stuffed the dragon back down, pulled his collar closed, and resumed his hike with Tak's body pressed against his chest and the jungle hunching over them. Rahkki inhaled, drinking in the conflicting scents that marked the rain forest—rotting leaves and fragrant flowers, dried bones and fresh blood, old bark and soft saplings.

He walked all day until the final glow of sunlight made it too dark to see. "We'll make camp here," he said to Tak, who was sleeping. Rahkki was frustrated that they hadn't reached a Sandwen travelway yet. He leaned against the colorful bark of a rainbow eucalyptus tree and woke Tak by lifting the young dragon out of his shirt and setting him on his shoulder.

Tak stretched his wings and coughed, clearing his lungs and spewing red sparks that sizzled when they met the falling rain. Then, with a forceful shove, the dragon pushed off. Worms had floated out of the saturated soil and Tak dived upon them, cooking them with his breath and swallowing them whole.

Saliva pooled in Rahkki's mouth. The night was too wet to start a fire, so he pounced upon the worms and began shoving them into his mouth. Normally, he enjoyed worms, but after eight days of delicious Gorlan soup, they tasted worse than dirt.

After his snack, Rahkki began stripping broad-leafed branches off the nearest trees and making a shelter. Next, he found a toppled balsa-wood trunk. He wove the branches through a framework of balsa wood and vines, creating a thin ceiling that repelled water. Tak returned and hovered above the tent, a curious glint in his eyes.

With raindrops running down his face, Rahkki

whittled a small spear to hunt larger game—tarantulas. The hairy spiders were big and easy to catch. They liked to hide beneath logs and large stones. Using his stick, Rahkki lifted up small trunks and rocks, moving quickly through the jungle before halting near a large gray boulder.

He rolled the stone just enough to startle out any snakes. When nothing emerged, he shoved the rock over. A thick-bodied, hairy tarantula skittered backward.

Rahkki stabbed, killing the spider instantly. "Yes," he rasped, holding it up. Tak swooped down from the sky. Remembering how his dragon had stolen the first catfish, Rahkki blocked him. "No, Tak!"

The dragon buzzed past, scorching the meal anyway.

"Sun and stars," Rahkki muttered, but then a slow smile etched his cheeks. "Hey, you cooked it!" Tak's fire had burned off all the spider's barb-like body hair. Rahkki tore off the crispy legs and plopped them into his mouth, chewing happily.

Prowling the undergrowth, he hunted and speared six more tarantulas, and Tak cooked those too. They shared the meal and settled beneath the woven leaves, listening to the rain.

Rahkki curled around his dragon, shivering from

being wet all day. Tomorrow, he hoped to find a Sandwen travelway. The wide smooth path would speed his journey home. What mattered was beating the hordes to his territory to prepare his clan for war.

16

THE LETTER

ECHOFROST STUDIED THE NEW STALLION, DRAEL.
He'd said little during the night, only that he'd brought
Rahkki's sister home and that the children's mother was
dead. Echofrost informed him that giants had captured
Rahkki and then Drael had retreated to be alone, but now
his curiosity about the wild steeds swelled. Drael trotted
closer and Storm Herd faced him, wings lifted. Overhead,
the clouds had recollected and darkened, and morning
sunrays poked between them, stabbing the grass.

"Who owns you?" Drael blurted, his eyes skidding
across their unkept hides and landing on the twin foals.
"Why aren't those two safe in the Ruk?"

Dewberry snorted. "Safe?" She stamped her hoof,

glancing furiously at Drael. "We're free pegasi. No one *owns* us." She collected her twins beneath her wings. Windheart and Thornblaze peeked at the stranger through her emerald feathers.

Drael nodded, but didn't seem to comprehend. "Did you escape from another clan?"

Dewberry huffed and Hazelwind intervened, explaining that Storm Herd had fled from their homeland and landed here, believing they'd be safe. He spoke about their capture, the Sandwen uprising, the giants, and Echofrost's Pairing with Rahkki.

Drael gaped at Echofrost. His feathers rattled softly, perhaps angrily. "You're Rahkki's Flier?"

She felt challenged and alarm rang through her muscles. "I am." Storm Herd trotted closer to Echofrost, their wings flared. Her tension had alerted all of them.

Drael seemed to realize his threatening posture. He smoothed his dark-amber feathers and folded his wings. "I belonged to Rahkki's mother, Reyella. I was her Flier." He spoke slowly, with great pride. He cast a look at Dewberry that said, *You will never understand.* And her eyes reflected the exact same sentiment.

After Drael lowered his wings, Storm Herd did the same. "I took Rahkki on his first flight," Drael continued.

"And I thought I took him on his last, but he's alive, you say?"

"He was when we last saw him," Hazelwind corrected. "The giants captured him."

Drael dipped his head and his light eyes glimmered. "I've come home too late."

Echofrost reared back. "You're not too late, you're just in time. We're going to rescue him."

Drael pricked his ears. "How? Kol said the Sandwen queen won't help Rahkki."

"She won't, but his family will, and they have us, and now you and Feylah."

Drael considered this, perplexed. "All of you will fight for Rahkki? I don't understand. If you're . . . free . . . why would you? And how did you become his Flier if you aren't a Sandwen steed?" Drael asked this without rancor.

"He won me in a contest," Echofrost answered. "But Rahkki knows he cannot keep me." Echofrost wasn't sure Rahkki knew this, but she believed he did. He did not command her obedience or lock her in a stall like the other Riders did with their Fliers. He understood that he did not *own* her. "Rahkki led an army to Mount Crim to save Storm Herd," Echofrost explained. "We aren't Sandwen, but Rahkki—he's one of us. We want to help him."

Fresh tears glimmered in Drael's eyes. "My boy was not a warrior when I escaped with Reyella. He slept in my stall and spent half his day staring at clouds." Drael nickered, amused. "Much has changed."

Echofrost nodded, because it was true. Much had changed.

Inside Darthan's hut, breakfast was over and I'Lenna watched Rahkki's sister produce a letter. She handed it to Brauk. "Our mother wrote this."

Brauk stared at it, his dark hair framing his cheeks, his golden eyes bright and unreadable against his black lashes.

Mut, Tam, and Ossi stood as one person. "We'll go check on the wild herd," Ossi said, and they left, giving the Stormrunners their privacy.

I'Lenna rose to join them, but Darthan shook his head. "Stay, I'Lenna."

She didn't want to stay—no good could come from this letter for her. It was like resurrecting a ghost. But there was no malice in Darthan's eyes, so she stayed.

"Our mom wrote it after I was born," Feylah said to Brauk, "right before she died. She instructed Tully to deliver it to Darthan when I turned twelve." Feylah pushed back her dark hair, a gesture that was exactly Brauk. "But when he saw Rahkki's name on that receipt, he knew he couldn't wait for me to turn twelve. Read it," she said.

Brauk handed it back, looking nervous. "Will you?"

"I'll read it," Darthan said, taking the letter. He broke the wax seal, opened the parchment, and paused at the sight of his sister's handwriting.

I'Lenna's breath came faster. The final words of the Pantheress breathed on that piece of yellowed parchment. Would she write about Lilliam—her killer? I'Lenna shivered, imagining Reyella's condemnation and fury spilling from the letter and into Darthan's hut. It would resurrect all the bad feelings that perhaps still bubbled below her truce with Brauk. I'Lenna felt sick. She wanted to say: *Don't read it. Please. Not while I'm here.* But she had no right to say anything.

She glanced at Brauk's flushed face. He seemed eager, heartbroken, and scared all at once.

"Hurry, Uncle," Brauk urged. The waiting was unbearable.

Holding the parchment close to the firelight, Darthan cleared his throat, and began.

My sons,

If you are reading this letter, then you are alive and my soul is singing. If the worst has befallen you, then we are together in the life-after-life, because by this time, I have passed over. And I'm sorry, my sons, to have failed you with such horrific splendor. As weakness shakes my fingers, I implore you to read my words and heed them.

Six days have passed since Lilliam stole my throne, and I am in Daakur. Thaan and Tully are turncoats, loyal to me. Please extend every kindness to them, my protectors. After Lilliam's attack, Thaan and Tully carried me into the jungle, where we searched and searched for you, my children. We found Drael, spun into the silk of those wretched spiders. Tully cut him loose, but you boys were gone. Simply gone.

I will die not knowing where you are or what happened to you. These tears you see on the parchment are caused by fury, bitterness, and desolation. My sons! My beautiful princes! Brauk the Fighter and Rahkki the Clever. I see your faces, your eyes, even now. You remain with me always.

My birthing time has come and gone and in

my arms I hold your bloodborn sister, my heir, the Crown Princess of the Fifth Clan. She is a ferocious golden-eyed babe, my sweet boys, but I am wounded, dying, and as I fall to dust, your sister will rise. I call her Feylah and the people will call her Feylah Stormrunner, Queen of the Fifth.

If you are alive, I know my brother will protect you and ask you not to seek revenge. I know these things as I know my brother. He will raise you to be noble and loyal to the crown, but I am your mother and I offer fresh counsel. Princes, you must fight back! Lilliam of the Second Clan will destroy the Fifth. She is a stringed doll, played by others to do great harm to our clan.

I know not who is controlling her, but I see their hand at work. You must cut the strings. Stand up, my princes, for your clan and for your sister. If your lives were spared in the jungle, then it was for this very purpose—to sit Feylah on my throne and to rid the Fifth Clan of my rival and my assassin, Queen Lilliam!

Heed my command, my princes, and forgive my bitter failings. Rahkki, my sweet, my stallion, Drael, belongs to you. Brauk, I bequeath you my sword. To

Feylah, orphan babe, I leave you my crown.

   Yours always and forever,

    your mother of highest love and devotion,

    Reyella Stormrunner

I'Lenna sank into her chair, her body cold to her toes. The letter was *worse* than what she'd imagined. Reyella had not only ranted about Lilliam and encouraged revenge, but she *knew* that someone was controlling I'Lenna's mother, just not who. I'Lenna tensed for interrogation, realizing that Lilliam's secret was going to come out, and soon—but Reyella's words had not completely sunk in yet with the people in the room.

Brauk sat back on his heels, his face stark. Darthan inhaled as though smoking a pipe, slow and thoughtful. "Read it again," Brauk said, and Darthan did, this time with tears streaming down his cheeks. When he finished, no one spoke for a long while.

Thaan, who wore two swords, unbuckled one. "This belongs to you," he said, bowing his head and offering the sheathed blade to Brauk.

Darthan's fire popped sparks as Brauk slid the weapon from its scabbard. His chest heaved. "Mother's sword. I remember it."

"It's a songsword," Feylah said. "Forged of Daakuran steel by the legendary Ruehem."

Brauk studied the markings engraved on the handle, and the runes on the blade. "I thought the Ruehem had all been destroyed."

"They were driven from the Culpash Mountains," Thaan answered. "And probably exterminated, but this is an old blade, infused with magic."

"Alchemy," Feylah corrected, smiling.

"What's the difference?" Thaan asked. "Anyway, it sings a nice tune in battle and it'll never need sharpening."

Brauk nodded to Thaan and buckled the sword to his waist. "This songsword didn't save my mother," he whispered, an afterthought that silenced everyone.

Ossi knocked on the door. "Can we come inside? It's raining again."

"Sure," Darthan answered, rising to meet them. Only then did I'Lenna notice the raindrops hitting Darthan's roof, smacking it like gigantic tears. Darthan shut the door and sat, studying the parchment, rereading it.

I'Lenna felt the hair on her neck rise when he glanced at her. "This letter implies a worse threat, I'Lenna," he said. "Who is pulling Lilliam's strings; do you have any idea what Reyella is talking about?"

Brauk, Feylah, and her guardians turned their attention to I'Lenna. She exhaled and nodded. It was time to confess everything. "It's my grandmother, Queen Tavara Whitehall of the Second. She sent Lilliam to the Fifth Clan to take the throne . . . and the treasury. My mother sends half your tithes to the Second Clan."

Stunned rage filled the shelter.

"She's *robbing* us?" Mut cried.

I'Lenna nodded.

Brauk rose to his feet, his golden eyes blazing. "She can't do that. She swore her loyalty to the Fifth. This is treason."

"This is why I started the rebellion," I'Lenna explained, finally justified. "To stop my mother *and* my grandmother."

"Did General Tsun know about this?" Ossi asked.

"Yes, but he agreed to keep it quiet if I helped him usurp her. I feared the clan would kill her if they found out."

Brauk rose to his feet, his face pinched with anger. He turned to his uncle. "My mother is right—it's time to fight back. Lilliam has been here too long. She took *everything* from us and she keeps on taking. She is not fit and not *authorized* to rule. Feylah is home, our rightful queen." He turned to his sister.

"Why fight Lilliam at all?" Ossi interjected. "When the people see Feylah, Lilliam will be marked as a false queen."

Darthan shook his head. "Harak and Lilliam have stolen the people's personal weapons and broken Clan Law. What's to stop them from denying Feylah, or killing her? They're in too deep to give up, and we can't protect her from Harak's army."

I'Lenna chewed the inside of her cheek, guessing he was right. "We need an army of our own to finish this," she said.

All eyes turned to her. "You don't have to fight your mother," Darthan said. "You can stay out of this."

I'Lenna rose from her chair. "I will help if you promise to banish my mother and not kill her. Please."

Brauk dropped his eyes. He clearly wasn't ready to promise anything, and I'Lenna felt a stab of fear.

"Where are we going to get an army?" Mut asked, glossing over their exchange. "The rebel warriors are locked in the Eighth Tower and the villagers don't have any weapons. If we could just get the rebels out," he mused.

"Maybe we can," I'Lenna said, a plan forming in her

mind. "If we can get to the fortress without being seen, I can get us inside and, I think, to the Eighth Tower. We can free the rebels through the secret passageways." Harak and his soldiers didn't know how to access the secret tunnels, only I'Lenna knew the trick. Her thoughts raced. The Eighth Tower had been a residence tower before Lilliam converted it to a prison; surely the tunnels reached it. I'Lenna could only hope.

Brauk flushed, warming to the idea. "Tuni's in the Eighth Tower. I'd love to fight Harak with her by my side." Ossi's eyes darted quickly toward Brauk, but he didn't notice. He paced, exercising his legs. "Maybe we can also free the Fliers that Harak locked in the Ruk. Then we'd have a winged army."

Darthan lit his pipe. "Let's focus on freeing the rebels first. We should go tonight, as soon as it's dark."

"We can try," I'Lenna said, listening to the pounding rain, "but this storm—the lower tunnels will be completely flooded. Perhaps we should wait until it's over."

"This is a monsoon, not a storm, and we don't have time to wait," Darthan said as he lipped his pipe. "We'll have to swim through, but this is good. A real plan is forming."

It was good, I'Lenna thought, for everyone except the

Whitehalls. What would happen to her siblings—Rayni, Jor, and K'Lar—if Lilliam didn't survive this battle? Would the Fifth Clan let the children stay? Or would I'Lenna be forced to raise them in Daakur by herself? At least she was educated; she could work at a museum or maybe as a teacher. She sighed; it was too much to think about. As Darthan had said, they needed to focus on freeing the rebels first.

As the Stormrunners and their friends collected supplies and decided on the most hidden jungle route to Fort Prowl, I'Lenna wondered what Rahkki was doing. His sister was alive! She wanted to tell him the good news, to watch his entire face light up. Rahkki deserved this and needed it. He'd never given up on his lost family. "Wherever you are," she whispered, "hang on. Your family is coming for you."

C 17 C

THE BET

BY EVENING, THE PEGASI HAD GROWN IMPATIENT and grumbling. "We can't stand in this rain another night," said Dewberry. "A dry Kihlara stall and a bucket of grain sound pretty good right now."

Kol brightened. "Yes, let's go to the barn!"

"I'm joking," Dewberry said, but Echofrost read the misery on her face. The twins were nursing all the nutrition right out of her. Dewberry ate voraciously but appeared thinner each day. Her sopping hair and feathers only added to her crankiness. "How long are we going to wait for these Landwalkers to do something? We should head to the jungle, to shelter."

"Just a bit longer," Echofrost nickered. "Please."

Dewberry whistled for her twins and moved them into Darthan's barn. The foals had spent the afternoon there also, avoiding the rain. Dewberry didn't care much for the structure, but her foals loved the barn.

Echofrost had watched the twins earlier. They delighted in the scent of Darthan's pigs and fowl, and they adored Lutegar, the swamp buffalo. Lutegar, who feared absolutely nothing, seemed as fascinated by the young pegasi as they were of her. She lured them into her stall by exchanging breath with them and then, once they were close enough, she nuzzled them like a mother.

When the twins fell asleep earlier today, curled against Lutegar's warm back, Dewberry had given up on trying to keep them away from the massive creature. She'd trotted out of the barn, her mane in disarray, and shrugged her wings. "Those two will make friends with *anybody*," she'd complained. "They're just like their sire."

Her statement had at first stunned Echofrost and then amused her, because it was true. Bumblewind had grown into a large, strong stallion, but his friendly, noncompetitive nature had set even foreign pegasi at ease. He'd fought side by side with Star in Anok, but that violence hadn't touched his gentle spirit. When the pegasi warriors weren't fighting, Bumblewind had always been the first to play a game or tell a joke. Echofrost snorted. Her brother was Dewberry's complete opposite, but their foals, especially Thornblaze, seemed to take after him.

Hazelwind and Shysong trotted to Echofrost's side, breaking into her thoughts. "Redfire should have returned from scouting by now," Hazelwind nickered.

Echofrost glanced at the eastern sky. "Maybe he's sheltering to avoid the lightning?"

"I hadn't considered that," said Hazelwind.

"I think Echofrost is right," Shysong agreed. "He's probably grounded somewhere or still scouting. If I know Redfire, he won't come back until he has some information about Rahkki, or what the giants are doing."

Hazelwind was not mollified. "I don't like it. We said we wouldn't split up."

"This is different," Echofrost said. "He's on a mission that only he can accomplish. None of us has learned to ride the jet streams."

"True," said Hazelwind. His long black forelock covered half his face and fresh rain droplets skidded across his curved muzzle. Her eyes traveled up his jawline and she saw that he was staring at her. Echofrost quickly looked away, feeling oddly pleased and nervous.

The friends huddled closer together, and Kol and Drael

joined them. While they waited for the Landwalkers to act, the pegasi shared stories about Anok, Kol shared stories about the Sky Guard, and Drael spoke fondly about Rahkki.

Echofrost was surprised to learn that her cub had loved to fly when he was a young child. "Rahkki was terrified of heights when I met him," she nickered.

Drael cocked his head. "My last flight with him was pretty terrifying. I almost died. I guess he thought I *was* dead."

"Everyone did," Kol confirmed.

Drael flicked the water off his wings. Even though he was soaked to the bone, Echofrost admired Drael's immaculate conformation, musculature, and coloring. *Sandwen breeding at its best*, she thought, feeling slightly sick about it. "Well, Rahkki is over his fears now," she said, as if she could take credit for the change in him.

Hot energy pulsed between her and Drael, and Echofrost realized they were jealous of each other. *By the Ancestors*, she thought, shaking her head, *I'm possessive over a Landwalker!*

Hazelwind nickered, his mirth shining in his dark eyes. He was laughing at her; she knew it. She nudged him with her wing and he nudged her back.

Just then Darthan's door popped open, spilling light and Landwalkers into the evening air. The group was dressed for travel, wearing boots and cloaks and carrying satchels brimming with supplies. It appeared to Echofrost that I'Lenna had borrowed Rahkki's clothing. She recognized his trousers and shirt, and his old, worn boots. Each Sandwen also wore a hooded rain cloak. Brauk whistled for Kol, and Feylah called for Drael.

"We'll travel overland to Fort Prowl through the jungle," Brauk said to the group.

Bedrest had thinned his legs and body, but he was young, and Echofrost guessed he'd recover quickly. She didn't know how he'd gone from paralyzed to walking so quickly, but it didn't surprise her. The Landwalkers were excellent healers, Brim had proved that when she repaired Echofrost's torn hide. The wound ached and itched in this awful rain, but not enough to impede her.

"Finally, something is happening," Dewberry muttered. She collected her twins from Lutegar. The foals whinnied with hunger and nursed off Dewberry from the air, hovering and stabbing at her like hummingbirds.

Brauk and his sister saddled and bridled their Kihlari

and fixed their supplies and weapons behind their saddles. They held the reins, ready to leave on foot. "Who will take care of your animals and crops?" Feylah asked her uncle.

"I hired an apprentice after Rahkki became a Rider," he said. "We'll be passing the village tonight; I'll get word to the girl to feed the animals tomorrow."

"And what about this wild herd?" I'Lenna asked, her eyes drifting to Echofrost. "Do we just leave them here?"

Brauk laughed. "I guess we'll find out right now if they're here to help us or if they're just hungry," he said. "I bet they stay and eat all Darthan's grain as soon as we're gone."

"Are you sure about that?" Ossi teased. "I bet you two dramals they follow us."

"You're on." Brauk and Ossi slapped hands and everyone laughed.

The group trekked off the porch and headed into the trees with Kol and Drael in tow.

Echofrost watched them go, feeling at a cross path. Rahkki's family was not walking east toward Mount Crim; they were heading toward the populated area of the Fifth Clan settlement, and some of them were armed. She had not changed her mind about helping them rescue Rahkki, but she felt more and more restless.

She'd come to this continent with a mission and had become entangled with Landwalkers and giants, but the urge to find a home was growing stronger every day, perhaps because of Dewberry's twins, perhaps because of her growing fondness for Hazelwind. She wondered what it would be like to fly with the buckskin stallion for any reason other than fear, battle, or escape. What would it be like to have a little fun?

"Are we following them or not?" Graystone asked.

Echofrost pinned her ears. "We are." She was getting ahead of herself. She would see Rahkki safely home, then she would find a home of her own.

"Anything is better than waiting in this rain," Dewberry nickered.

The pegasi turned as one and followed the Landwalkers into the jungle. Echofrost felt good; they were taking action and they were together.

Ossi Finn glanced back, saw the wild herd trailing them, and shoved Brauk. "You owe me two dramals."

18

DRAGONFIRE

AFTER ESCAPING THE WARREN, RAHKKI HAD trekked all day, camped overnight, and now it was daylight again. His ankle had begun to throb, he still hadn't found a Sandwen travelway home, and the clouds were still dumping rain. "I'm lost," he moaned to Tak.

The little dragon hummed as Rahkki absently stroked him. Rahkki was no longer afraid of the dragon's sharp teeth or barbed tail. Tak was annoying—he often nipped Rahkki for attention—but he was also affectionate. Tak pressed into the boy's fingers, his eyes drowsy with pleasure.

Rahkki sat on a log, frustrated and wet. The monsoon

rains hadn't let up long enough for the sun to dry him since he'd left the warren. His fingers and toes were soggy. His clothes had begun to fray and tear at the seams. Thankfully, Tak's dragonfire was impervious to water. He cooked Rahkki's food and, last night, he lit a small, warming campfire out of a pile of moist sticks that Rahkki had stacked.

"Sandwens don't get lost," Rahkki complained as he rested. The incessant clouds shielded the stars, and the tall trees blocked his view of landmarks. Rahkki hadn't traveled much as a kid, and when he had gone anywhere, it had been aboard Kol with Brauk. Navigating was easy in the heights, where he could see everything spread below him like a living map.

A map! Rahkki decided to draw one from memory. It might help him decide which way to walk. He grabbed a fallen branch, smoothed the soil below his bare feet, and began to draw.

Mount Crim, the River Tsallan, Cinder Bay, and the travelways. He placed a mark where he thought he was right now, and then looked around and sighed. He still had no idea which direction to go.

Tak winged overhead, gliding between the trees like a

tiny Kihlara, and Rahkki got another idea. "*Mushka!*" he said, *idiot*. If he climbed the highest tree, he might be able to see a travelway.

As he searched for the best climbing tree, the hairs on his arms lifted. He paused. Other than the soft pelting rain, utter silence had befallen the jungle—it was so out of place that the quiet seemed louder than the usual noise. He closed his eyes and sent his ears out into the jungle, listening.

Clack. Clackety-clack. Clack.

He recognized the soft clapping of hard-shelled legs—an ant army. Rahkki normally might have ignored this—ant armies were easily avoided—but this one was gigantic; he could tell by the sheer volume of noise building in the distance.

He spun in a circle—how far away were they?

Then, to his horror, the soil around him shifted and a red, antennae-crowned head emerged from the mud. The rat-sized ant dragged itself out of the dirt and clapped its legs. The jungle floor seemed to roll as a thousand more ants hatched, full grown and starving. They snapped their sharp jaws and reached their razor-haired legs toward him.

Bile filled Rahkki's mouth. These weren't regular ants;

they were monsoon ants! The eggs lay dormant all year until the monsoon rains flooded the soil and activated them to hatch. Rahkki must have stumbled upon one of their birthing grounds. Hundreds, maybe thousands, were erupting out of the dirt all around this part of the jungle. No creature was too large for the army to swarm and eat. They turned their bright heads toward Rahkki.

He leaped to the nearest branch and pulled himself into a tree, his heart galloping. Rahkki despised ants, but monsoon ants were the worst. "Tak!" he cried in a panic.

The dragon landed on his head and screeched angrily at the insects.

The jungle floor heaved and shifted as even more hibernating ants awakened. Decaying plants, carcasses, and living creatures—everything in their path would be devoured by morning.

Rahkki was about to climb higher when a soft growl reached his ears. Peeking through his lashes, he spotted a frightened panther crouched above him. She was small, probably a female, and also hiding from the ants. Her yellow eyes narrowed in warning. Her jaws parted in a silent hiss.

Tak flapped off Rahkki's shoulder and spit hot flames at the cat while Rahkki eased his way down the tree trunk. The panther swiped at the dragon and missed. She stepped down one branch and whipped her tail, her muscles rippling beneath her wet fur. Her eyes locked on Rahkki.

Bloody rain, he thought. The cat wiggled slightly, testing the steadiness of the tree, preparing to pounce.

Below marched thousands of the huge aggressive ants.

Rahkki would have to choose—die by fang and claw, or get chewed to death by ants the size of his fist? The panther sprang. Rahkki let go and fell toward the jungle floor. The panther's claws raked his outer tunic, ripping the fabric.

Rahkki landed on top of the ants. His foot squashed one and slid across another. A shrill, primal scream rose in his throat. The ant tide turned toward him. Rahkki sprinted away, his heart pounding faster than his bare feet. Tak glided overhead, chortling at the insects as if scolding them.

Rahkki's eyes swept the muddy terrain and he skipped over as many ants as he could. A female emerged right in front of him, her spiked legs straining as she pulled herself headfirst out of the ground. Swiveling her shiny antennae, she spotted Rahkki and began a ferocious clapping with her front legs. The jungle floor bubbled and more giant ants pushed out.

Disgust churned his gut. "Help me, Tak!"

The golden burner soared through the raindrops and dived toward the insects, shooting blue flames, his hottest. Ants caught fire and exploded. Their disembodied legs and shells spiraled into the sky.

A jointed leg stuck to Rahkki's wet skin and he had to swipe it off with his hand. Bile rose again in his throat, but he gagged it back down. Meanwhile, Tak scorched the earth. His golden eyes turned black and his juvenile barbs glowed. Panting, he fed his fire with the jungle air, creating hotter and hotter flames and sending the ants scurrying into retreat.

"Good boy, Tak!" Rahkki cried. The burner puffed his chest and extended his frills.

Rahkki sprinted through the trees, leaping over ants as they continued to shove out of the dirt, their jaws gaping for food. Tak glided lower, shooting firebolts at them when they popped out of the ground. The jungle filled with smoke, broken red shells, and sizzling flames.

But for all that, the ants caught up to Rahkki and swarmed his legs. He drew Miah's dagger and attacked, knocking the ants off his skin and skewering them. Tak squalled, flaming the brush around Rahkki, creating smoke that confused the swarm. The rain and fire formed hot steam that rose like tendrils toward the sky.

The ants kept coming. They scurried up Rahkki's legs, clamped their mandibles around his flesh, and then jammed him with their stingers. The venom burned as it shot through his body. *Land to skies, why ants! Is this a nightmare? Am I still asleep?* Rahkki became disoriented. The hungry insects reared up and rubbed their front legs together, calling more ants to the meal. Thousands of shiny heads streamed toward the boy from every direction.

Climb! Get off the ground, Rahkki's mind screamed. The panther had driven him out of one tree, but there were others! He leaped onto a banyan, a desperate cry rising in his throat. But a gang of monkeys had already claimed this tree. They screamed at Rahkki and rattled the branches. He tried another—it housed a viper. He ran, panic swelling. Tak followed, shooting flames.

The ants flowed faster toward him, their antennae circling, their legs blurring, their jaws clacking. He leaped onto another tree, this one full of vultures. They hissed and spread their wings.

"Let me up!" he screamed at them, spurting saliva. "I'm not leaving this tree."

The vultures attacked and pecked his arms.

Rahkki fell backward and slammed onto the ground again. The savage ants flowed over him. He flailed. His death would be painful but quick, like a piranha attack.

Suddenly, wingbeats whooshed overhead and a shadow fell over the boy.

He peered up. A copper-coated Kihlara stallion dived from the clouds, ears pricked forward.

"Here, I'm here!" Rahkki cried.

The stallion spotted him and angled his wings. Rahkki rolled out of the way as the Kihlara landed and stomped the ants surrounding him. Tak helped by singeing the squished insects.

Rahkki dimly recognized the stallion as belonging to Sula's herd. The giants had brought him to their parlay with the Fifth Clan. He dragged himself onto the stallion's back like a sailor onto a life raft. The wild Kihlara lifted off and flapped toward the clouds with Tak trailing behind him. Rahkki used Miah's dagger to flick off the last remaining ants. Once free of them, he pulled himself tight against the stallion's dark-gold wings.

The wild steed swiveled his neck to look at Rahkki,

and he nickered, as if in greeting.

"Th-thanks," Rahkki stuttered. The ant's venom flowed through his veins, making everything blurry. Welts appeared across his arms and legs. His lips felt numb. Rahkki leaned over the stallion's neck, oblivious to where they were going, and not caring. His chest hurt and he felt dizzy.

They flew for what seemed a long time. When the stallion needed to rest, he sank toward a lake and plunked into it, spreading his wings and paddling to stay afloat. Tak joined them, swimming with only his eyes and nostrils showing above the water, like a crocodile.

Rahkki slipped into the lake and allowed the water to clean and soothe his bites, but he was clumsy and couldn't stay afloat. As he began to sink, the stallion's gentle jaws gripped his collar and tugged him to the surface. Rahkki crawled back aboard and closed his eyes. Cold sweat leaked from his skin.

The monsoon ants surrounded the lake, scavenging and devouring plants, eggshells, reptiles, and other insects. As they scoured, they left behind picked-clean skeletons and a path devoid of debris and rot.

Rahkki and the battle-scarred stallion floated until the ant swarm had passed them by. Then the Kihlara paddled to shore and walked out of the lake with Rahkki seated haphazardly on his back. He trotted overland, perhaps sensing that his rider was not stable enough to fly. When Rahkki almost bounced off his back, the winged horse shifted into a smoother gait, a slow, rolling lope. His hooves slapped the muddy trails and the rain continued to fall. Tak followed them, gliding easily and trailing twin lines of smoke from his nostrils.

Feeling hot but shivering violently, Rahkki gripped the stallion's red mane as tight as he could. His welts itched to the point of maddening him, his stomach had soured, and dehydration cramps gripped his legs so hard he had to bite his lip to keep from calling out. The ride on the winged horse was torture with every hoof fall.

When Tak grew tired, he rode on the winged steed's neck. The copper stallion didn't like that. He snorted and shook his mane, but Tak just batted at the flying hair as if it were a game. After a time, the steed accepted the young dragon.

Now the wild Kihlara nickered and Rahkki heard an urgent tone to his voice. The exhausted boy lifted his head and was shocked to see they'd arrived at the edge of the fallows in the Fifth Clan territory. It was early afternoon and Rahkki was almost home.

His stomach lurched and saliva flooded his mouth. He slid off the stallion and vomited into the bushes. The copper steed pranced, seeming upset. Rahkki wiped his mouth, fell over, and stared up at the sky. He couldn't stand without retching. The stallion nuzzled him, his dark eyes round with concern. He tried to lift the boy, and Rahkki spewed bile all over him. "I'm sorry," Rahkki whispered.

The stallion glanced toward the Fifth Clan settlement, then back at Rahkki, and then he lifted off and flew away. Rahkki sank into the dirt, unable to move. The ants had already passed through this area and Rahkki was as safe as anyone could be in the jungle. Tak remained with him, nestled against his chest.

Rahkki must have slept for a long time, because when he woke, it was evening and the nausea had passed. But *something* had wakened him, a noise. Rahkki stilled, again sending his ears into the forest.

Voices wafted toward him. "You hear that?" asked a man.

A woman answered. "If you're talking about your grumbling belly, yeah, I hear it."

Between the trees, Rahkki glimpsed two Fifth Clan

soldiers walking through the forest. He clutched Tak, willing the little dragon to be quiet. When Tak began to struggle, Rahkki let him go. Tak tore into the night sky and disappeared.

The soldiers strolled closer.

Rahkki spread himself flat in the mud and let the thick evening mist roll over him like a blanket. He concentrated on becoming invisible, on blending into his surroundings, a trick he'd learned when he was a stable groom.

"How are we supposed to patrol when our queen barely feeds us?" the male soldier asked.

The woman snorted. "Harak Nightseer eats well enough. Saw him gulping down a bowl of buffalo stew on my way to the armory."

"General Tsun would have shared his rations. Harak cares only about himself."

"And Lilliam."

"I don't know about that," said the man. "I wonder if he's using her too. Charmed her like a snake, he did."

"Or she charmed him," the woman countered. "Two of a kind, they are."

The male clucked his tongue. "The queen should worry more about feeding us. We're all that's keeping her safe from the villagers. They're starting to turn against her, you know. Started as soon as the food stores and the crop-lands flooded, just like I said it would. Land to skies, this early monsoon is killing us."

The soldiers paused and Rahkki heard one pull an arrow from a quiver. "Shh." It was the female soldier. "Just ahead, you see that?" she whispered.

"Yeah, I see him," the man whispered back.

Rahkki held his breath. Had they spotted him? He heard the creaking of a bow drawn tight. The two soldiers crept closer and Rahkki braced. Their footsteps sent bee-tles scuttling his way. One crawled into his trousers and marched up his bare leg, inflaming his welts. He squeezed shut his eyes. The soldiers were so close that he could hear the male's rumbling belly and the woman's soft breaths. They halted right beside him.

"Shoot him in the neck," the woman commanded.

Rahkki's gut clenched. Should he beg for mercy or run?

The man loosed the arrow. *Twang!*

The shaft shot from its bow, whistled through the air, and then the squeal of a wild boar rang through the trees.

"Got him!" cheered the male soldier.

The two ran past him and one of their boots clunked Rahkki in the head. They were so focused on the boar that neither noticed the hiding boy. Rahkki exhaled and scooted out of the mud. The injured boar stumbled away, chased by the soldiers. Seconds later, a sharp oink marked the end of the pig's life. He heard the soldiers gutting it right where it had fallen.

Urgency shoved Rahkki to his feet. He had to get out of the jungle, now. Odds were that boar had been hunting *him*. Rahkki wiped the rain from his eyes and the bugs from his body. Ducking low, he skirted the path, waded through the flooded fallows, and wound his way toward his settlement.

Tak returned and landed on his arm with a satisfied, smoky burp. Rahkki needed to get to Darthan's farm, but he knew he'd never make it that far. The ant venom had numbed his tongue and made breathing difficult. Brim Carver's animal clinic loomed into view.

He dropped and crawled toward it. Upon reaching her shed, Rahkki stopped and listened. He heard her humming and shuffling around inside. Deciding she was alone, he pushed her door open without knocking.

"Oh!" She whirled around, holding a pot of batter in her hands.

Rahkki stared back at her, suddenly dizzy with hunger.

"Rahkki!" Brim dropped her pot and grabbed him,

keeping a wary eye on the small fire-breathing dragon perched upon his arm. "You're okay, you're safe," she breathed.

"I—I." He collapsed into her open arms just as his throat closed shut.

19

NO MERCY

BRIM CLAMPED HER STRONG ARMS AROUND
Rahkki's body and dragged him onto a cot. She spied the
welts on his lower legs. "Monsoon ants," she stated, shaking her head.

He flailed his arms as he tried to take a breath.

"All right, it's okay. You're going to be fine. I have an
antidote, don't move!"

Rahkki swatted and struck Tak. The burner hissed
and fired green smoke, filling the hut. Rahkki heard Brim
cough as she shuffled through her medicine jars.

"Up, up," she said, lifting Rahkki's torso off the cot.
"Drink." She forced a cup to his lips and lukewarm liquid

seeped into his mouth. He choked. "Relax and drink," she said, tilting back his head. He fought her, but Brim had a grip like a python.

Some liquid dribbled down his throat and his airway began to open. He drank more and his vision cleared. He lay back and let his eyes drift closed.

He didn't sleep. He listened to Brim work and as he began to feel better, he slowly opened his eyes and looked out the window. The birds had stopped singing for the night and moonlight streaked between the clouds in silver stripes. He smacked his lips and wiped his face. "I'm thirsty," he rasped.

Brim brought him a mug of juice and a bowl of soup. He drank, but just stared at the soup. The memory of what he'd done to Fire Horde reared in his mind.

Stroking his hand, Brim prodded him with questions. "Did you escape from the giants, Rahkki, or did they let you go?"

"I escaped." Rahkki's palms turned clammy. "Is I'Lenna home? Is she okay?"

"You haven't heard?"

"I don't know anything. I just got back."

Brim nodded. "The Borla sentenced her to the Sunstone."

Rahkki's jaw clamped shut.

"Don't worry, she escaped! I'Lenna is alive, no thanks to her mother. They called a dragon and one came, but I saw Koko yesterday. She was sneaking around that night with Mut, Tam, and Jul. They loosed some goats to distract the beast." Brim pursed her lips. "Lilliam has gone too far."

Rahkki nodded, his heart racing as he imagined I'Lenna fighting off a hungry drooler. "Where is she now?"

"She left with Mut and Tam to find Darthan, but I haven't heard anything new. No one is talking. Harak has ears everywhere."

Rahkki met Brim's warm blue eyes. "I have to find her, and I have to warn the clan. The giants are angry, Brim. I—I made them angry."

She arched her gray brows. "We've been at war with the Gorlanders for a thousand years, Rahkki. I doubt you've made things worse."

He laughed. Brim always made him feel better. "That's true, but I think I did. I struck a truce with all three hordes and they offered to help me fight Queen Lilliam, but then I ruined Fire Horde's soup." He shrugged helplessly. "Now they're sending three armies to finish us off for good. That's worse, isn't it?"

There was a long silence marked only by Tak's claws clicking on the floor as he chased a beetle. "Is he killing that bug or playing with it?" Brim asked, momentarily avoiding the subject of the giants.

"Both," Rahkki said. As if on cue, Tak froze the beetle with his cold purple fire, turning him into an icy snack.

Brim clucked her tongue and then returned her attention to Rahkki. "Did the giants hurt you for ruining their soup?" she asked. "I've treated the ant bites, but your arms are heavily bruised."

Rahkki rolled up his sleeves and saw blue, black, and purple colors blooming across his skin. "No," he said, crinkling his brow, "giants are strong, that's all."

She hissed softly between her teeth. "And they're going to destroy us because you ruined their dinner?"

Rahkki shook his head. "Not exactly. I spoiled a very old soup by throwing a catfish into it. Did you know that giants don't eat meat? That all the stories about them eating Sandwen children aren't true?"

Brim squinted and took a chair. "Are you sure?"

He nodded. "We have to warn the clan that they're coming."

"I'll get the word out," she promised, "but you must stay hidden. I heard about the trick you pulled, putting the giants to sleep instead of killing them during the battle for the wild herd. Quite clever, but Harak thinks you're a deathlifter." Her brief, proud smile faded fast. "He's ordered his soldiers to capture you on sight. And he's offered a full round to anyone who turns you in."

"A full round!" A Sandwen could live for years on that much coin.

She nodded. "No one but your family can know you're back. And you need to rest. I'll make you a tea and cut some fruit. You tell me more about these giants."

Moments later Brim placed a steaming cup of tea and a plate of mangoes and sweetened bread in front of Rahkki. He dug in with his filthy fingers, cramming the delicious bread into his mouth and slurping the hot tea while he explained the giants to Brim.

She laughed out loud when he talked about the antics of Miah and her brothers. She listened with wide eyes as he described the warren and the healers' tent. "Where do all the terrible stories come from if they aren't true?" Brim wondered.

"From parents trying to scare their kids," Rahkki guessed, and she smiled.

Rahkki rubbed his tired eyes. "If the clan had just talked with the hordes sooner, I think we could have come to terms. My mother always wanted to, but now I've ruined any chance of an alliance."

Brim stood and collected their plates. "It was a misunderstanding, Rahkki."

He shook his head. "There's no excuse for what I did."

She clucked and poured more tea. "I have some news that might cheer you up. Sula came to me after the battle. Much like you, she was injured and needed some attention. I stitched her back together and she stayed for a few days, and then she and her herd flew away."

A wide grin cracked Rahkki's face. His princess had escaped the Sunstone and his Flier was alive. "That's good. Thank you! I hope the wild steeds fly far away from here."

Brim smiled at that. "You've grown more than a pinch since I last saw you."

"It's the Gorlan soup," Rahkki said, explaining his theory that it was special, that it healed and caused rapid growth. "I feel bigger and stronger."

Brim agreed. "I think it probably saved your life. That many monsoon ant stings should have killed you."

"So what now?" Rahkki asked, feeling replete after his meal.

"I'll get the word out about the giants," Brim said.

"Perhaps the news will unite the clan—greater enemy and whatnot. The Fifth is in horrible shape. Harak Nightseer stripped the villagers of their weapons, the crops are underwater, and the few food stores that didn't get soaked are diminishing quickly. If Queen Lilliam has any coin left in our treasury, she's not spending it on food. The clan is hungry. Everyone's hunting, but the rains are making that difficult. I've enough rice stored to last one moon cycle, and then I'm out. When do you think the giants will arrive?"

"They can't be too far behind me. Maybe four or five days, maybe longer? I flew most of the way home."

"Flew?"

He grinned. "A wild steed carried me."

"You don't say?" She clucked her tongue again, straightened, and glowered east. "The hordes might not eat animals or children, but they're still giants, Rahkki. They won't show mercy."

"I know." He stretched his arms, feeling exhausted.

Brim stroked his hair and Tak flew down from the rafters. He inserted himself between them and hummed, puffing white smoke. Brim chuckled and her bright-blue eyes met Rahkki's. "Why don't you and your dragon friend rest now?"

Rahkki touched her arm, a lump rising in his throat. Brim's wrinkled face and hands, her kind eyes, and her singsong voice soothed him more than any of her medicines or teas. He hugged her tight. "Thank you for always helping me and Sula."

"You're welcome," the old doctor said in her gentlest voice.

Rahkki's eyes grew heavy and Brim made up a private bed in an empty stall for him. He trudged toward it and sank into the furs with Tak snuggling close. "This is all my fault." Rahkki swept his hand over his head, indicating the magnitude of the Fifth Clan's current troubles.

Brim pulled the blankets up to his chest. "No, Rahkki, you did your best to fix things." She extinguished her oil lamp. "Any harm that comes from helping is fate, not failure."

As sleep wrapped him in its arms, Rahkki's thoughts swirled with images of angry giants. *They won't show mercy*, Brim had said. Rahkki imagined the giants storming his clan's territory, destroying the village, ripping down the Kihlari stable, and crushing the Sandwens. Their roars filled his ears as if they were in Brim's hut.

He moaned, halfway between sleep and wakefulness.

How could his people fight three hordes at once, especially when the Fifth Clan was divided and half their warriors were locked in the Eighth Tower? The answer was terrifying: they couldn't.

20

DARTHAN'S QUESTION

I'LENNA TIGHTENED HER RAIN CLOAK AROUND
her body. After leaving Darthan's hut, Brauk had led
their group as long as he could before everyone noticed
that his legs were too weak to handle trudging through
dense underbrush.

"Will you please ride Kol?" Ossi had insisted, her face
worried.

"No one else is riding," he'd answered.

"You're slowing us down," Darthan said, and this had
finally goaded Brauk into mounting his stallion. Now Kol
twitched with pleasure at carrying his Rider. I'Lenna
guessed he'd been pretty lonely cooped up in his stall after
Brauk's injury.

They were on their way to free the rebels locked in the Eighth Tower. Thaan and Tully marched beside Feylah. Darthan and Tam took up the rear. And Ossi stayed close to Brauk, whispering with him. Mut strode beside a huge furry wild stallion, grinning from ear to ear. "This is a fine Kihlara," he said, openly admiring the creature. "I've always wanted a big Flier like this."

"We aren't keeping these wild steeds," I'Lenna said.

Mut frowned. "But I can't afford to buy one," he complained. "Most of my friends can't either, so why not keep them? I'll never have another chance to fly."

Feylah interrupted. "That's going to change when I'm queen."

"What do you mean?" Brauk asked.

"I don't think it's right that Kihlari are so expensive. You shouldn't have to be rich to fly."

"Yes," Mut cheered. "I like your thinking."

Feylah's golden eyes warmed. "I'm going to open a school. Riders will train for the right to Pair and if a Rider or Flier dies, they'll have the chance to Pair again. It's a waste to retire them when one dies." She patted Drael's bay neck and Brauk eyed her sharply. "Don't you agree?" she asked.

Darthan cleared his throat. "I do," he said, "but the

clan is used to doing things a certain way. Change will take time."

Feylah grinned. "We'll see."

I'Lenna listened to the conversation and tried to hide the fact that her entire body was shaking. The trembling had begun last night and she suspected she had a fever, but the clan's and Rahkki's future depended on freeing the rebels. She didn't have time to be sick.

"Are you cold?" Tam asked her.

"I'm fine, just wet," she answered quickly, and she followed as the group threaded between the palms. The rain pattered against the leaves, masking their footfalls.

"We're parallel with the village," Darthan said, halting. "Wait here while I visit my apprentice." Darthan crept away to give his worker instructions to watch the rice farm.

The group settled beneath the broad foliage to wait, sheltering as best they could from the rain. The wild herd stretched their wings and grazed on wet plants. I'Lenna watched Darthan vanish into the mist, but before he'd gone too far, soldiers' voices stopped him. "You there! Halt."

Her heart thudded as she and the others exchanged worried glances. Darthan must have bumped into a patrol. "Don't move," Brauk mouthed. They were shrouded in darkness and hidden by brush, but close enough to the soldiers that a small cough or a snapping branch would give them all away. The wild herd seemed to sense the danger and they ceased grazing and went as still as the trees.

"What are you doing in the jungle?" a guard asked Darthan.

"Hunting," he lied. "You know there isn't enough food."

There was a brief silence, an acknowledgment of that truth, I'Lenna guessed. Then the guard said, "It's past curfew."

"Curfew?" Darthan asked, surprised.

"Sunset to sunrise," he answered. "General Nightseer announced it in the village this morning."

I'Lenna fumed at the men calling Harak *general*. Her mother had appointed him after General Tsun died, and it annoyed her that Lilliam favored the blond Headwind beyond his actual worth and abilities.

"Some of the best hunting is at night," Darthan returned, which was true.

"That's the way it is though," replied the guard.

"But why issue a curfew now?" Darthan pressed. "The people haven't done anything wrong and the rebels are locked up."

I'Lenna watched Brauk shake his head, silently scolding his uncle for questioning the soldiers.

"Orders are orders," the patrolling guard answered, his tone bristling. "I don't know why. The people are restless maybe."

"They're hungry," Darthan muttered.

"Get back to your farm, Stormrunner," the man said. "Or I'll report you to the general."

I'Lenna shifted her weight and almost fell over. Tam reached to steady her, and cold sweat began to trickle down her forehead. "I'm okay," she mouthed.

"Will you pass a message to Harak?" Darthan asked, refusing to use his new title.

The patrolman huffed. "Fine, what is it?"

"Ask him who Lilliam burned on my sister's funeral pyre, because it wasn't Reyella."

Stunned silence followed Darthan's remark. In the jungle, Brauk's eyes widened in shock. Feylah sucked in her breath.

"Are you suggesting that Lilliam isn't our rightful queen?" the soldier whispered.

"Just ask him, will you?" Darthan said. "Tell him Darthan wants to know."

The patrolling soldier sighed. "All right, but he's not going to like that question. Now get back to your farm or stay in the village tonight."

"I'll stay in the village with friends. Thank you."

"Have a good evening," said the soldier.

I'Lenna listened as he and his patrol marched away. Darthan continued into the village to meet with his apprentice. The people and the Kihlari steeds relaxed and waited for what felt like forever—then Darthan doubled back and rejoined them.

"What was all that about?" Brauk hissed. "Harak already knows Reyella escaped that night. You're just poking a snake, asking questions like that."

The group had gathered around Darthan, who shook his head. "I don't think he knows anything," Darthan answered. "If Harak suspected that Lilliam was a false queen or that she was robbing the Fifth for her mother, I don't think he'd be so keen to help her. I knew Harak when he was just a pup. He might be a snake, as you call him, but he believes in Clan Law and the chain of command. I don't believe Lilliam has been honest with him."

Darthan glanced toward the fortress. "If I'm right, my question will cause a rift between Harak and Lilliam. If

I'm wrong, and he already knows my sister escaped that night, then he'll understand we know it too. Either way, if we can seed doubt between Harak and Lilliam, their alliance will begin to unravel."

Brauk's jaw muscles fluttered as he considered this. "I see your point," he said.

Darthan nodded and the group continued their hike south, approaching Fort Prowl and the prison tower.

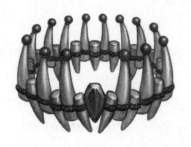

21

THE EIGHTH TOWER

AS BRAUK RODE KOL THROUGH THE SOGGY DROOP-ing rain forest, Firo and Sula left the wild herd to walk beside I'Lenna. Firo nickered and fussed, as if sensing that I'Lenna didn't feel well. I'Lenna wanted to ride the roan, but she didn't want anyone to know how tired and sick she felt.

Sula pranced anxiously. Her silver coat appeared gray in the darkness and her eyes shimmered like wet stars. Her white mane lay flat and matted against her neck and her tail swished as she moved. The brand on her shoul-der flexed with her muscles, a dark mark against her lighter coat. I'Lenna felt a surge of admiration. Sula had returned to help her Rider when she could have fled the Realm forever.

The group reached the stand of trees that bordered the south side of the fortress. The night was quiet. A few half-hearted soldiers lined the high fortress walls and guarded the gates. Thick clouds scudded across the pale moon overhead.

"Here it is," I'Lenna said, pointing at a metal grid. Water gushed from the drainage ditch and flowed in rivulets down the hill.

Darthan assessed the tunnel. "It's flooded. Is there another way inside?"

"All the lower tunnels will be flooded," I'Lenna explained. "We'll have to swim through."

"What about the Kihlari?" Mut asked.

"Drael will wait for me," Feylah said, turning him loose.

"So will Kol," Brauk agreed. He dismounted but left the stallion's saddlebags attached. He stroked Kol's red muzzle. "Be back soon as I can." The stallion shoved his head into Brauk's chest and nickered.

"Tam and I can stay with the Kihlari," Mut said. "If trouble comes, we can get at least Kol, Drael, and the wild steeds out of here."

Brauk nodded and turned to Darthan. "Where should we go if—no *when*—we break the rebels out of the tower?"

Darthan grimaced. "The Western Wilds," he said.

"Gah!" Mut cried. "Black magna territory? Are you trying to get us killed?"

"It's the best place to hide so many people." Darthan's expression said he was serious.

"You have to admit, no one will look for us there," Tam agreed.

"The spiders hate rain," Brauk added. "We should be okay."

"What could go wrong?" Mut chided.

"You didn't just say that!" Brauk moaned, plugging his ears.

"Say what?"

Ossi explained. "The second you ask what can go wrong, the world shows you."

"Bah!" Mut huffed. "That's a Rider's superstition, like spitting every time someone says *giant*."

The entire group leaned over and spit on the ground.

"See," Mut said, gesturing. "Does spitting actually keep giants away? No. So like I said, what could go wrong with hiding out in black magna territory? Sounds perfectly safe to me."

"You and Tam just wait here and keep your mouth shut," Ossi said to her brother, rolling her eyes.

The rest of the group walked toward the fortress drainage grate. I'Lenna moved to unlock it and Feylah appeared beside her. "Show me how you do it," she said.

Feylah was the true queen and I'Lenna knew she needed this knowledge. The tunnels had been engineered for the monarch's escape, after all. "Of course," I'Lenna said, nodding. With their backs turned to the group, I'Lenna slid out her blackstone necklace. "This acts as a key," she explained quietly, and she pressed the stone against a worn spot on the hidden metal lock. It clicked and the rushing water pushed the grate opened.

Feylah studied the necklace. "It's a magnet," she whispered, frowning. "How obvious."

"Not to our people," I'Lenna said. "We don't have magnets in the Realm."

"Then who built these secret doors and tunnels?"

"Daakurans built the fortress for the Fifth Clan," I'Lenna explained. "Only queens know how to use the magnets. Reyella would have learned the secret from her mother, but my mother doesn't know, since she wasn't born to the Fifth and didn't, you know, inherit the throne." I'Lenna swallowed those last words, guilt rising in her chest for what Lilliam had done to Feylah's mom.

"How did *you* find out then?" Feylah asked, her golden eyes piercing.

"I found an old set of Fort Prowl's plans in a Daakuran museum," I'Lenna answered. "I wanted to find my room on the plans, and while I was looking for it, I noticed the tunnels and false fireplace doors. The magnet part I figured out later. Daakurans use them a lot, so when I couldn't find a key or keyhole to open the doors, I tried this magnet my little sister bought for me when I was seven."

"I see." The two girls studied each other a moment.

"What's taking so long?" Brauk whispered, interrupting them.

I'Lenna tucked the blackstone necklace back into her dress and turned to the group. "The gate's open," she said.

They all pressed into the tunnel, fighting the rushing current. Tully grabbed Feylah's hand as the water pushed the child off her feet. Within moments, it was too deep for any of them to walk through. I'Lenna struck out, paddling like a dog. The group swam against the current and the passageway grew dimmer. "Keep going," I'Lenna urged.

The stone walls wept rainwater, and moss slicked the sides of the tunnel. After snaking through the long watery passageway, they finally reached a ledge pathway above the water level. The group pulled themselves onto it to rest and dry out.

"I keep a tinderbox and candles tucked away in several landing spots," I'Lenna said, feeling along the wall until her fingers located a natural depression. She found the box and handed it to Tully, who was closest to her. "Will you light it?" she asked. Her injured thumb prevented dexterous work like starting fires.

Tully struck the flint against the steel. It took a few tries, but soon he shot a spark that set the tinder burning. He blew softly on the flame and when it swelled, he lit candles, handing one to each of them. The firelight blinded them after the darkness of the lower tunnels.

The group was above the waterline now and the ledge path was slippery as they resumed walking. I'Lenna whispered directions. "Turn right. Now left. Watch your heads. Go straight."

Ossi grunted when her arm smacked against a protruding rock. Her candle fell and extinguished, then rolled away. I'Lenna's small flame battled hard against the darkness, casting dim light.

"I think that passage leads to the Eighth Tower," I'Lenna said, pointing at a hoof-shaped tunnel carved off the main passageway. "It's been years since I explored it."

Truth was, the mostly deserted prison tower had always frightened I'Lenna.

Ducking, the group entered the passageway and slowed as they encountered a circular ascending walkway. "This is it," I'Lenna said, "the Eighth Tower."

They passed several false fireplace doors. "These lead to the guards' quarters," she whispered. "We won't be able to access the prison cells directly, since they don't have fireplaces, but if we can find a set of keys in one of these guards' rooms, we can unlock the cells from the main hallway."

Brauk chose the closest secret door and tried to pry it open. Thaan and Tully rushed to help.

"I'll open it," I'Lenna whispered. "But be careful. It might not be empty." She took a breath and unlocked the hinged back of the fireplace with her magnet. The guard's room was vacant and they crept into the small chamber.

A bed, a dresser, a chair, and an aged table stood against each wall. Thick furs covered the floor. The bed-covers were rumpled, and a few items of clothing—a pair of sandals and worn tunics—were scattered around the room. Brauk, Ossi, Mut, and Tam rifled through the guard's belongings, looking for keys.

A large man charged into the room. "Ay, what's this?"

Brauk shot up and struck the guard with the back of his elbow, knocking him unconscious before he could draw his weapon. The man toppled. Thaan and Tully quickly searched his pockets and found keys. The others let out their breath.

A woman's voice drifted toward them from the hallway leading to the cells. "Who's there?" she asked, her voice muffled. "What's going on?"

"It's Tuni," Brauk whispered. He raced into the hallway toward the sound of the Headwind's voice and located her cell. I'Lenna and the others followed

"Brauk?" Tuni whispered.

He nodded, unlocked her door with the keys, and dragged her into a breathless embrace. "Are you hurt?" Brauk touched her face and stroked her hair. His golden eyes swept over her. I'Lenna and the others held back, watching.

"I'm fine," Tuni rasped.

But she didn't look fine. Her dark-red hair hung limp, her face was pinched, and her clothing hung off her body, frayed and torn. She looked years older since Harak arrested her and a Sandwen soldier shot her Flier with an arrow. I'Lenna had heard that Rizah was as good as dead.

Tuni's once-sparkling brown eyes, now as dull as mud,

swept up Brauk's legs. "You're walking?"

"Yeah," he said, lips curving gently. "I'Lenna gave me the Queen's Elixir."

Tuni smiled wanly at I'Lenna, then leaned against Brauk, her voice tight. "Get me out of here," she said. "Please, get all of us out of here."

"We're working on it," he said, kissing the top of her head.

Feylah interrupted them. "Where are the other rebels?"

Tuni gaped at the girl, the female replica of Brauk and Rahkki, and pointed. "That way."

"Let's release them," Feylah said, and exited the chamber.

"Turns out I have a sister," Brauk said, smiling, and Tuni's eyes lit with a hope that Brauk quickly extinguished. "My mother didn't survive. I'll explain later, let's go."

The group raced out and jogged up the hallway, with Thaan using the keys they'd retrieved off the prison guard to unlock the iron doors. Captured rebels from both the Sky Guard and Land Guard armies poured out of their cells. Grateful expressions marked their thin faces and soft cheers erupted from their lips.

As they prepared to return to the tunnels, Tully spoke.

"Hold up. Does anyone smell smoke?"

I'Lenna scented the air. Yes, she smelled it—smoke. "Where's it coming from?"

"The tunnels are blocked," Brauk cried. "Someone has started a fire in them."

Now I'Lenna heard voices. "Add more wood, smoke the vermin out, yeah." It was Harak. "My man followed you to these tunnels, Darthan," he snarled. "Did you think you could fool my guards? Hunting? What a lie, yeah? Everyone knows you're not starving on that farm of yours."

Darthan's hands crushed into fists and disappointment lined his face.

"I've got soldiers at the main entrance and fire in the tunnels. You're trapped," Harak snarled.

"If we don't get out of here, we'll die," Brauk said, beginning to cough.

I'Lenna's voice cracked as she spoke. "You heard him—soldiers are waiting for us at the main door and we can't go back the way we came. The windows are the only way out, but we're too high up to jump."

Tully glanced outside. "She's right. Can we get lower?"

"I hear you talking, you traitors!" Harak shouted.

Far below, his soldiers threw open the main door to the Eighth Tower and began tromping up the spiral stairs.

I'Lenna's group could not get lower and the smoke was billowing deeper into the hall. "We are truly trapped," Darthan said, also coughing now. They all lifted their tunics and shirts and tried to cover their faces.

Tuni spoke, her eyes watering. "Break open the shutters. We need fresh air."

The freed rebels grabbed old chairs and stools and used them to batter open the shuttered windows in the main outer hallway. A sudden draft of air swept toward them all.

"But how will we get *out*?" asked a rebel Rider. "We can't scale the tower walls without rope."

Feylah sheathed her sword. "I have an idea; we'll fly out. I'll call my stallion. Ossi, you yell for Mut. We need him to bring those wild steeds here."

Feylah leaned out the window and whistled for Drael. Brauk called for Kol, and Ossi shouted Mut's name. Their whistles and cries carried over the drenched forestland. A fortress guard, seeing smoke pouring from the Eighth Tower, began to clang the alarm bells. Ringing noise ruptured the cool night air, waking sleepy villagers and rousing unaware guards.

"So much for a secret rescue," Brauk said.

Meanwhile, smoke from the tunnels continued to fill

the hallways. I'Lenna leaned out the broken-shuttered window. "Firo! Firo!" she shouted. The roan mare had saved her when Rahkki had pushed her off the cliff at Mount Crim. Surely the mare would save her again!

Brauk joined her, whistling and yelling for Kol.

"Do you think the Kihlari can hear us?" I'Lenna asked, choking on smoke.

"If not, we'll have to fight our way out."

They'd come so far; it couldn't end like this! The two yelled louder and watched the sky for wings.

22

RESCUE

ECHOFROST HAD WATCHED WITH PINNED EARS as I'Lenna and the Landwalkers snuck off and disappeared into the fortress. "What are they doing?" she'd asked.

No steed answered because no one knew what the Landwalkers were doing. Mut and Tam had stayed behind, but she couldn't ask them.

Echofrost paced. Since landing here and getting captured, she'd been frustrated by her inability to communicate with the Sandwens. And now, watching them creep toward danger and not knowing why, her stomach churned with worry. If they were caught and imprisoned, how would they rescue Rahkki from the giants? She pranced in small circles to ease her mind.

Hazelwind assigned sentries to watch for dragons and other predators, and the rest of the pegasi grazed to ease their nerves. Mut whittled a branch with his hunting knife, and Tam leaned against a rubberwood tree. Dewberry's twins suckled. "Do the foals look thin to you?" Echofrost whispered to Hazelwind.

He peered at her through his thick, matted forelock. "You're worrying."

"Of course I am," she said, stamping her hoof. She faced north, toward Anok. "What do you think is going on at home? Do you think Star won the final battle against Nightwing? Do you think Anok is safe?"

Hazelwind swallowed. "Do you want to return home?"

"No. I'm just . . . frustrated. I feel blind."

"Maybe after we settle, Redfire could ride the jet streams home and find out what's happening there," Hazelwind suggested.

"Yes. That's a good idea," Echofrost nickered. She resumed prancing, her hooves splashing in pools of rainwater that the soaked soil could no longer absorb. The usual clatter of insects, birds, and monkeys seemed subdued by the rain, which had lessened to a soft drizzle.

Graystone preened his feathers, Shysong grazed, and the twins continued to nurse while Dewberry drowsed. Shysong pricked her ears. "I hear I'Lenna calling."

The pegasi lifted their heads.

The whistle sound came again, sharp and coasting over the trees.

"Feylah is calling too," Drael whinnied.

Alerted by the swiveling ears of the pegasi, Mut and Tam stood and listened. "I think I hear my sister," Mut said.

Graystone neighed. "There's smoke rising over the fortress."

"Formation," Hazelwind whinnied. The pegasi galloped together.

"Mount up," Mut said to Tam. "I'll take Drael, you ride Kol. Something's wrong at the tower." He climbed onto Drael's saddle and urged him into the sky. For a brief moment, Mut's entire face lit up with a white-toothed grin. "I'm flying!"

Tam leaped atop Kol and followed him into the sky. "How do I steer?" he cried.

"I don't know," Mut said, tugging on Drael's reins. "Like you would a horse, I guess."

Behind them, the Storm Herd pegasi lifted off and

followed the two teens. The moon's gentle rays set their rain-washed feathers aglow as they all cruised over the treetops.

"That tower looks like it's on fire!" Graystone whinnied.

Echofrost squinted and her focus sharpened. She spied Princess I'Lenna and Rahkki's sister leaning out a high window, waving their arms. Smoke billowed around them. More Landwalkers leaned out of other windows that spiraled around the tower. Desperation rounded their eyes.

"That's the rebel army that Harak imprisoned," Echofrost whinnied.

"Whatever I'Lenna's plan was, I think it failed," Dewberry said, adding a haughty flick of her tail. She flew low with her foals fluttering beside her, their eyes huge in the darkness.

"We're going to have to fly the Landwalkers out," Echofrost said. "Keep the twins away from the smoke."

The pegasi flinched.

"This is the army that will free Rahkki," she whinnied. "Let's get them down from there."

Hazelwind nickered agreement and the herd swooped toward the tower, the wind screaming through their feathers. On the ground, villagers swarmed out of their huts. "Kihlari!" they shouted.

I'Lenna's lips curved into a huge grin when she spied her mare rocketing toward her. "Firo!"

The trapped Landwalkers cheered and Echofrost studied the disaster ahead of her. The Sandwens might be able to tame fire, but it seemed they'd lost control of this one. She pinned her ears. So they weren't *all*-powerful; she stored that information away.

Storm Herd whisked around the tower, their wings sweeping the hard stone walls. Rebel warriors stood on windowsills, ready to jump.

"Here," I'Lenna called.

Shysong darted to the sill and I'Lenna leaped onto her back. Rahkki's sister landed behind Mut, riding Drael double. They soared out of the way, allowing room for new steeds to approach and catch the next Landwalkers. All around the tower, people jumped onto the backs of pegasi.

Echofrost spotted a female with dark-red hair and recognized Tuni. Smoke stung Echofrost's eyes and drifted down her throat as she coasted toward the woman. Tuni's eyelids sprang wide. "Sula!" The silver mare dropped below the windowsill and Tuni jumped, landing hard on Echofrost's spine. Echofrost spun out of control.

Tuni purred encouragement into Echofrost's ears and,

using her body as a counterbalance, she helped Echofrost right herself. They cruised toward the heights.

Bells clanged from the fortress, drawing the rest of the clan. "FIRE!" a guard screamed. Soldiers, Riders, and villagers raced to form two lines from Leshi Creek to Fort Prowl. Buckets were dunked into the raging waters and passed person to person down the line.

The Sky Guard Riders and Fliers cast nasty glances at the escaping prisoners, but the fire was the larger threat. The entire fortress could burn if they didn't put it out. More soldiers raced inside the Eighth Tower, attacking the flames from within.

Harak Nightseer staggered out of a lower tower door, covered in soot. He collapsed, coughing and screaming. His ash-filled yellow hair puffed around his face like a lion's mane. The Borla came with a stretcher and Harak shoved him away. His eyes drifted up and spotted the escaping rebels. He spit ashes from his mouth, his green eyes blazing.

Tuni's legs gripped Echofrost as she twisted around. "I'll be back for you, Harak Nightseer!" she screamed at him.

The pegasi and the rebels banked left and flew toward the southern mountains, allowing Tuni to lead the way.

"When we're out of sight, turn west," Brauk told her. He had landed on Graystone. The white stallion flew with pinned ears, and Echofrost felt sudden, overwhelming gratitude for his help.

Behind them, the fire raged. The villagers, land soldiers, and Riders worked together, shouting instructions and tossing water on the flames. No one could risk leaving the fire to chase Storm Herd. As soon as they were out of sight, Tuni urged Echofrost to bank right and fly west, away from the sun that had just begun to rise over Mount Crim.

23

THE TEAM

"RAHKKI, WAKE UP!" IT WAS BRIM'S VOICE, AND she was shaking him.

"I'm awake," he said, wiping his crusty eyes. Dawn light streaked through the cracks in the horse stall where he'd slept. Tak roused also and stretched his golden wings.

"Sula and her friends are back," Brim said.

Rahkki sat up and swayed. "What? Where?" he cried.

Brim twitched with excitement. "I'Lenna and your brother broke the rebels out of the Eighth Tower just before dawn. Sula and her herd helped them."

"Wait." He blinked, confused. "Did you say my *brother*? How? He can't walk."

"He's healed!" Brim paced the floor, trousers swishing.

Rahkki threw off his blankets. "Why didn't you wake me sooner?"

"I wasn't here. I left to spread the word about the giants. Then Harak's soldiers stopped me. They were questioning every single person in the village about the breakout. Harak is beside himself. He's shouting at his army, the villagers, even at the queen. He's cracking, Rahkki."

Rahkki swallowed. "Everything is happening so fast. Which way did my brother fly?"

"Witnesses said he flew south, but once he was out of sight, he could have gone anywhere."

Rahkki glanced from the stall, back to Brim, and then looked down at himself. He noticed an old pair of boots next to the cot, about his size.

"Those are for you," Brim explained, nodding toward his filthy bare feet.

He pulled them on and left the stall, which opened to Brim's clinic. Confusion had scattered his thoughts. "So, Brauk is walking?"

"Not just walking, he's flying Kol." Brim's cherry cheeks rounded as she smiled. "Once the rebels regroup, they'll come back and fight Harak and Lilliam. I know it. The villagers are preparing, sharpening hunting knives,

whittling new spears, stockpiling what food they can."
Brim's excitement wilted with her next comment. "The
timing is terrible for a Gorlan attack."

Tak swooped up to the rafters and chortled at them.

Rahkki paced. "I need to find the team General Tsun
assigned to me on Mount Crim—Mut, Koko, Jul, and Tam.
If I'm going to find my brother, I'll need help. Can you get
a message to them?"

Brim frowned. "Mut and Tam were with I'Lenna," she
said. "Koko and Jul are still around, but do you think you
can trust them, Rahkki? Remember, Harak is offering a
full round for your capture."

A smile crossed his face as he remembered scouting
giants with his team. "Yeah, I can trust them. Anyway, I've
got no one else. I mean, beside you and Tak." He shrugged
and she smiled. "Ask them to bring camping gear, a few
days' supply of food, and some horses. My brother won't be
easy to find."

"Koko is at the stable," Brim said. "I'll give her your
message and she can fetch Jul. I'll collect some old warhorses for you to ride. If I bring a few to the hut for their
medical exams, no one will question it." She tied back her
hair and moved to leave.

"Brim, wait," Rahkki called, stopping the animal doctor just as she was closing the door. "I—I don't want to put you in danger."

The animal healer winked at him. "Don't fret, young warrior, everyone underestimates an old person."

While Rahkki waited for his friends, he wove together random pieces of leather, wondering how his brother's legs had healed so fast. The last time he'd seen Brauk his brother couldn't walk at all. Tak stretched and flew out Brim's window to hunt.

Soon after, footsteps approached. Rahkki bolted into the horse stall and hid as Brim's back door opened. "Ay?" came a soft voice.

"Rahkki?" asked another. It was Koko and Jul.

Relieved, Rahkki stepped into view. When Jul saw him, he leaped at Rahkki and shook him playfully. "You're alive," he said, adding a brisk hug. "And taller."

Koko was next. "Ay, Stormrunner." She threw a jab at Rahkki's chest, and her strength sent him stumbling into a table.

"Sorry," she said, her lips twitching into a smile.

Rahkki righted himself and grinned. "It's good to see you both."

Questions exploded as the three caught up on all that had happened since they'd last seen one another. "Everyone thinks the giants ate you," Jul said.

Rahkki burst out laughing. "I'd be dead if they did."

"Yuh used ta be too small ta eat," Koko teased. "No' anymore."

Rahkki quickly explained about the soup—what was in it and what was not.

"Tha' can't be," Koko said. "I 'eard the stories since I was a tot. Giants eat kids."

"Not true. They're peaceful." Flashes of roaring, stomping giants filled Rahkki's mind. "Maybe not peaceful," he corrected, "but they don't hunt us." Then he explained about their sacred land and how Rahkki had spoiled Fire Horde's soup.

"You did this *after* they offered us three armies?" Jul asked.

Rahkki grimaced. "Yeah, and now they're coming to kill us, hopefully not until after the rains though. Did you get the camping gear? Will you help me find my brother? He'll know what to do about the giants."

Koko nodded at their satchels. "We snatched up wha' we could. No' much food left, an' no good weapons."

Jul produced a Daakuran hammer and Koko held up her pitchfork. "Harak took all the real ones," Jul explained.

"I have this." Rahkki showed them Miah's wooden-handled dagger, which was the size of a small sword in his hands, and he chose one of Brim's old shovels.

Brim entered the hut, whistling a song. "I got three warhorses tied outside," she said. "They're old, but they're well trained."

Rahkki grabbed Brim and hugged her tight. "I—" He didn't know what to say.

She hugged him back. "I know," she whispered, eyes crinkling as she released him. "Go on now, find your brother and your princess. And here, wear this hat." She plopped a frayed old sunbonnet on his head. "It'll hide your face."

"Thanks," Rahkki said, and he slid through Brim's door with his friends, keeping to the jungle side of her hut. They found the horses ground tied in the shelter of a palm cluster. Koko sorted through Brim's meager tack supply and they outfitted the horses, adjusting bridles and saddles to fit them. Koko chose the chestnut stallion.

Jul picked the gray mare, and that left Rahkki with the biggest horse, a solid-black stallion that was as thick as a bull. The retired warhorses, while long in tooth, were strong and willing. Rahkki stroked the black's wet mane as he mounted. "Don't buck me off," he said.

The experienced stallion accepted Rahkki's weight without fidgeting.

"You look like a gardener, not a fighter," Jul said, laughing at the hat. "But it'll do. With your mucked-up clothes, hand-me-down boots, and bonnet, you look like any other shoddy village kid."

"Except I have a dragon," Rahkki said. He turned his face to the clouds and chortled, imitating Tak. The burner never flew too far from Rahkki and his hearing was excellent. Within a few moments, Tak appeared, diving through the rain.

"Is that a Gorlan burner?" Jul asked, openmouthed.

Rahkki nodded. "Yeah, his flight picks on him, so he hangs out with me now." Tak swooped over their heads, releasing dragon pellets in a neat circle, before landing on Rahkki's shoulder. "Crawk!" he shrieked proudly. Jul and Koko clapped their hands.

"Yuh tamed 'im good," Koko said.

Rahkki shrugged. "He tamed himself. His name's Tak."

Jul snorted. "You've got some way with animals, Rahkki. Wild animals don't tame themselves for me."

"Me either," Koko said. "Most try ta eat me." They all burst out laughing.

With that, the team trotted into the jungle. They would swing wide to avoid the Fifth Clan boundary and then head south to look for Brauk.

24

WESTERN WILDS

AFTER COASTING THROUGH A CLOUD BANK, Brauk yelled over his shoulder, "There it is, the Western Wilds."

I'Lenna lifted her eyes and squinted between Firo's ears. After the rebel army had been freed, Tuni had led the group south to confuse the Sky Guard. But as soon as they were out of view, the group had dropped into the forest canopy and angled west. The wild herd had helped with the rescue and many carried rebels on their backs. Tuni had landed aboard Sula, and Brauk was riding a gigantic white stallion with furry legs.

Tuni guided Sula closer to Brauk and they spoke,

catching up and plotting their revenge against Harak and Lilliam. Ossi dragged behind, looking unhappy, and Feylah carried the rear, taking in everything. The freed rebels balanced on their wild mounts, looking awestruck, and the herd flew in a formation that put I'Lenna in mind of migrating birds. The twin foals glided on their mother's wake, looking tired but determined.

Firo's powerful wings gripped the wind as the group soared across the sky. I'Lenna knew very little about the Western Wilds and had never seen them. The woods ahead were plain and dark, as if a fire had roared through them and burned out all the colors. The soaring black-wood trees grew out of brown mud and their hard trunks were smooth barked and unpalatable, even to termites. Silver foliage decorated the cold and impervious branches, which reached out like frozen tentacles.

I'Lenna searched the looming forest for glints of silk that would indicate a black magna colony, and noticed the treetops were preternaturally silent. "Where are the birds?" she asked.

Brauk turned his head around. "They avoid the Wilds."

"Does anything live here beside the black magnas?"

Brauk peered at her. "You have more tutors than teeth,

I'Lenna; didn't they teach you about the Realm?"

"They're from Daakur," she huffed. "They teach letters, culture, Gorlish, and mathematics."

"None of that will help you here," he scoffed.

"Look," she said, frowning now. "A crown princess has armed soldiers for fighting, private guards for traveling, and wranglers to deal with wild animals. We're taught to *lead*, not to tangle with common threats. As the future rulers of our clans, we must be protected, much like your helmet protects you. Without the head, the body is useless, no?" She glanced across the sky at Feylah, the true crown princess.

"I didn't say you knew nothing," Brauk groused.

"But you implied I know nothing *useful*." Her spine grew tighter. "No, you didn't imply it, you said it outright."

"You did," Feylah agreed, smirking at her brother.

Leaning over the white stallion's neck, Brauk tossed each of them a lopsided grin. "My apologies."

"Thank you. Now please answer my question. What else lives here?" I'Lenna pressed, her voice carrying on the wind.

"War hares, gophers, and deer," he answered. "They thrive on these silver plants and leaves."

I'Lenna tensed at the mention of war hares. She'd read plenty of stories about them in a series of popular Daakuran children's books. The fighting rabbits were as large as Sandwen dogs and meaner than weasels. Highly territorial, they attacked all creatures that came near their hidden warrens.

"War hares are the spiders' favorite meal," Brauk added.

"Oh," she breathed. "That doesn't bode well for us." I'Lenna hugged Firo's glossy neck and peered down at the rain-soaked jungle. A wet, mulchy odor steamed up from the forest floor, mixing with the cooler air. They flew over a pile of bones, gray-white and ravaged clean by monsoon ants. I'Lenna recognized the skull, a stag's.

"Gah!" Mut cried, jabbing his finger west and twisting around on Drael's back. "There's a colony! Look at it!"

I'Lenna spotted the glimmer of rain-wet silk far off toward the horizon. Only the uppermost levels of the colony were visible from where they flew.

"Black magna webs span across acres and acres of blackwood trees," Brauk called out to the group. "It's how I imagine the capital city in the empire—planned and layered like a grid. The different levels are all connected by silk ladders, and every black magna citizen has a job."

"A job? What do you mean?" Ossi asked. I'Lenna noticed that her playfulness toward Brauk had cooled since he'd reunited with Tuni.

Brauk answered her question, oblivious to the change in her. "Like they've got scouts, sentries, and soldiers for the armies. And at the web, they have spinners to make new levels and repair old ones, babysitters for their spiderlings, breeders to make more of the little brats, and a slew of teachers, medics, and cleaners. But they despise rain, which is good for us."

"Do they hibernate?" Mut asked. He'd never ridden a Flier before and his tall body perched awkwardly on Drael's back.

"No, they're awake, but their scouts won't venture far until the ground is drier. We should be fine."

Should be fine? I'Lenna had never heard less soothing words.

Brauk tugged gently on the white stallion's mane, urging him to hold steady. The stallion complied, shaking his head and stomping the sky with his hooves. It was obvious he didn't like to be ridden. The entire group joined Brauk, hovering near the treetops. The Kihlari had also spotted the thick silk cords and, with their superior eyesight, could probably make out the inhabitants as well.

"We're landing here," Brauk shouted over his shoulder. The wind billowed his tunic and slapped his wet hair against his face.

Grateful to get out of the weather, I'Lenna nudged Firo to descend. The mare tucked her black-edged feathers and dropped altitude.

When they touched down between the trees, the riders dismounted. Brauk released the wild stallion with a friendly pat, and his golden eyes seemed brighter against the colorless gray clouds. He addressed the freed rebels and introduced Feylah, his sister. He explained how their mother had escaped and then died.

"You're our true queen," one rebel said to Feylah, and the warriors dipped their heads to her in awe.

I'Lenna flushed and stepped back, still unsure of her place in all this.

Brauk continued. "The Sky Guard has mapped out three black magna colonies over the years," he said. "There might be more we don't know about, but this spot is as far from the three known webs as we can get. Let's make camp. Be as quiet as you can."

The group and the freed rebels broke apart to construct shelters, weave groundcover, itemize their meager supply of weapons, and ration their food supply. Around them, the wild and tame Kihlari grazed, flicking their ears at every noise.

Mut peered at the desolate blackwood trees. "Without birds or monkeys to warn us, how will we know if there's danger?"

"We have better sentries," Feylah answered, eyeing the wary winged horses.

Brauk, Thaan, and Ossi withdrew their hunting knives and went out with several rebel soldiers to gather food. Just as they disappeared, the overfull clouds let loose fresh rain. When the group returned, they scooted beneath the newly fashioned overhangs the others had built. They all shared a meal of squirming grubs. "It was all we could find," Ossi said in apology.

The Kihlari spread their glossy feathers to deflect the falling water droplets, and the twin foals sheltered beneath their dam's large wings.

The Stormrunners—Darthan, Brauk, and Feylah—called a meeting with Tuni and the rebel soldiers. "We need to make weapons and prepare," Brauk began. "Harak will be expecting our return."

Tuni nodded. "But his armies are hungry—Lilliam's not feeding them well—and nothing erodes loyalty faster than hunger. If we make a strong show, more warriors may join us before the battle is over. Especially when they see your sister."

"She's not fighting," Brauk said. "And I won't risk exposing her. Harak and Lilliam are not following Clan Law. They won't respect her authority."

Feylah twirled her sword. "I'm a *warrior* queen, Brother. I am fighting."

His eyes snapped to Thaan and Tully. "I thought you taught her our ways? Women are fighters, true, but not princesses and not queens. Feylah is a ruler. We protect *her*, not the other way around."

"Tell *her* that," Thaan said with the resigned look of someone used to losing arguments with Feylah Stormrunner.

Brauk swiped back his long hair and turned to his sister. "You're serious? You want to fight?"

"We train almost every day," she said, glancing at her guardians. "I've been preparing for my return to the Fifth Clan since I learned to walk."

Brauk considered this, and then shook his head. "No. You're too young and too important," he stated. "Anyway, you have to be twelve to fly with the Sky Guard. That's the law, and as the queen, you must obey it."

Feylah lifted her chin. "That's not fair—"

"I won't argue with you." The two faced off, male and female reflections of each other, and Brauk's posture did not waver.

Feylah finally dropped her eyes and nodded, but she was clearly disappointed.

"And we're not riding these wild steeds," Brauk told the group. "They're unpredictable and untrained." He glanced at the Sky Guard Riders. "Your Fliers are locked in the Ruk. We'll break into the barn and free them. If you lost your Flier during the battle on Mount Crim, you can choose a retired steed."

I'Lenna watched Tuni swallow hard as tears filled her eyes. She was probably thinking of her lost Flier, Rizah.

Brauk brushed Tuni's arm and continued. "The soldiers will fight from the ground. The wild herd can do as they like."

The plans and arguments continued, and I'Lenna tuned them out. She leaned against a tree as shivers rolled through her body. Exhaustion threatened to pull her into sleep.

Firo, who grazed nearby, turned her ice-blue eyes toward the princess. Droplets of water wet the mare's long, dark eyelashes, and her mottled blue hide was as clean as a fresh-laid egg.

With a great sigh, I'Lenna turned her thoughts to Rahkki. He was clever enough to escape the giants; she knew it. But if he had escaped, then where was he? Why hadn't he come home? Tears gathered behind her closed eyelids.

Brauk noticed her sad face and sidled away from the meeting to check on her. "What is it?" he asked.

"Rahkki" was all she could say. Her throat was so tight it hurt.

Brauk touched her shoulder, briefly and gently. "I miss him too," he whispered. "Don't worry, we'll find him."

She stared out of the shelter at the falling rain, took a long breath, and let it out.

Brauk touched her forehead and chewed his lip. "Are you sick?"

"I'm fine."

"Darthan! Tully!" he called. "Come here, I'Lenna's burning up."

Rahkki's uncle trotted to her side, touched her forehead, and felt her pulse. "Why didn't you say something?" he asked, his face pinched.

She shrugged her shoulders.

"I brought medicine," Darthan said, heading for his supplies.

Brauk sat next to I'Lenna, his golden eyes raking over her trembling limbs. "It's almost over now."

She gazed up at him. He was talking about the uprising against her mother. Didn't he realize that afterward, she'd be marooned without a family? The Whitehalls would be banished—or worse—and her mother would denounce her for helping Brauk.

He seemed to read her thoughts. "The clan is your family, I'Lenna. We'll take care of you. All of us, especially the Stormrunners."

"You can't promise that."

He shrugged and repeated one half of an ancient Sandwen proverb. "They say a promise born is a promise dying, right? So give me a chance to show you I'm serious."

She nodded and her unbraided hair shifted across her shoulders.

"Good. My uncle will give you something for the fever. Stay strong and speak up when you need help, okay?"

With a smile that reminded her of Rahkki, and a quick wink that was all Brauk, he returned to the meeting.

Darthan appeared next with medicine and I'Lenna swallowed it. He offered her a dry bedroll and she climbed inside, feeling utterly alone as she imagined a future without her mother.

25

REDFIRE'S DISCOVERY

SEVERAL DAYS PASSED IN THE WESTERN WILDS after the rescue mission. While the Landwalkers prepared by fashioning weapons, Dewberry taught a group of small mares the ancient skill of sky herding. She'd learned it in Anok from Mountain Herd mares, and now she was teaching her agile team the secret language and herding maneuvers that they would use to drive enemy pegasi out of the sky. Hazelwind taught Kol and Drael how to sharpen their hooves.

Intermittent rainfall had kept the black magnas web bound, but now silver rays of moonlight broke apart the clouds and stretched toward the soil. A bright dawn sky loomed on the horizon.

Echofrost stretched her wings to ruffle her plumage, then folded them back. The Landwalkers were up early too, donning their makeshift spears and vine-woven shields, and Echofrost nickered approval. The humans had also been preparing for battle, and a sense of anticipation filled the air.

Kol watched Tuni strap on her belt and wondered about the woman's Flier. "I hope Rizah's alive somewhere," he nickered.

The stallion hadn't been groomed in days. His tail hung in swirling snarls, his feathers were crumpled, and sweat streaked his hide; but Echofrost guessed that Kol's lackluster appearance had more to do with his grief over Rizah than his hygiene. The palomino pinto mare had been Kol's best friend, next to Brauk, and seeing Tuni without her partner upset Kol very much.

Now Graystone's heavy hooves thudded across the soil and the pegasi glowered at him for trotting and making so much noise. "Sorry," he nickered, slowing to a walk. Kol had warned them that black magna webs were anchored to trees *and* soil. When the spiders felt foreign vibrations through their silk ties, they investigated. So far, Storm Herd hadn't seen any spiders up close, and they wanted to keep it that way.

As they were all glaring at Graystone, the sound of wingbeats filled their ears. "Dewberry and the sky herders must be back," Echofrost nickered, yawning.

But it was a lone steed who descended from the sky. "That's not Dewberry," warned Hazelwind.

Rattling their feathers, the pegasi collected to confront the stranger. The Landwalkers startled and looked up.

The approaching stallion landed in a pool of fading moonlight. His copper coat appeared almost white in the silver glow.

"Redfire!" Shysong glided to his side and Storm Herd pressed in closer. They all exchanged breath. The Landwalkers also relaxed when they saw the wild herd greet him with such affection.

Echofrost felt a burst of relief to see that he was unharmed. "Did you find Rahkki?" she asked.

Redfire stretched his wings, and everyone stepped back. "I had more trouble finding you all. What kind of forest is this? It's so . . . bleak."

"So you did find him?" Echofrost pressed. The vein in her neck began to pulse with worry.

Redfire nickered. "I found him loose in the jungle. Somehow, he'd freed himself from the giants."

Pride rose in Echofrost's chest, and the other pegasi

nickered at her, as though praising Echofrost for Pairing with such a clever cub.

"He seemed unharmed, except he was being attacked by huge, vicious ants," Redfire continued. "I tossed him onto my back and tried to fly him home, but he was acting strange, like he was delirious. So we traveled overland the rest of the way. We stopped just outside his territory and he was very sick by then. I left him and went to find you, but you weren't at the farm. When I flew back for Rahkki, he was gone."

"Gone?" Hazelwind asked.

Redfire shrugged his wings. "Yes, so I followed his scent to a small hut, the healer's den, I think, because it smelled like her. I could hear them talking inside and I knew he was safe. I left to search for you and now here I am. Finally."

"Brim will take care of him," Shysong nickered, and then brightened. "If Rahkki's back, then we don't have to fight the giants! We can leave."

"Wait," Echofrost said, raising her wing. "He's still in danger from Queen Lilliam. And not just Rahkki, but his entire clan. And what's to stop her from tracking us down and trying to catch us again? We need to see this through until everyone is safe."

"She's right," Hazelwind said.

"I'm just anxious to find a home," Shysong nickered. "We still don't know where we're going, or where we'll end up. We need a place to raise the twins."

Everyone glanced at Windheart and Thornblaze. The foals were trying to graze on the silver foliage and making horrible faces at the taste. Windheart gagged and tried again but Thornblaze quickly gave up and dived into Dewberry's flank to nurse. "He's just like his sire," Echofrost murmured, remembering Bumblewind.

"Actually, I might know where we're going," Redfire interjected, and the pegasi turned their long necks toward him. "When I didn't find you waiting at Darthan's farm, I decided to do some exploring. I took a jet stream past the southern mountains and discovered a territory where I think we can live." He sighed so deeply and contentedly that the entire herd leaned toward him.

"Tell us about it," Shysong urged.

"I saw beautiful green meadows and wide, clear lakes. A deep river winds through it and there are thick shade trees and rolling foothills." His eyes widened, remembering. "It's perfect for us. The hills will protect us from the wind, and there's plenty of open grazing land and enough coverage to shelter us from rain and sun. I don't think I could imagine a better place to settle."

"What lives there?" Hazelwind asked. "Did you notice signs of Landwalkers or dragons?"

"I didn't stay long," he admitted, shaking his red mane. "I landed to inspect the meadow. I first suspected it might be marshland, but it wasn't. The soil was firm, even in this weather."

Storm Herd nickered, growing excited and rattling their feathers.

"I spotted forestland to the east and more grazing pastures farther south. I flew a spiral around the territory and didn't see any signs of Landwalkers. Plenty of creatures though—elephants, buffalo, and horned animals."

"There will be dragons nearby," Shysong guessed.

"Every good territory attracts predators," Graystone said, and they all nodded.

"How far away is it?"

Redfire continued. "I rode the jet streams, but it will take the herd six or seven days to fly there and much longer if we travel overland because we'll have to cross the mountains."

"The twins aren't ready to fly over a gusty pass," Dewberry groused. She flashed Redfire an annoyed glance as though he had purposely discovered a homeland that was inconvenient.

The copper stallion went on, unfazed. "Then we'll walk there. What do we have if not time? Once Rahkki and his clan are safe, I'll lead you there and any tame steeds who want to join us." He glanced at Kol and Drael.

"What's he talking about?" Drael asked.

Hazelwind filled him in. "Your kind fled the same homeland we did four hundred years ago. The Sandwens captured and tamed you, but you're meant to live free, like us. You can come if you want."

Drael flicked his ears at Kol. "Is this true? Are you going?"

"I don't want to live wild," Kol said, casting a miserable glance at his tangled tail. "And I don't know if it's true."

"Why would I leave the clan?" Drael asked.

"Tell me," Dewberry said, "how did you feel when your clan sold you away from your mother?"

Drael recoiled and his wings sagged to the ground.

"Do you remember?" Dewberry pressed.

"I do," he rasped. Unpleasant memories swam in his eyes. "I—I didn't like it."

"That's why you should leave, so you can have a family and keep it." She drew her twins, Windheart and

Thornblaze, closer. "We're going to rescue the Ruk steeds and their foals too before we leave here. You two can do what you want."

Echofrost's heart squeezed. She wasn't sure it would be that easy, but she also wanted to rescue the dams and foals and retired steeds. She turned to Redfire. "The land you discovered sounds perfect for us."

He puffed his chest at that, and Echofrost felt lighter, a huge burden released. Crossing another ocean to a new continent would have been daunting. She was glad Redfire had found suitable land here, but far from the Landwalkers. She'd rather deal with dragons than people.

To the east, the sun crawled into the sky, spreading a hazy glow across the land. "It's going to be dry today," Echofrost nickered, welcoming the change.

"And the spiders will leave their webs," Kol pointed out.

All of Storm Herd groaned. "At least our feathers will finally dry out," Graystone said, and the herd dispersed to graze and wait.

Echofrost watched Brauk snatch up a spear, a cheerful expression on his face. "The sun is out. I'm going to the pond for a proper bath."

Darthan smiled. "You haven't had enough of being wet?"

Brauk tossed back his hair and laughed, his spirits rising with the sun. "I'm muddy. I'll be back soon. Anyone else want to come?"

Ossi joined him, followed quickly by her brother, and they darted into the black woods.

Echofrost watched them go, wondering if today was the day they'd take action. She hoped Rahkki would stay with Brim, where he was safe. The Landwalkers would be ready soon, very soon, and then all this would be over. The pegasi would trek to this land Redfire had found, and perhaps it would become their new home. She nudged Hazelwind. "The territory Redfire described reminds me of Dawn Meadow, where we were born."

He nodded. "I was thinking the exact same thing." He gazed deeply at her and she sighed, anxious to settle and leave the world of Landwalkers behind. When he dropped his head to graze, she peered south, dreaming of their future.

∽26∼

THE POND

"YOU HAVE TO HOLD HIM STILL, KOKO," RAHKKI
grumbled. He, Koko, and Jul had been exploring the
southern rain forest for days and found no sign of I'Lenna,
Sula, or Rahkki's family.

"If I 'old 'im any tighter, I'll hurt 'im."

Koko had pinned Jul to the ground and wrapped her
legs around his body to hold him still. Now Rahkki was
bent over him, scraping bee stingers out of his skin while
the boy thrashed. Jul had spotted a gigantic beehive in
the trees and, against Rahkki's warnings, had climbed up
to steal some honeycomb. The insects had attacked.

"I hope you're not allergic to bees," Rahkki said. Using
Koko's hoof pick, he hooked the stingers and yanked them

out. The faster he did it, the less poison would infect Jul's blood. Next he sliced open the aloe leaves he'd collected and smeared the gel across the wounds. Jul groaned against the pain.

"'E didn't even get any honeycomb," Koko moaned, gazing longingly at the hive. Nothing was sweeter than bee honey for kids who couldn't afford candy, and Rahkki wished for some too. Also, he was hungry. Because of the rains, hunting had been difficult. Tak kept them alive, scorching snails and charring insects, but Rahkki was tired of eating bugs and slugs.

"I don' think yur brother's 'ere in the south," Koko said.

Rahkki had to agree with her. He yanked out the last stinger and Jul lurched upright. His face was a mask of swollen welts. "Where is he then?" the Rider's apprentice asked.

Rahkki considered the possibilities. The wild herd and the rebels were with Brauk, so he'd need space to hide that many people and animals. He wouldn't fly east toward the giants and the Fifth Clan was north. Since he didn't appear to be here in the south, Brauk had to be hiding in the west, but that was black magna territory. Sandwens didn't travel there, not if they wanted to live. *But they might go there if they wanted to hide!* Rahkki's scalp tingled. "I think I know where Brauk is, but you're not going to like it." He explained and then glanced at Jul's swollen hands. "Can you ride?"

"I don't know."

"Yuh can ride wit me," Koko offered.

Moments later, they were all riding west on their borrowed warhorses. Tak snuggled inside Rahkki's shirt and slept, humming softly. If his dreams turned scary, he'd shriek or shoot flames—Rahkki had several holes in his clothes as a result of Tak's worst nightmares—so he stroked the dragon to keep him calm.

"I can't believe we're going into the Wilds," Jul said, licking his lips and wiping one hand nervously on his pants. The other was wrapped around Koko's waist, and she led his gray warhorse by the reins. Koko clutched her pitchfork tightly in her hand.

"You don't have to come with me," Rahkki said.

Koko snorted and Jul glanced balefully toward home, but they continued riding west. The sun had just dawned and the day promised to be sunny. In the distance, Rahkki heard the roar of a waterfall. The steady rain had filled the Realm's lakes, rivers, and creeks to overflowing.

Flooding, mudslides, and falling trees would cause problems for the seven clans until this early monsoon season ended.

Since they'd camped near the western borderlands last night, the trip into the Wilds was relatively short. Rahkki knew they'd arrived when the green foliage was replaced by silver plants, the swaying palm trees replaced by upright blackwoods, and the chattering birds replaced by deafening silence.

Jul gazed up at the dark trees, his eyes searching for spiders. "Sun and stars," he whispered. "Even birds avoid this place." Koko shivered, though the morning was warm and muggy.

"Tssh," Rahkki hissed. "Hear that? Something is splashing."

Koko lifted her pitchfork, Jul peeked over her shoulder, and Tak poked his head out of Rahkki's collar. "Whatever it is, it's not a spider. They don't swim," Jul said.

Rahkki dismounted and so did the others. Tak stared at his surroundings, and Rahkki felt his tiny heart beating faster and faster. Then his eyes narrowed and he pushed out of the boy's shirt and coasted overhead, shooting his sparkling white fire into the air. He dived and circled as if attacking invisible enemies.

"What's gotten into him?" Jul asked.

"He's scared," Rahkki explained. "So he's showing off."

Koko narrowed her eyes. "Did 'e tell yuh all tha'?" she asked.

Heat glided to Rahkki's cheeks. People thought he could speak to animals, but that wasn't it. He observed and paid attention. As head groom of the Kihlara stable, Koko should understand that. "Course not," he muttered.

The splashing grew louder as they walked the warhorses closer to the noise. It wasn't a leaping fish, a waterfall, or a hunting alligator. It sounded like a person. Rahkki's heart fluttered hopefully.

They crept toward the noise, placing each foot carefully and slowly in front of the other. Rahkki drew Miah's dagger and held it in front of him in case he was wrong. "Tie the horses here," he whispered. They wound the reins around low branches, then resumed stalking toward the water. The well-trained battle horses stood were they were tied, silent and waiting.

Rahkki crouched and rounded a wide blackwood tree. The first person he saw had red, springing curls—Ossi Finn—and then he spotted a tall red-haired teen—Mut Finn. They'd stripped to their undergarments and Mut was splashing his sister. They were laughing. A third person swam underwater, fast and graceful, lean and tan. Rahkki straightened.

Ossi spotted him across the pond and her rosy lips fell wide open. Mut scratched his head. "Rahkki?" he asked as though not believing what he saw.

Rahkki grinned.

Then the swimming man emerged and flung back his wet hair. He wiped the water from his golden eyes.

"Brauk!" Rahkki cried. His throat closed painfully on the word. Every feeling, every fear, and every terror he'd squished down since his capture welled within him at the sight of his brother. Hot tears filled his eyes. His nose began to run. If he moved at all, he'd break into sobs.

But Brauk did not look happy to see him. His eyes rounded. His face drooped into an ugly grimace. "Rah-kki!" he shouted. "Run!"

27

SCOUT

RAHKKI FROZE. *RUN? WHERE?* THEN A SILK thread lassoed his waist and yanked him off his feet. The world turned upside down. He faced the sky, rising swiftly toward the uppermost branches of a blackwood tree. Eight glittering eyes peered down at him as a lone black magna scout hauled him toward its mouth.

Rahkki heard loud, guttural screaming—his own voice. He thrashed at the silk line with Miah's dagger, but his hand was empty. He'd dropped the knife. He tried to kick the silk away from him, but it stuck to his legs.

He threw back his head. Far below, Brauk, Mut, and Ossi raced toward him. "Help!" he cried. Koko hurled her pitchfork like a spear, just missing the spider. Jul began to climb the tree.

The spider grew excited. It danced on the branch as it reeled Rahkki in like a fish. Rahkki grabbed the silk and tried to break it, but the sticky thread wrapped around his hands, further entangling him.

Tak dived from the sky, cawing like a crow. He blasted the spider with his hottest blue fire. The creature ducked and then shot a flurry of silk that splattered across the dragon, disabling his wings. Tak dropped like a stone. The spider clicked its singed legs, shaking with fury.

Rahkki heard Tak hit the ground with a thud as the spider dragged him up the last few lengths. It grabbed him with its front four legs and patted Rahkki down as if searching for a weapon. Then it rolled him, shooting more thread from its abdomen and winding it around the boy's body.

"Brauk," Rahkki yelled.

Jul was halfway up the tree, but he'd never make it to Rahkki in time. Once his prey was secure, this scout would clack its front legs together and call the spider army to carry Rahkki back to the colony. They'd feed him to their spiderlings. A wave of dizziness washed through him as he spun around and around. "Hurry," he wheezed.

Brauk had reached the base of the tree and found Miah's dropped dagger. He gripped the handle to hurl it, and hesitated. Brauk could easily miss the spider and strike Rahkki. Rahkki glimpsed this in pieces as the world spun with him. "Do it!" he urged.

Brauk nodded and then flung the dagger. It whirled end over end toward him. The metal glinted. Rahkki held his breath. The dagger slammed into the spider's belly. Blue blood squirted from the wound and splattered Rahkki and the tree. A hiss of air seemed to whoosh from the huge creature, its eight eyes locked on Brauk—then it fell out of the tree, dragging Rahkki with it.

His belly floated as his body dropped. Brauk raced to get under him. Koko retrieved her pitchfork. Rahkki and the wounded spider fell fast. Mut swept Tak out of the way and cradled the frightened dragon to his chest.

Rahkki smacked into Brauk's waiting arms and they crashed onto their sides. The spider landed upside down. It hissed, injured and furious, its legs kicked the air.

Koko lifted her pitchfork.

"Don't kill it," Ossi cried. She leaped onto the injured spider and began wrestling with its thin, razored legs.

"Hold the head," she gasped. Without questioning her, Koko dropped her weapon and put the spider into a headlock.

Rahkki and Brauk sat up, watching in shock as Ossi reached into the spider's wounded belly and pushed her hand up toward its throat. The overturned spider thrashed its eight legs, fighting for its life. Ossi grabbed something inside the beast, set her jaw, and yanked it out. She held her prize triumphantly over her head—the venom sack, the Queen's Elixir. "Now you can kill it," she said to Koko.

Koko gave the spider's head a hard, fast jerk, killing it instantly.

Ossi wiped her forehead with a clean section of her arm. "The venom's only good if you collect it while the spider's alive," she reminded everyone.

Mut gaped at her. "You're brilliant, Ossi."

She flushed and they all turned to check on Rahkki. Brauk touched him all over, like the spider had done. "Are you okay? Is anything broken?" he asked, his voice cracking.

Rahkki wasn't sure. Everything hurt.

Brauk sat back and studied Rahkki's face, his eyes

swallowing him whole. "I can't believe you're here. You got away from the giants?"

Then he pulled Rahkki close, hugging him tight. His chest heaved from the aftermath of the spider attack, and something else. Some emotion he refused to let Rahkki see. Everyone caught their breath while the brothers reunited.

Mut squinted down at the dragon cradled in his arms. "Is this burner friendly?" he asked Rahkki. "Or am I holding a wild dragon right now?"

Rahkki smiled. "Tak's friendly."

Looking somewhat doubtful, Mut carried Tak to the water to wash the sticky silk off his body and wings.

Brauk stood and pulled Rahkki to his feet. "It's true," Rahkki said. "You're healed." Relief filled the boy. He'd relied on Brauk's strength since their mother died when he was four years old. His brother was the sun to him, and after Sula accidentally paralyzed Brauk, it was as if both their worlds had darkened.

Brauk grinned. "I'Lenna healed me." He explained about the Queen's Elixir I'Lenna had stolen.

I'Lenna, Rahkki thought. The image of her quick smile and shining eyes filled his mind. "Is she with you?"

Brauk grinned and hugged Rahkki again. "Yes, let's go see her." He pulled away. "Wash the spider's blood off first," he said to Rahkki, Koko, and Ossi. "The spider army might be able to track the smell."

"I'll get the horses," Jul said, and Brauk threw him a quizzical look. "We borrowed them from the clan," he explained, and Jul vanished into the blackwoods, returning with three warhorses.

"Our camp isn't far from here," Brauk said. "We'll ride these horses of yours back." He helped Rahkki out of the pond, suddenly beaming. "I have a surprise for you," he said.

A surprise sounded nice to Rahkki, but he felt sick and bruised from his close encounter and his fall, so he simply nodded.

Mut handed Tak back to him. The little burner was clean and trembling, but seemed uninjured. Rahkki held him tight and rubbed noses with him. The gesture soothed Tak. Rahkki felt the dragon's heartbeat slow as he settled close to Rahkki's skin.

Brauk watched this with an amused expression. "A wild Kihlara mare and now a young dragon, what's next, a pet jaguar?"

Rahkki grinned and the group mounted the three horses, each riding double, and Brauk steered Rahkki's large black stallion away from the pond and toward his camp, and toward I'Lenna.

28

REUNITED

WHEN ECHOFROST SPOTTED RAHKKI ENTERING camp on a land horse, she blinked in astonishment. Kol was the first to greet her cub. The winged chestnut glided to his side, snuffling Rahkki's hair and lipping at his pockets. One of the miniature volcanic dragons, a burner, lay nestled in Rahkki's arms. It chortled at Kol, then ignored him. The stallion pressed his muzzle into Rahkki's belly and nickered happily.

"I don't have anything for you," Rahkki said, smiling.

Then the Landwalkers surrounded Rahkki, overwhelming him with hugs and greetings. Animated speech flowed from their mouths. Smiles lit their faces. They touched his skin and his hair, pet his dragon, and lifted him off the horse.

As Echofrost watched, she felt the eyes of Storm Herd watching her. This was her Rider, the one they'd come to save. Matching brands marked his flesh and hers. This boy had ridden on her back and taught her to trust him. She studied him with fresh eyes, watching how his people pressed their faces to his, how they inhaled his scent, and how they needed to touch him. A herd would greet a foal who had been lost in much the same manner.

The longing to inhale her cub's scent filled Echofrost, suddenly and fiercely. She nickered a high-pitched greeting.

He turned and spotted her. "Sula!" He dived away from his friends and rushed her. His worried face broke into a sharp-toothed grin. Startled, his little dragon lifted off and landed on a tree branch. Rahkki launched himself against Echofrost's chest, jostling her onto her hind hooves.

Storm Herd backed away, also startled by his enthusiasm.

Rahkki's past wariness with Echofrost had vanished. He wrapped his arms around her neck and squeezed. "Sula," he whispered.

She closed her eyes, inhaling his essence deep into her nostrils. He was filthy and full of odors she couldn't place, but his woody, spiced breath was familiar. She stretched her wings and then wrapped her purple feathers around his body, creating a warm cocoon for him. She used to be so afraid of this boy. His scent had filled her with such revulsion; his touch had sent fury down her spine. Now she couldn't imagine fearing this small, brave creature.

He stepped back and touched the arrow wound that Brim had stitched for her. "Did you come back for me?" he asked, turning his eyes to hers.

She saw bruises up and down his arms, no doubt made by the giants. Healing welts covered his skin, probably insect bites, and he was taller, stronger. New, wiry muscles defined his arms. His voice had deepened. Her cub was growing up, and somehow this eased her mind, for their time together was coming quickly to an end.

Storm Herd would finish this battle against Rahkki's enemy, Queen Lilliam, and then their detour into the Sandwen Realm would be over forever. Storm Herd would migrate south, to the lands that Redfire had discovered.

She nuzzled Rahkki as Brauk and Darthan approached them.

"Is this my surprise?" Rahkki asked, smiling up at Echofrost.

Brauk studied them both, his old fury at her now gone from his eyes. "It is not," he answered. He put his arms on Rahkki's shoulders. "I need to talk to you about our mother."

Rahkki's body stilled, while his pulse sped up. "You found her, didn't you?" he said, but felt gutted. "You found her bones." He said *bones* because Rahkki knew in his heart that his mother was dead. He'd known it the day I'Lenna had asked him, *If you're mother's alive, then why hasn't she returned?* This question had tumbled around and around Rahkki's mind, but there was only one answer, only one reason why a pantheress would not return for her cubs. Reyella was gone.

"Not her bones," Brauk answered, and he explained how their mother had died. "We found this." He and Darthan moved aside, allowing a short Daakuran warrior to approach.

"Actually, I found you," the warrior said. Her voice was high and sweet.

Rahkki blinked. This was not a soldier; this was a girl. She pushed back her dark hair, exposing golden eyes, tan skin, and long black lashes. Rahkki felt confused, dizzy. He knew her but he didn't know her.

Darthan smiled and cried at the same time. "Rahkki, meet your sister. This is Feylah Stormrunner."

The girl gazed up at him, as wonderstruck as he. "So you're the one who sold the Kihlara blanket?"

"What?" Rahkki stared at the girl who was dressed in clothing from the empire, feeling more confused than ever. "You're my *sister*?"

She nodded and joy burst in Rahkki's chest. He felt like he'd just been shoved into the sunlight after a lifetime of living in cold fog. He gaped from Darthan, to Brauk, to Feylah. "My sister," he repeated, shaking his head in disbelief.

She cocked her head and grinned, looking exactly like Brauk.

Rahkki grabbed her and hugged her. He couldn't speak. For eight years, he'd had a hole in his stomach. His sister's return filled it somehow, even though he hadn't known she existed. "I can't believe it," he said. "My sister."

She grinned, then squeaked—he was hugging her too tight.

That's when Rahkki spotted the bay stallion. His breath caught and the ground shifted below him. He hadn't seen this stallion since he was four years old, but Rahkki would know him anywhere. "Drael," he whispered.

Everyone backed a step away as the bay stallion pricked his ears and trotted to the boy. "You're alive," Rahkki said. His knees buckled and Brauk rushed to help him, explaining how Thaan and Tully had freed Drael from the spiders. Rahkki regained his legs and pressed his forehead to Drael's. "Dee Dee," he cried, using his childhood nickname for the bay. Drael nickered and sighed with contentment. Rahkki wrapped his arms around his neck.

"We're all together now," Darthan said. He and Brauk and Feylah joined the hug. Rahkki's friends and several soldiers wiped their eyes as the Stormrunner family reunited.

After a long embrace, they broke apart and retreated into the shade. Darthan produced slices of fish jerky and skins of water. Ravenous and thirsty, Rahkki, Jul, and Koko gulped the jerky and quenched their thirst. Rahkki chatted with his sister about life in Daakur and she questioned him about his time with the giants.

"Where's I'Lenna?" Rahkki asked, surprised and hurt

that she hadn't rushed to greet him like the rest of the crowd.

"She's sleeping. She's been sick with fever," Darthan said.

Tuni approached. "Hey, Sunchaser," she said, using her nickname for him.

"Tuni!" He grabbed her hands, suddenly bursting with his unspoken news. "The giants have Rizah. She's alive."

Tuni bent over, gasping. "Alive?"

"Yes. The giants have healers like we do. They were helping her."

"Which horde?" she asked, breathless. Color flooded her wan features, like a statue coming to life.

"Highland," he answered. Rahkki went on to explain how he'd ruined Fire Horde's soup and how the three Gorlan armies would soon leave Mount Crim to attack the Fifth Clan. The hordes had their own rivalries and had never joined forces before. The news was devastating. "I'm sorry," he finished.

"Stinkin' giants," Brauk said, and everyone spit on the ground.

"We need to deal with Lilliam and Harak before the giants get here," Tuni said. "If they catch our clan divided, we'll lose to them for sure. Even united, fighting three hordes will be challenging." The rebel soldiers nodded.

But Rahkki felt hopeful. His team from Mount Crim was reunited, Sula stood beside him, his brother could walk again, and his sister was home. The only thing missing was his best friend. "Is I'Lenna *still* sleeping?" he wondered aloud, surprised that all the talking hadn't roused her.

Darthan rose to his feet. "I'll wake her. She's going to be so happy to see you." He retreated into the shadows and then returned a moment later, his face ashen. "I'Lenna's gone."

"What?" Rahkki's insides crumbled.

"Maybe she's with Firo," Tuni guessed.

"Her satchel and bedroll are gone too," Darthan said. "I think she's been gone for a while, probably left some-time last night."

"Why would she leave?" Mut asked.

Rahkki grimaced. "I can guess why." Everyone turned to him. "We're plotting to destroy her family, aren't we?"

The group went silent a moment. Then Mut spoke. "But she's the one who started the rebellion against her mother."

Rahkki stood, tugging on his hair. "I know, but she was in charge of it then, and she believed her mother would go peacefully. Now the rebellion is out of I'Lenna's hands. I—I mean, how can we expect her to help us? I don't blame her for running off."

"Will she give us up?" Tully asked.

"No!" Anger sharpened Rahkki's reply. "She would *never* give us up." He paced, putting himself in I'Lenna's mind. Where would she go? Not to the fortress. Not to the village, where Harak might spot her. He turned to Darthan. "You said she's sick?"

"She was feverish last night."

Rahkki grimaced. "She may not be thinking straight. Did she leave any tracks?"

The group searched the area. To Rahkki's chagrin, Firo stood with the wild herd. That meant I'Lenna had left on foot, and a sick girl alone in the jungle could quickly attract predators. The soil was so trampled by his family and the rebel soldiers that no one could make out I'Lenna's tracks.

"Where would she go?" Darthan wondered.

"There's only one way to find out," Rahkki said.

Brauk and Darthan exchanged a look. "Rahkki," Brauk warned.

"You know I'm going after her," he replied, belting his Gorlan dagger. "I'll take Sula."

"What?" Feylah said, her eyes rounding. "I just found you. We're finally together." Her bottom lip trembled, reminding Rahkki how young she was in spite of the gleaming sword strapped to her belt.

"I'm sorry, but I'Lenna is my best friend." Rahkki regretted leaving his sister so soon too. "I'll be safe on Sula's back."

Brauk's jaw clenched and Darthan sighed.

Rahkki fidgeted anxiously. "I'Lenna can't have gone far yet. The sooner I fly out, the better. When will you attack the fortress?"

"Tomorrow morning," Brauk said. "We'll finish making weapons and shields today. Our first stop tomorrow will be at the Ruk to free the Fliers kept there. I'm not sure these wild steeds are safe to ride."

Rahkki nodded. "If I find I'Lenna today, I'll meet you back here. If it takes longer, I'll meet you at the Ruk tomorrow at dawn."

"I'm sending soldiers with you," Brauk said.

Rahkki laughed. "I'm flying, Brauk, and you just said these wild steeds aren't safe to ride. Unless you lend out Kol or Drael, you'll have to send foot soldiers, and they'll slow me down."

Brauk hesitated and Tuni spoke to him in a lowered

voice. "Let Rahkki go after his friend," she said. "He commanded a dragon, put an army of giants asleep, slayed the Mother of Serpents, tamed a wild Kihlara, and escaped from Fire Horde's warren—all without help."

Brauk rolled his eyes and loosed a long breath.

Rahkki offered a thin smile. "I didn't really—"

"Tssh," Brauk interrupted. "Never dispute your own legend." The brothers hugged and Rahkki felt Brauk's continued reluctance in his tight embrace, but his acceptance too. Brauk wasn't going to stop him. "Keep your eyes on your path," he said. It was a Rider's phrase.

Rahkki nodded. "I will."

Darthan packed a satchel of supplies and handed Rahkki a whittled spear to go with the dagger he'd stolen from Miah. "Fly low and fast," he said. "When you find I'Lenna, take her to my farm. She can hide there, and tell her that she and her siblings can live with the Stormrunners, always. We won't abandon them."

Rahkki nodded. Now he just had to convince his silver mare to let him fly her. He approached Sula, his eyes gliding over her shaded purple wings and small back. She nickered at him, but instead of flinching away as he expected, Sula trotted forward.

Rahkki leaped swiftly onto her, slipped his legs tight below her wings, and gripped her sparkling white mane in one hand. "Thank you," he whispered. Then he whistled for I'Lenna's mare to join them. These two brayas, while wild, were familiar enough with Sandwen ways to understand what Rahkki wanted, and Firo flew to his side.

Rahkki nudged Sula off the ground, reveling in the lush drop of his belly as she lifted off. Firo flapped beside them, and golden Tak soared above. The wild herd pranced anxiously. Sula whinnied and the buckskin stallion lifted off, also joining them. The rest of the herd settled.

Rahkki hugged Sula's neck as they soared away. Riding her felt like another kind of homecoming. He thrived on the lush beat of her wings, the powerful bunching of her muscles, and the bite of her mane against his cheek.

As they flew, he kept his eyes down, searching for I'Lenna. His friend was good at sneaking around unseen, but Darthan had said she was sick. Rahkki was counting on that to slow I'Lenna down. He was pretty sure he could find her, but not as sure he could convince her to stay in the Realm.

I'Lenna couldn't watch the rebels destroy her mother, he understood that, but what if they could save Lilliam?

Rahkki clenched his jaw. He had a very terrible idea, but somehow, it also felt like the right one. If he could just find I'Lenna, he could tell her, and maybe she would stay and help him.

29

THE RIVER

I'LENNA RACED THROUGH THE BLACKWOOD FOR-
est, heart pounding. *Don't run in the jungle*, she chided
herself. She knew better! But her feet didn't listen. They
skipped faster, hurtling her *away*.

After Brauk rescued the rebel army from the prison
tower, everything had changed for her. When she'd begun
the rebellion with General Tsun, she'd been in charge of
it. She'd demanded protection for her mother and her siblings and safe passage to the empire where they would
live in exile. General Tsun had even agreed to pay Lilliam
a small allowance for one year that would help her rent
rooms and find work. The thought of her mother *actually*
working was as incongruous as a tiger wearing clothing,

but I'Lenna had remained hopeful.

Now Brauk was in charge. He knew Lilliam was stealing from the clan, and Lilliam had proved she would not accept defeat. I'Lenna had watched the rebels prepare for attack with growing trepidation. The pile of sharpened spears made her feel sicker than she already was. She couldn't stop what was to come, but it had struck her early this morning that she couldn't watch it either. She decided to go.

I'Lenna ducked beneath a silver-leafed blackwood branch. She needed to get out of the Wilds before a black magna spotted her. She had a hunting knife, a small ration of food, a bedroll, and a rain cloak.

She was heading to Darthan's farm. She'd borrow more supplies there and pay him back after reaching Daakur. A few precious gems decorated her ankle bracelet and she planned to sell them to Willa Green at the trading post. She'd buy a ferry ride across Cinder Bay to the Daakuran Empire and lease a room there. With her expensive education, I'Lenna could find work to support herself.

Tears rolled down her cheeks as she imagined living alone. Truth was, she couldn't imagine it, not really; she'd just have to experience it. She wiped her eyes. The sun was rising fast, too fast. Tomorrow Brauk would lead the attack on Fort Prowl. She hoped to be in Daakur by then.

I'Lenna paused for a breath. Her body shuddered with grief and weakness. Her fever had finally broken and she felt light, empty. Perhaps as soon as tomorrow night, Feylah Stormrunner would be sitting upon her rightful throne, her ancient crown upon her head. I'Lenna's lips twitched into a brief smile. A huge wrong would be made right—well, maybe not made right, but resolved anyway.

And even though Brauk and Darthan had assured I'Lenna she had a place in the Fifth Clan, she could not accept it. Lilliam's reign was a lie. I'Lenna's jewelry, clothing, her education—were all stolen from the true crown princess. Heat rushed to her cheeks as the shame of it struck her anew. I'Lenna deserved to live on foreign soil, far from her people, as Feylah had been forced to live. Her spine stiffened with resolve and she resumed running.

By midday, I'Lenna had reached the River Tsallan. "Sun and stars," she cried. The banks had disappeared and the muddy river had reached the tops of them. Dead branches and debris sped downriver. I'Lenna hiked closer to the river's edge and stared into the water. It would be impossible to cross it. But there was no way to get to Darthan's farm and then Daakur *without* crossing. She teetered and began to laugh. "I'm stuck here." She laughed harder, realizing she was exhausted and perhaps hysterical. Sudden dizziness overcame her. *I need to sit down,* she thought.

I'Lenna took a step, but in the wrong direction. Her foot hovered and then touched water. *Oh!* Her body tipped forward. Her arms flailed. She tumbled into the river.

Rahkki and Sula glided between the trees. He kept his eyes down, trying to find I'Lenna's boot prints. Firo, the buckskin stallion, and his dragon trailed behind, silent and watchful.

The Wilds were dense, the soil as dark as the trees, and every odd mark on the ground was as likely to be a shadow as a boot print, but Rahkki had spotted a consistent line of smudges that looked like tracks.

He urged Sula down, slid off her back, and examined the marks. He grinned, pleased. Yes, these were boot prints—I'Lenna couldn't be far. He leaped back aboard Sula and asked her to trot. They were about to exit the Wilds, and Harak's patrols could be anywhere. Better to stay on the ground, Rahkki decided.

Sula trotted, and then eased into a smooth canter, and Tak flew down to rest on Rahkki's shoulder. Firo and the buckskin galloped between the trees beside them. Rahkki noticed how quiet they were for such large creatures. They leaped overgrown bushes and jumped small logs with the aid of their wings.

Appreciation filled Rahkki's heart. Cantering Sula reminded him of riding horses. The beat of her hooves wound up from her body to his, staking them to the land and to each other.

The sun arced overhead and its beams pierced the trees, splaying like fingers to the ground. Reptiles slithered out of the shade to rest on hot stones. Some bolted out of Rahkki and Sula's way, others held their ground, hissing. Monkeys screeched at the Pair, excited by their speed, and mosquitoes flew in black swarms.

As the rain forest rolled by, white froth broke out along Sula's neck and chest. Rahkki leaned forward to relieve the pressure on her back. Ahead he heard the rushing sound of the River Tsallan.

They burst out of the trees and onto the high, wet banks of the river. The water, ready to spill over, sped past him, muddy and ferocious. Sula and Firo each whinnied and reared. The buckskin pawed the mud. Rahkki leaned forward and grabbed his mare's neck before he slid off her back. Upset by the commotion, Tak darted off his shoulder and shot toward the clouds. "What is it?" Rahkki asked the winged horses.

Firo leaped off the bank and glided in an anxious circle. Using one hand to block the sun from his eyes, Rahkki scanned the forest on the other side of the river and saw nothing unusual.

Then he noticed that I'Lenna's boot prints ended at the very edge of the water. "Land to skies!" He urged Sula into the sky. Had I'Lenna tried to swim across?

They soared over the water, following the current. Anxiety bloomed in his chest. He glimpsed no boot prints on the other side of the river. "Where is she?" he asked the three Kihlari, as if they could answer him. That's when he spotted a small head bobbing in the water, rushing toward the ocean. "I'Lenna!" he screamed.

She didn't hear. Her eyes were fixed on the shore, her arms and legs paddled furiously, and exhaustion lined her small face. She grabbed hold of a rolling log, but it only whipped her faster downriver. She let go and churned toward the river bank.

Without thinking, Rahkki stood and dived off Sula's back into the water. Pulling hard with his hands and kicking rapidly with his legs, he cruised toward I'Lenna, swimming with the flow of the current. The princess struggled, sinking between breaths. Sula and Firo dived toward her, whinnying frantically.

Loose debris—branches, leaves, and garbage from the village—drifted alongside, clunking into Rahkki. "I'Lenna," he gasped as he drew closer.

She heard him and shifted her head in his direction. Their eyes met and she blinked, looking stunned. He floated fifty lengths behind her, maybe less. "Rahkki?" she mouthed.

He kicked harder, jetting toward her and then bumping into her. As he grabbed her thin body, he felt overcome by relief and exhaustion. Sula and Firo reached them and bit into their clothing, dragging them through the water toward shore.

They reached Darthan's levy. He'd built it to protect the Sandwen lowlands from flooding during monsoon season. It also enabled him to divert water to irrigate his rice fields. Rahkki and I'Lenna climbed it. The levy bulged, damaged by time and pressure, ready to break. They exited the water, and then tramped across the mud and into the cover of the jungle. They collapsed on their backs and wheezed for breath.

The three Kihlari stood over them. Firo snuffled I'Lenna's skin, and Sula leaned against the buckskin stallion, keeping one eye on Rahkki.

I'Lenna wasn't still for long. She propped herself onto her elbows and stared at him. Her lips trembled, blue with shock. "You're back," she said. "You got away from the giants?"

"Somehow I did." He stared into her dark eyes. The last time he'd seen her, Harak had been chasing her through the clouds to arrest her.

I'Lenna scanned his body. "Did the giants hurt you?"

His throat tightened. He shook his head. She flopped back down, touching her shoulder to his, still out of breath. They rested, worn out. "I heard you've been sick," Rahkki said.

She frowned. "I'm fine."

"I'Lenna," he chided. Her wet clothing clung to her, showing how thin she'd become since her arrest. Her eyes gleamed like dark marbles and her normally tan skin had lost all color.

But I'Lenna just smiled. It was that quick grin Rahkki had learned meant anything from *I am truly fine* to *I am truly not fine but I'm going to pretend that I am anyway.* "So you talked to Darthan, which means you've seen your brother and met your sister?" she asked, brightening a bit. "I've been with them since I escaped the Sunstone."

Anger roared through Rahkki at the mention of the Sunstone, and I'Lenna must have read the sudden fury in his eyes. She held up her hand. "I don't want to talk about me," she warned him. "Just you."

Rahkki wished she weren't so stubborn. "Yes," he finally answered, "I saw my brother and Drael, and I met Feylah. I—I still can't believe I have a sister and that Drael is alive."

I'Lenna intertwined her fingers with his. "Feylah is going to make a fine queen."

"She will," Rahkki agreed, and a real smile formed on his lips. "And Brauk is healed, thanks to you!"

She laughed, waving off his gratitude. "I think he's finally forgiven Sula for kicking him." She glanced at the wild steeds that stood over them like sentries. "They came back for you, we think. They flew to Darthan's farm and just . . . waited. They followed us into the Wilds." I'Lenna shook her head. "The rumors about your power over animals will grow."

Rahkki grinned. "Wait until you meet my dragon."

I'Lenna blinked. "You have a dragon?"

Where was Tak? His golden friend liked to explore and

hunt but he was never too far away. Rahkki whistled for him and, a few moments later, the burner jetted from the clouds and thumped onto the ground between them, burping green smoke.

"Oh," I'Lenna cried, mesmerized. "You weren't joking."

Rahkki stroked Tak's scales. "I am the Commander of Dragons, after all."

I'Lenna shoved Rahkki as playfully as she could in her weakened state. "And the Slayer of Serpents."

He pushed her back, softer. "And a Saver of Princesses too."

I'Lenna laughed, a true happy giggle. "Ah, Rahkki, you're home," she whispered, tears glistening in her eyes. "Your family is together. I'm so happy for you."

They enjoyed a quiet moment listening to the river before he remembered that he was there to collect her. "Why did you run off?" he asked, though he believed he already knew the answer.

I'Lenna stood and stroked Firo's mottled blue hide. "I'm leaving the Realm. The Whitehalls don't belong here."

Rahkki stood also. "Nothing your mother has done is your fault. You were three years old when she took over the Fifth Clan!"

"I know that," she said.

His shoulders drooped. Of course she knew that. "Look, Darthan suggested you hide at his place. Why don't we go there together and just . . . wait for all this to be over." Rahkki's eyes searched her face. Could they ignore what was happening? Just let their families sort it out without them? He enjoyed the fantasy. "I'll cook the food and we'll play stones and hide from the world." He reached for her hand, noticing he'd grown taller than her.

I'Lenna gazed up at him. "I can't be here for this battle, Rahkki. I'm leaving."

Rahkki's earlier idea floated up in his mind. The rebels would be furious if he followed through with it, but he suddenly didn't care. He only cared about I'Lenna and the awful past that still lived between them. "What if you and I could save your mother?"

Her jaw gaped open and Rahkki felt immense satisfaction to have tongue-tied I'Lenna Whitehall. "So are you in?" he asked.

She blinked and found her voice. "I'm listening."

30

DAWN

THE TWO CUBS FINALLY RECOVERED FROM THEIR disastrous swim and stood. Rahkki climbed onto Echofrost's back and I'Lenna onto Shysong's. They lifted off and Rahkki guided Echofrost through the jungle to Darthan's farm. Hazelwind flew between the trees, following them like a shadow.

When they arrived, Echofrost scented a stranger. Someone had come to tend Darthan's animals and rice crop. Their sandal prints and cloying smell lingered all over the farm, but the stranger was no longer present.

I'Lenna stumbled into Darthan's hut while Rahkki entered the barn and returned with a rich mixture of grain. "Here," he said, offering it to the three pegasi.

The golden dragon danced on his shoulder, chortling with excitement and filling the air around him in green smoke.

"Rahkki's made a new friend," Echofrost nickered to Hazelwind.

"A loud friend," Hazelwind added.

Rahkki stroked Echofrost's neck, then joined I'Lenna inside the hut. Soon a low fire burned in Darthan's hearth and their soft voices filtered from the open window. Tak darted toward the heights, enjoying a rare dry sky. He flew loops and dived at dizzying speeds. He shot five shades of fire at imaginary enemies. He raked his claws across the dark clouds.

Echofrost inhaled a deep breath of jungle mulch and salt-tinged sea air. If she pointed her ears north and closed her eyes, she could hear waves lapping the shore of the Dark Water ocean. Overhead, fresh storm clouds marched across the sky, shrouding the sun. Thunder boomed in the east, drawing closer. "A new storm is coming," she nickered to her friends. "I expect we'll have more rain tomorrow."

"The battle is tomorrow," Hazelwind said as he scratched his neck with his back hoof. "I can tell by the excitement in the Landwalkers' eyes. They are not so different from us."

"That's true," Shysong agreed. "They're warriors and

they've had enough with I'Lenna's mother. This is an old fight, not as old as ours with Nightwing, but old enough that the course cannot be changed." She angled a mournful glance toward the hut. "What do you think will happen to I'Lenna if they drive her mother out?"

Echofrost smoothed her plumage. "What will happen to the clan if they don't? The Fifth has no choice."

Hazelwind trotted between them. "You're both getting too involved. Lilliam is a bad ruler, like Petalcloud was in Anok. But once the clan is free of her, what they do next is their business." He flung back his thick forelock.

Echofrost nickered. Hazelwind was right. Freedom was about choices. Making right ones or wrong ones was a separate consideration. They ate the grain and rested for the remainder of the day. As evening dawned, Echofrost grew agitated. "Is Rahkki going to take us to the fight?" she wondered aloud. "We're far from Fort Prowl and Brauk's army. I don't want to leave my cub, but I won't let Storm Herd fight without us."

Hazelwind glanced at the sloppy wet rice fields, the cozy barn, and Darthan's hut. Smoke rose from the peaked roof as the cubs cooked their meat. "I don't think those two are going *anywhere* tonight. Let's see what dawn brings."

Hazelwind settled to preen his jade feathers. Shysong and Echofrost finished the last of the grain Rahkki had left them. The sweet, nutrient-rich mixture restored Echofrost's tired muscles and hungry belly.

While the clouds piled higher and the air grew thicker, the pegasi stood head to tail, swatting evening mosquitoes, and they drifted into sleep.

At dawn, Echofrost woke when Rahkki and I'Lenna emerged from Darthan's hut. They stretched and yawned in the languorous, unhurried manner of youth. The burner that Rahkki called Tak flew out and up, scorching the thick fog with red dragonfire. Blearily, the two cubs entered the barn where Lutegar the swamp buffalo lived and came out with arms full of saddles and bridles.

Hazelwind flinched and Echofrost felt a familiar wave of dizziness at the sight of the oppressive gear. Rahkki set down his load, went back inside, and returned carrying her set of armor. Brim must have delivered it to the farm after removing it from Echofrost in the woods. The heavy stuff hadn't exactly protected her, but then she remembered how many arrows the armor had *deflected*. Yes, one got through, but the armor *had* saved her life. I'Lenna approached Shysong with an old horse saddle and bridle in her arms.

Shysong touched her wing to Echofrost's shoulder. "We can wear this tack one more time," she nickered, encouraging her friend. "For them." She nodded toward the cubs, and Hazelwind nickered approval.

Rahkki and I'Lenna plopped everything on the ground. I'Lenna went back for another huge bucket of grain, which she placed at their hooves. As the pegasi munched breakfast, the cubs dressed Echofrost and Shysong in their tack. I'Lenna made several adjustments to get the horse saddle to fit behind Shysong's wings. When they were finished, they mounted and galloped the pegasi overland, heading south, riding between the trees where they would not be spotted.

Echofrost assumed they were heading to Fort Prowl, but Rahkki halted her in a thick cluster of palms near the Ruk. Soon after, Brauk and his army appeared, over a hundred warriors, slinking through the shadows. Storm Herd walked with them, and when they spied Echofrost, Hazelwind, and Shysong, they flared their wings in greeting. Rahkki and Brauk must have set up this meeting place yesterday, before her cub took off to find I'Lenna.

Brauk leaped off Kol's back and hugged Rahkki and smiled at I'Lenna. "You found each other," he said. Rahkki nodded and the brothers pressed their foreheads together. Brauk pointed at them. "You two stick to the rear with Feylah," he said. "I don't want her fighting. I don't want *any* of you fighting."

Rahkki nodded.

"Thaan and I won't leave Feylah's side," Tully said. "Don't worry about her."

Brauk climbed back aboard Kol.

Scanning the Fifth Clan structures and settlement in the distance, Echofrost saw that all was quiet. Smoke piped from the huts, but otherwise, the villagers and soldiers were asleep. If the Sky Guard Dawn Patrol was out flying, it was over the jungle somewhere else, not here. The morning air was full of moist fog and even the crickets seemed depressed by it, singing halfheartedly. Lightning flickered overhead, followed quickly by thunder, and the clouds bulged, full of rain. The weather today would be nasty.

The rebel Landwalkers donned their makeshift shields and spears, and Echofrost rattled her feathers. Hazelwind moved closer and touched his muzzle to hers, making her heart thud harder. "Are you ready for this?" he asked, brushing his wing against her healing wound.

"I'm ready," she answered.

Storm Herd collected, watching the Landwalkers with mounting excitement.

Windheart and Thornblaze scampered from beneath Dewberry's wings, chasing insects. Echofrost gaped at the pinto. "You brought the twins?"

"What was I supposed to do with them?" Dewberry asked. Feathers shed from her wings like emerald tears. Stress creased her forehead.

Echofrost had never seen Dewberry look frightened before. "Take them to the coast. Wait for us there."

Dewberry shook her head. "I spent the last few days training the sky herders, but they're not ready to fight without me. I have to lead them." She stamped her hoof in frustration. "In Anok, the elders would watch the twins for me, but we have no elders."

Echofrost closed her eyes, thinking. *Who could watch the foals?* Then her eyes sprang open. "Lutegar will protect them!"

Dewberry snorted. "That old swamp buffalo?"

"Lutegar adores them and they trust her. They'll be safe in Darthan's barn."

At that moment, a fast breeze rushed through the jungle, almost knocking Windheart over. "They can't stay here," Echofrost whinnied.

"All right," Dewberry agreed. "I'll take them now. It's not far." She gave a low whistle and the twins lifted off and glided obediently to her side. They soared toward Darthan's barn, flying low with their hooves skimming the underbrush. The foals' tiny wings flapped at twice the speed of Dewberry's.

Echofrost turned her attention to the Landwalkers. They were speaking rapidly to one another; gesturing toward the Ruk. The rebels adjusted their branch-woven shields and lifted their wooden spears. When they were ready, Brauk whistled the command to go. The Landwalkers and the pegasi marched forward, treading as softly as possible.

The group crept between the trees, heading directly toward the Ruk. A calm settled in Echofrost's heart, as it always did before battle. Pegasi were born warriors. Even Dewberry's foals knew how to bite and kick and rear, and unlike most hooved animals, pegasi did not run from danger.

Echofrost's muscles stretched and bunched as she assessed her health. She felt rested, strong, and alert. Her threaded scar was flat, the skin closed tight. She drew a breath, filling her lungs. It still hurt to breathe deeply, and she swallowed the slight gasp that rose to her lips.

Dewberry soon returned and caught up to them. "The twins are safe," she said. "You know, if that Lutegar had wings, she'd make a pretty good warrior."

Echofrost nickered, imagining Lutegar's large body flying with Storm Herd. Meanwhile, the sun rose in the east and tried to poke holes through the heavy wet clouds.

"Follow Brauk's lead," Echofrost instructed Storm Herd. "Fight his enemies."

The pegasi rattled their feathers and flattened their ears as they all marched toward the Ruk.

31

THE RUK

IN THE HUSH THAT PRECEDED DAWN, THE REBEL army reached the Ruk. Echofrost spied Harak's Sky Guard patrolling over the eastern forest, too far away to easily notice them.

"So this barn is where the mares and foals are kept?" Dewberry whispered.

"Yes," Echofrost answered. "And the Fliers of the imprisoned Riders we freed are also inside."

Brauk dismounted and forced open the huge sliding wood doors. He, Tuni, and the others slipped inside, followed by Dewberry, Echofrost, Hazelwind, Shysong, Redfire, and Graystone. Muffled cries arose from the Sandwen grooms who worked at the Ruk. Tuni, Ossi, and

Mut snatched the grooms and clapped their hands over their mouths. "Shhh," Tuni warned them.

When the grooms saw how many rebel soldiers had entered the barn, they ceased struggling and the Landwalkers released them. "Your Fliers are that way," one said. He pointed down an aisleway. The eldest groom flattened herself against the wall as the Landwalkers and the wild steeds marched past her.

A jungle breeze blew through the doors, carrying the pegasi's scents deep into the Ruk. The Kihlari breeding stallions reacted first, blaring piercing challenges to the strange steeds in their midst.

Hazelwind could not resist their calls to battle and he bugled back at them, stamping his hooves. Echofrost exhaled, sensing how fast this situation could unravel.

"These wild Kihlari are upsetting our sires," a groom said, full of concern for his tame charges. Thunderous pounding filled the Ruk as the breeding stallions kicked their stall walls.

"We'll be quick," Brauk said. He hurried to release the trapped Fliers. They nickered with joy when they saw their Riders coming.

As Echofrost passed rows and rows of Kihlari stalls,

her heart twirled in her chest. She counted fifteen foals, each bright eyed and well formed with perfect wings and glossy feathers. They watched her, bleating curiously. Some reared to better see over their stall doors. The mothers whickered and pranced, nervous at the influx of wild steeds.

"Look at them," Dewberry whispered. "They're beautiful."

Unlike the foals in Anok, who were lean and dusty and feather crumpled from playing—these grain-fed colts and fillies were round bodied and sleek. Their dams had clear, soft eyes. They seemed gentle yet fearless. Their physical conformation was perfect. In Anok, any mare could have a foal. Here, only the best were allowed.

The angry stallions kicked their doors so hard the walls shook.

"Come for our mares, have you?" one stallion blared at Hazelwind. "You'll have to kill us first."

Hazelwind pranced side by side with Graystone and Redfire. Their feathers had puffed, making their wings appear twice their normal size. Their muscles rippled like hot fluid beneath their hides, and they could not tear their focus off the braying challenges of the foreign stallions.

Echofrost nudged her friends. "We're not here to fight with these steeds."

Redfire blew hard out his nostrils. "But they're calling us out!"

"No they aren't," she assured him. "They've never lived in a proper herd. They don't understand what their challenges mean to us."

"I think they do," Hazelwind snorted, but he lowered his wings.

Outside, Echofrost heard many pairs of boots tramping through mud.

Tuni heard them too. "Soldiers are coming," she warned.

The oldest groom shouted at Brauk and the rebels. "Get your Fliers and get out of here before our sires tear down the Ruk!"

The Landwalkers quickly freed their trapped Fliers and chose several retired Kihlari to fill out their ranks. The thumping boots moved closer. Shouts sounded and Echofrost heard the clang of metal. "We're going to get trapped in here if Brauk and Tuni don't hurry up." She glanced at Dewberry. "If you want to free the dams, you'd better do it now."

Dewberry reared and whinnied to the breeding mares and stallions. "Steeds of the Ruk!" she called. "Listen to me. You descend from the ancient Lake Herd pegasi of Anok, the legendary wind surfers of the Flatlands. You aren't meant to live locked in stalls. Your ancestors lived free. Come with us and join our herd. Live untamed, as pegasi are meant to do!"

The stallions quieted and the Ruk went still. Echofrost lashed her tail, ears pricked toward the Landwalkers approaching the Ruk. She heard low voices outside.

Dewberry continued. "With us, you can choose your own mates, fly when you want, and raise your foals. You don't have to watch them get sold when they're yearlings. In our herd, mares and stallions join for life. You'll always have protection and you'll never be alone." All ears pricked toward Dewberry. "But you have to *want* freedom. It's your choice." She glanced at Hazelwind and he nodded to her.

Using her wings, Dewberry began unlatching stall doors and flinging them open. "Go!" she cried to the mothers. "Live free!" Then she dived out of their way.

The Kihlari breeders blinked at her from inside their open stalls.

"Go on," Dewberry urged. A colt bleated and hid behind

his mother's wing. Not one steed moved.

Dewberry faced Storm Herd and shrugged her wings in disappointment. "I was expecting a bigger moment," she nickered.

Hazelwind shuffled his hooves. "The soldiers are rounding this barn," he whinnied.

"Think about joining us," Echofrost finished, glancing at the pampered Kihlari foals. "We'll teach you our ways."

A soldier's voice sounded, giving orders. "Surround the barn," she commanded. She and her patrol had approached the Ruk from the south.

"Let's go!" Echofrost whinnied, and the urgent tone in her voice electrified her friends. They galloped toward the exit.

Brauk and his Riders mounted their steeds, riding bareback. Those who didn't own Fliers chose retired Ruk steeds to ride, a mix of older mares and stallions. And they all exited the Ruk.

The female groom flattened herself against the wall again as they loped past. "Land to skies," she whispered.

Echofrost galloped out of the barn just as the sun breached a cloud, casting the winged army in golden light. The pegasi leaped into the sky, over the heads of the angry soldiers.

"Call General Nightseer!" a soldier cried.

Brauk's Flier, Kol, trumpeted an over-stallion's call to battle.

The final war for the clan had begun.

32

DESCENT

RAHKKI GUIDED SULA OVER THE VILLAGE AS THE fortress bells began to ring, calling the Sky Guard army. His pulse thrummed and his muscles twitched. The wind ruffled Sula's purple feathers, carrying their dry scent to his nostrils. She pumped her wings and whinnied, and the sound vibrated her rib cage. She glanced back. Her eyes were dark shining pools. Her teeth were bared. Rahkki gripped her mane tighter, preparing.

"Head to the fortress," Brauk commanded.

Sloppy puddles marked the terrain below and massive cloud drifts layered the sky, tumbling upward in dark billowing clumps that drifted south, pushed by the breeze.

It was a perfect day for sheltering by a hearth and telling stories, playing stones by candlelight, or fighting beetles with the other Riders—but none of this was to be. The fortress bells had clanged, tolling the onset of battle.

The villagers poured out of their huts, armed with shovels and hammers and covered in thick hides to protect their bodies. They cheered when they spotted Brauk. I'Lenna, disguised in her rain cloak, flew beside Rahkki. Feylah flew with Thaan and Tully, hidden by her helmet.

"Land to skies," I'Lenna hissed. "My mother has pushed this too far."

Harak's soldiers spotted the villagers. "Get back inside!" They rushed in to escort the villagers to their huts.

"We won't hide from you!" shouted the clan blacksmith. He raced toward the soldiers, hammer lifted over his head. The adult villagers charged with him. They swarmed the soldiers, who seemed frozen with shock.

One of the captains shouted. "Fight back!"

Another yelled, "But these are our people!"

"No. They're traitors to the crown!"

This got the soldiers going. Not all of Lilliam's forces respected her, but they were loyal to her throne. Rahkki watched as they lifted their sawa swords and pressed into the villagers, cutting and arresting.

"Brauk!" Rahkki screamed over the rising wind. "We've got to help the people."

A curt nod from his brother and then Brauk was descending. The fortress and the queen would have to wait.

At the sound of Rahkki's voice, the villagers cheered. "It's Sula and Rahkki, the Commander of Dragons!" shouted a villager. "They aren't dead!" The soldiers hesitated, and the villagers gained ground on them.

Brauk shot Rahkki a triumphant grin. Maybe rumors weren't so awful, Rahkki thought.

But his musings were squashed a moment later when Harak's soldiers attacked with renewed vigor. They lit firebrands and tossed them at the huts, setting thatched roofs on fire. Smoke quickly rose and the Kihlari had to dodge it or risk inhaling it.

Tuni's mother, Kashik Hightower, blasted out of her home wielding one of Tuni's old practice swords. Tuni landed her borrowed Ruk stallion beside her mother and they fought together. "We're your *clanmates*," Kashik yelled at the soldiers.

Several soldiers focused on arresting villagers rather than fighting them. Others had switched into battle mode and saw only enemies. They struck and parried and burned more huts.

The rebels landed to help the villagers. They fought the soldiers from the ground. I'Lenna ducked as a sword grazed past her head. "Get into the sky," Brauk snapped at her. "You're not protected."

I'Lenna, who had no shield or armor, nodded. She and Firo glided out of the melee and joined Feylah, Thaan, and Tully, who watched helplessly.

Brauk leaped off Kol's back. He twirled and thrust his sword. Kol reared, clubbing soldiers with his hooves. The wild herd dived from the sky, striking Harak's soldiers, who were no match for their speed and strength. Coughing on smoke, Rahkki balanced on Sula as she landed and galloped into the fray.

"Get to the jungle," Tuni screamed to Kashik and the other villagers.

Rahkki watched in horror as Sandwens attacked Sandwens. Young mothers sprinted away, carrying their babies into the rain forest. The jungle should not be safer than the village. This was wrong, all wrong. But at least the soldiers didn't bother to chase them there. Animals had broken free from their pens, and Sula leaped over a squealing pig as it scrambled across their path.

Anger, hot and pulsing, roared to life in Rahkki's chest. "Stop fighting your own people," he screamed at the soldiers. They ignored him.

Brauk leaped aboard Kol and flew him over everyone's heads. He raised his hand. "Halt," he commanded with such bloodborn authority that everyone obeyed him.

The bleating of animals and crackling of flames provided the undercurrent for what he was about to say. Beyond him, Rahkki heard the Kihlari stable's ceiling opening. The Sky Guard would be upon them in seconds, but in this breath of a moment, Brauk spoke to the villagers and soldiers alike. "Queen Lilliam sends half your tithes to Queen Tavara of the Second Clan. She's stealing from you."

The villagers gaped at him.

Harak's battalion leader shifted and her armor creaked. "Prove it."

Brauk's gaze was indulgent. "You know it's true. You're living it. Why can't Lilliam afford to feed her army? Why does she charge for medicine? Why can't she afford war with the giants?" His jaw muscles fluttered angrily. "Lilliam's own general turned on her. Have you wondered *why*?" His golden eyes swept across everyone present.

His words sent shock waves through the villagers and the soldiers.

"Don't fight us," Brauk implored Harak's battalion of soldiers. "Help us."

Sudden hollering and whinnying filled the sky. "Incoming!" Tuni shouted.

Rahkki snapped his head toward the noise and watched the Sky Guard Riders fly up and out of the Kihlari barn, Harak in the lead. The villagers sagged at the sight of them.

The Riders, fresh and hostile, were well fed because they'd been hunting off the backs of their winged steeds, which was much easier than hunting on foot. Now, with their squeaky-clean armor sparkling and their weapons gleaming, Rahkki's heart sank.

"Well?" Brauk urged the battalion leader. "Which side are you on?"

Her eyes bounced from the poorly armed rebels to the glossy and well-fed Sky Guard army. The battalion leader heaved a breath. "I'm on the side of the throne."

Brauk twirled his songsword, creating a soft yet violent hum. "Lilliam is using that throne to rob the clan. Help us take it back."

The woman shook her head. "No. We're not traitors. We fight for the queen."

Just then a shining bay steed dropped from the clouds and Brauk grimaced. It was his sister, Feylah. She was supposed to stay hidden and safe until the battle was over. She glided toward the small battalion of soldiers and ripped off her helmet. "My mother was the Pantheress, Reyella Stormrunner," she said, sweeping her golden eyes over them. "I am Feylah Stormrunner, her heir and your rightful queen."

The soldiers and villagers gaped at her, confused.

Brauk rushed his sister, his face hard with anger. "Put your helmet on, Feylah. You're only the queen if you're alive. I can't fight Harak and protect you at the same time."

"They need to know I'm here."

"Not at the expense of your life!"

Feylah thumped her helmet angrily back onto her head. At a nod from Brauk, Tuni flew up and whisked her into the center of Brauk's army while Brauk faced the battalion leader. "If you won't fight for me, will you fight for her?"

"The Pantheress had a daughter? When?" she asked, staring at him openmouthed.

Harak and his Sky Guard soared closer.

"I don't have time to explain," Brauk shouted. "But I tell you the truth, that is my sister. Now you are either with us or against us. Which is it?"

The battalion leader glanced at her soldiers, read something in their eyes, and made a decision. She nodded. "We're with you, Stormrunner."

Brauk grinned. "To Fort Prowl." He rallied everyone. "Down with Lilliam!"

The attack on the villagers ceased and Brauk's forces, combined now with one of Harak's battalions, marched and flew to the iron gates that protected the queen.

Rahkki glided to I'Lenna's side. "Get to the rendez-vous spot we talked about last night. I'll meet you there as soon as I can." They had formed their own plan that Brauk knew nothing about, and Rahkki's heart raced thinking about it. He reached between their two mares and grabbed I'Lenna's hand, squeezing it gently.

Smoke from the burning huts and the cries of Sandwen

children came into sharp focus as she nodded.

"We'll save your mom, I'Lenna, I promise! Does a dragon drool?"

She smiled and wiped her eyes, but Rahkki heard her whispered response: "Not a dead dragon."

∽33∽

STORM HERD

THUNDER CRACKED THE SKY AND THE STORM clouds shuddered, finally releasing the rain that had swelled within them. The Sky Guard Fliers swooped beneath the weeping clouds, shouting battle cries at the rebel forces.

"Formation!" Hazelwind neighed. Storm Herd collected as they would in Anok—the largest steeds flanking each winged captain, the sprinters in the front and the endurance fliers in the rear, creating striated offensive lines with pegasi poised at various altitudes, like an angled stack. A pegasus battle was as much about stamina as skill. The first herd to drive the other to the ground would triumph—and all battles ended on the ground eventually.

By contrast, the Sky Guard army flew in a flat square of straight lines.

Dewberry celebrated. "My sky herders will easily drive them apart."

"Show us!" Echofrost whinnied.

Dewberry led her mares into the fight. She'd taught her small, agile mares how to drive pegasi toward land and how to divide their battle formations. They'd also practiced the secret language of sky herders, which was an unfathomable series of clicks and whistles to the untrained ear. Now Echofrost would see if the time they'd spent training produced results.

Rahkki leaned and adjusted as she flew, as if he were part of her. He didn't attempt to steer her; rather he drew his blade and shield, ready for anything. Tak glided beside them, shooting electric white fire into the sky. I'Lenna had guided Shysong toward the fortress and Echofrost had lost sight of them.

Another peal of thunder shook Echofrost's ears. It wasn't safe to fly in this storm, but not one pegasus, wild or tame, seemed to care. The two armies clashed above the fortress walls.

Echofrost ducked, narrowly avoiding a collision with a

Sky Guard Flier. Then all thought left her as Harak's stallion, Ilan, pinned his ears and led his larger army toward hers. The rebels gripped their spears and Harak shouted orders that were unintelligible to the wild herd. But whatever Harak had said, the meaning was clear—his Riders would not spare any Kihlari, wild or tame, just because they were sacred to the clan. Their hooded eyes promised death. Their sharp blades craved blood.

But satisfaction bubbled in Echofrost's gut. Finally, Storm Herd would show these pampered steeds how to fight, and how to fly! She threw back her head and rallied Storm Herd by recalling their homeland. "In the Trap, we defeated two armies. In the Flatlands of Anok, we fooled the Destroyer. This *army*"—she snorted at the Sky Guard—"cannot touch us!" All the savage fury she'd tamped down since being captured surged through Echofrost's veins. Her pulse pounded, her feathers rattled.

Around her, the wild steeds buzzed their wings as they charged forward.

Ilan flattened his neck and bared his teeth. Harak pushed him to fly faster.

Brauk leaned over Kol's neck, his lips pulled into a snarl. Kol's muscles rippled with savage power, his eyes beamed at his enemies, his hooves struck the clouds with deadly fury, and Echofrost remembered the first day she'd met him. He'd terrified her. She'd learned later that he was vain and spoiled and ignorant—but his Anokian roots shone in battle, and she was pleased.

The flying armies collided. Riders swung their swords, hooves struck hides, and teeth tore into skin. Grunts and snorts, squeals and shrieks filled the sky. The self-selected captains, Echofrost, Hazelwind, Redfire, and Graystone, trumpeted commands.

"Drop!" Dewberry whinnied. Her sky herders followed her down and then up into the center of the Sky Guard. They broke apart the bulky formation, then formed a circle, each facing out. As Fliers charged them, they reared up and clubbed the Kihlari's foreheads. In Anok, this would have killed them, but here the steeds wore helmets.

Echofrost spiraled down, her chosen squad diving with her. Rahkki clung like a burr to her back as she circled to the rear of Harak's army. Hazelwind's group joined hers and half the Sky Guard was forced to turn around to fight them. The other half faced Redfire's and Graystone's squadrons.

Divide, confuse, destroy—that's what Thundersky had taught his Sun Herd captains in Anok. Hazelwind and Echofrost knew the strategy because they'd been born to Sun Herd. The Desert Herd stallion Redfire used speed and altitude to attack, and Graystone, who hailed from Snow Herd, used blunt and shocking force—battling head-on. With their combined skills, they overwhelmed Rahkki's enemies.

The Sky Guard had a fighting style all their own. They preferred maximum early effort and a quick win— but that would not work with Storm Herd. The wild pegasi groups were too agile, too fast, and too fit.

Ilan shot toward her and Echofrost dodged him. She tipped sideways and raked her sharpened hooves across his exposed ribs, drawing blood. He lunged and bit into her upper leg.

Ilan's Rider, Harak, swung his sawa sword at Rahkki, his green eyes raging behind his helmet. Echofrost darted higher. The spotted stallion flipped around, but too fast, and Harak almost slid off his back. Ilan steadied for the sake of his Rider, and in that heartbeat, Echofrost kicked his wing, stinging the muscles. Ilan stalled and plummeted toward land, regaining his balance just moments before he and Harak would have struck the ground.

Beside Echofrost, Hazelwind battled three steeds at once. His mane blew in the wind; his jaw twitched into a grimace. The length of his muscles rippled as he spun, dived, bit, and clubbed his assailants. It was like watching Thundersky when he was alive—as if the sire and the son had combined into one mighty warrior. Hazelwind made short work of his three Kihlari, sending two to the ground and one into retreat.

The Riders hollered to one another and sliced at the wild pegasi with their glinting swords. The rebels returned the attack, using their whittled spears. Redfire's wounded shoulder gushed blood. Long gashes marked Hazelwind's flanks. And several Storm Herd steeds had gone to ground, too injured to fly. Echofrost noticed all this in a breath, and then she singled out a dun Kihlara mare and rejoined the attack. As she and the mare flew tight circles, biting and kicking, Dewberry's sharp whinny reached her.

"Drive the Sky Guard down!" Dewberry commanded the sky herders. The mares re-collected and charged back into the fray. The tiny mares, a blur of bright feathers, exploded into the remaining ranks of the Sky Guard and dashed their formation to pieces. As she shot past Echofrost, Dewberry whinnied with pleasure. "Lovely day for a battle, don't you think?"

Echofrost snorted in rebuff. Some steeds were too

aggressive for their own good, and Dewberry was one of them. But the tide had turned to Storm Herd's favor. The Kihlari, laden with saddles, armor, and Riders, were too heavy and slow to defend themselves against unencumbered pegasi warriors. And Harak's Riders couldn't shoot their arrows effectively in such close combat.

"Press the advantage," Hazelwind neighed to Storm Herd.

"Attack the Riders," Echofrost brayed. She'd noticed that once a Rider fell off his or her Kihlara, the Kihlara stopped fighting.

The pegasi of Anok descended upon the Sandwens, and the Landwalkers lifted their shields and weapons. These people who'd abandoned Rahkki to the giants, who'd enslaved wild pegasi, and who'd imprisoned Echofrost in a stall and cut her flight feathers were locked in her sights. The sky washed bright red as anger blinded Echofrost. She drew a breath. *No!* This battle wasn't for revenge; it was for freedom—for Rahkki's people and for the Kihlari—and freedom, unlike revenge, was worth fighting for.

She exhaled and charged.

34

CHASE

I'LENNA DUG HER HEELS INTO FIRO'S SIDES AND they fled the battle. She would meet Rahkki at the drainage grate as planned, near the southern tunnel that led into Fort Prowl. When a clan was under attack or siege, the monarch and her family retreated to her private chambers. Her personal guards would protect the entrance. Her acting general would defend the fortress. This was a siege of sorts and I'Lenna imagined Lilliam would follow the same safety protocols, especially since she had recently birthed Prince K'Lar.

If the battle swung in Brauk's favor, Rahkki would meet her and they'd sneak through the tunnels to Lilliam's chambers and enter through the false door in her fireplace. They'd offer Lilliam one last chance to flee the Realm or risk death at the hands of the enraged rebels. If the tide swung toward Harak's forces, and it looked like Lilliam would keep her power, Rahkki would meet I'Lenna and help her escape to Daakur.

Now I'Lenna flew through the steam and fog, heading toward the drainage grate. Her rain cloak billowed around her, shrouding her head and body. She felt much stronger after her night of rest and warmth in Darthan's hut. Behind her, Brauk's forces swarmed toward the fortress. She hoped no one would notice her, a lone rider aboard a small roan mare.

But it was her beautiful braya that gave I'Lenna away.

"That's Firo!" one of Harak's Riders shouted. It was Headwind Meela Swift. "Who's riding her?" she asked. "The princess is dead."

I'Lenna had just flown past the Kihlari training yard. She leaned over her mare's neck, as though she could hide them both.

"Catch whoever it is and bring them to me, yeah," Harak's voice commanded. "Hurry!"

I'Lenna glanced back in time to see Meela drop out of

formation. Their eyes locked and Meela squinted, unable to recognize I'Lenna beneath the cloak. "Halt, you," she shouted.

I'Lenna's heart stuttered. She couldn't get caught now! "Go!" she whispered to Firo. She squeezed the mare's sides and rose lightly in her stirrups, taking her weight off Firo's back. The roan surged ahead.

"You're gonna regret running," Meela snarled aboard her Flier, Jax.

Jax's wingbeats filled I'Lenna's ears. Between fearful looks back, I'Lenna fed Firo the reins, length by length. The mare's wings carved the wind. She flew faster. I'Lenna guided her south. It didn't matter which way they went, they just had to lose Meela, and then they could circle back.

They soared past Fort Prowl. She glimpsed land soldiers and guards swarming the courtyard, slamming doors, locking the iron gates, and ringing the bells. The wet wind blew I'Lenna's hair into her eyes. Lightning snaked above her. She wiped her hair off her forehead and her cloak's hood slid backward, revealing her face. At that very moment, she spotted her mother on the tower wall.

Lilliam stood with her guards, preparing to retreat to her quarters. The flying blue roan outside the spiked gates had caught her attention. Other than a sharp flicker in her eyes, Lilliam did not seem surprised to see that the dragon had not eaten I'Lenna. Resigned maybe, but not surprised. Her hand floated to the baby she held in a sling across her chest. She graced I'Lenna with a curt nod, and then whirled and vanished down the steps toward her private chambers.

I'Lenna and Firo winged across Leshi Creek, which gushed like a river, and into the jungle. Meela surged closer. "You don't have to do this!" I'Lenna screamed over her shoulder.

Meela bent over Jax's neck and urged him to fly faster. She recognized the princess now that her hood was off. "I can't let you go, I'Lenna." Riders, like soldiers, swore blood oaths to protect their monarch, for better or for worse, and Meela was loyal. She had not seen Feylah and didn't know Lilliam was a false queen. Harak had commanded her to catch I'Lenna, and Meela would be worthless to all future leaders if she failed to obey the orders of her sworn queen's general.

Heart thumping, I'Lenna guided Firo into a dive toward the jungle. She'd have to lose Meela in the trees. Firo was light and agile. Jax and his Rider were armored.

"Stop," Meela repeated.

Firo dropped into a stand of trees and rocketed forward. I'Lenna briefly floated out of the saddle and Firo slowed. *Sun and stars*, I'Lenna thought, *Firo is holding back so I don't fall off! But I need* all *her speed.*

Jax powered up behind them, his breath on Firo's tail. Desperate, I'Lenna wondered how she could make Firo fly at her top speed. Her braya seemed more bent on protecting I'Lenna than escaping Jax. "Go, Firo, go!" I'Lenna urged. She loosened the reins all the way, but Firo continued to fly carefully.

She must stop worrying about me! They hurtled, dodging skinny palms and larger eucalypti. I'Lenna's next thought, however, was more sobering—Firo was going to crash! They were racing straight toward a section of impenetrable vines and foliage. I'Lenna leaned over the roan's neck and closed her eyes. Firo notched her wings, tucked her legs, and plunked straight through, creating her own hole.

Sharp twigs scraped I'Lenna's skin and tore her clothing. She slid dangerously toward Firo's rump. It took all the strength in her arms to haul herself back up beneath Firo's black-edged wings.

Meela and Jax burst through the same hole, making it bigger. Jax regained his speed. His neck reached Firo's rump. Meela leaned forward, grabbed I'Lenna's cloak, and tried to yank the girl off Firo's back.

The cloak ripped off and hurled into the wind.

"Faster," I'Lenna begged, and Firo flicked back her ears, listening. Was this as fast as the roan could fly? If so, I'Lenna knew it was over. They were as good as caught.

But Jax was tiring. He slipped behind Firo, then flapped hard to catch up again. He grew frustrated and angry. He eyed Firo's mottled flank and opened his jaw.

"Don't do it," Meela screamed at him, tugging back on her reins. But Jax couldn't resist Firo's exposed hide. He leaned in and bit her flank—hard—drawing blood.

His bite electrified Firo! She dug into the wind and rocketed forward, her wings a blue-black blur. I'Lenna almost slid off, but Firo only flew faster. She lowered her neck, tucked her legs, and hurtled between the trees, twisting sideways, ducking below some branches, soaring over others. All thought for I'Lenna's safety seemed to have vanished. Firo flew as though losing this stallion was all that mattered in the world.

"Yes," I'Lenna hissed. "Give it all you've got, girl!" The mare pumped her wings even harder with the praise. Her muscles shimmered and the veins in her neck bulged. I'Lenna balanced on Firo's back, moving in rhythm to her wingbeats. Her heart pounded. Her hands and legs ached from holding on.

She glanced back. Jax shrank in the background, evaporating into the mist. Meela's expression filled with awe and anger all at once. Then Meela and Jax vanished when Firo reached a waterfall, arrowed her wings, and dived hundreds of lengths straight down.

A huge smile spread across I'Lenna's face. "Yaweeeeh!" she cried, jingling the bells on her ankles. They snapped out of the dive and Firo glided over the unnamed river, casting no shadow in the gray morning light.

I'Lenna sat up and stroked her mare's sweaty and rain-soaked neck. They landed and I'Lenna dismounted to allow Firo to catch her breath. After a cooling walk, they both drank carefully from the rushing river. I'Lenna rinsed her face and hands.

Firo lipped at a few plants, her ears swiveling warily. I'Lenna leaned against her chest, feeling Firo's strong, steady heartbeat. It was time to fly back and wait for Rahkki. "I'm going to miss you when this is over," I'Lenna said as sudden sadness welled within her breast.

Firo nuzzled her while I'Lenna stroked her jagged blaze and soft, dark muzzle. If it weren't for Firo and Sula, she'd never have become friends with Rahkki that first day in the Kihlari stable. Even though their friendship had caused them both a lot of trouble, she was grateful for it. "You ready to head back?" I'Lenna asked.

Firo blinked at her, and I'Lenna imagined that her ice-blue eyes were full of thoughts and dreams and wonderings. I'Lenna hugged the mare and then climbed onto her saddle.

Firo lifted off and they cruised low, skirting open areas. When they reached Leshi Creek, Firo touched down and let I'Lenna guide her to the drainage grate. I'Lenna dismounted and the pair waited at the edge of the jungle for Rahkki to appear. Around the front side of the fortress, clanging swords, shouts, and the whir of arrows filled the air. "Granak, Father of Dragons," I'Lenna whispered. "Please protect your people."

C∽35∾

SHOWDOWN

ECHOFROST SWOOPED AROUND, ASSESSING THE battle. Rahkki's little dragon soared with them, searing the feathers of any enemy Kihlara who flew near. "Dewberry, take your sky herders to the walls and stop the archers!" she whinnied.

"What's an archer?"

"The Landwalkers with the shooting sticks!"

"Got it." The pinto whistled for her clever mares. The sky herders flocked together and then parted quickly, whistling and clicking. They glided up the sides of the walls toward the archers.

"Loose!" one of the Landwalkers shouted.

A hundred arrows arced from the fortress guards. The mares twirled and dodged. Feathers exploded when one was hit, but she flew on, ignoring the pain in her wing. An arrow struck another mare in the flank. She twisted her neck, grabbed the shank, and jerked it out.

Dewberry piped instructions, sending her team faster to the top of the wall. She arrived first and flew sideways, legs coiled back. Her sky herders followed and they glided in a line, kicking archers in the chest as they nocked their second set of arrows. Tak joined the line and scorched the archers with gleeful chortling.

The targeted Landwalkers tumbled backward, falling into the courtyard. When they struck land, Echofrost heard the sickening crunch of broken bones. Rapid cursing and shouting followed.

Echofrost flexed her wings and pointed her muzzle down, planning to glide straight into Fort Prowl. Rahkki leaned forward and patted her neck, encouraging her. Mut, Ossi, and Mut's friends had landed inside the gates with a band of rebels. There they battled the guards. The furious villagers stood outside, shouting, "Down with Lilliam!"

A short fight with the surprised guards ended with

the massive gates sprawling open. Rebel soldiers and angry villagers spilled into the courtyard. "Yes!" Rahkki cheered. Tuni rushed toward the queen's chambers and proceeded to batter at the locked doors. A stream of rebels protected her. Brauk leaped off Kol's back to fight soldiers on the ground. His body twirled and his sword hummed, a blur of leather and steel. Kol reared beside him, clobbering Brauk's enemies.

Echofrost whinnied to Redfire. "Help Tuni get to the queen. The sooner they root her out the faster this will be over."

The copper chestnut nodded and sank toward Tuni.

"Let's go," Rahkki said, squeezing her ribs with his legs.

But Echofrost broke her dive and hovered, panting. *Think first, don't just react*, she told herself. Graystone and Hazelwind joined her. "Your tactic is working," Graystone nickered. "The Kihlari worry so much about their Riders they can't fight us properly."

They were about to descend upon a group of winged warriors when Echofrost noticed that the courtyard had grown very quiet. "Look," she whinnied.

A thundering bray rattled her ears. Hazelwind,

Redfire, and Graystone jerked their heads toward the noise. Dewberry and the sky herders had reconnoitered for another pass at the archers. Rahkki loosed a breath.

The paths of Brauk Stormrunner and Harak Night-seer had finally collided.

Below him, Rahkki watched Brauk and Harak face off in the courtyard, each man surrounded by his most loyal warriors. Kol trumpeted and Ilan screamed an answering challenge. The two stallions flared their wings and reared. Tuni charged to Brauk's side, her ferocious eyes locked on Harak. Uncle Darthan joined them, his lean body ready to pounce, but they held back because this was a showdown.

Sometimes a war shrank to a fight between two leaders, with the winner taking all. If Brauk won, Harak's forces would submit to his authority. He would control the Sky Guard and Land Guard completely, and through them, the throne. If Harak won, Brauk and the rebels would submit their fates to him. Rahkki licked his lips, which had gone suddenly dry.

Thaan and Tully circled overhead with Feylah, who

remained disguised by her helmet. Only a handful of Harak's soldiers had seen her earlier and Brauk would signal when it was time to reveal her identity to everyone, but he wanted the tide of battle heartily on his side before he risked exposing their sister.

"Surrender, *General*," Brauk said to Harak. His condescending tone made the title sound ridiculous, and someone snickered.

Harak grimaced, noticing that some of his own soldiers now stood with Brauk. "My forces outnumber yours, Stormrunner," he replied.

Brauk shrugged. "Mice outnumber jaguars, so what?" He flashed his mirthless grin.

Red fury crawled up Harak's neck and spread across his face.

Rahkki guided Sula lower and his heart swelled as Brauk danced on the balls of his feet, twirling their mother's songsword. The brother who had carried Rahkki on his shoulders, taught him to play stones, and protected him from Lilliam was back, fully restored.

Tak dropped from the clouds and landed on Rahkki's saddle. The little dragon watched the two men below, as if he understood that what happened between them was all that mattered now.

Brauk glanced up, winked at Rahkki, and the hum of his singing blade filled the courtyard. Next he beckoned Harak and taunted him. "Come closer, mouse."

The two circled each other in the center of the court-yard, weapons raised. The fighting around them had ceased. Villagers, rebels, and loyalists stood side by side, hopeful that this fight between many could be resolved with a fight between two.

Blade clashed against blade as Harak and Brauk lunged at the same time. Tuni drew her warriors to the queen's chamber doors and waited. "The end is near," Rahkki heard her say to them.

Harak drove his sword toward Brauk's chest. Brauk dodged it, trusting his newly healed legs, but Rahkki noticed his brother still wasn't as quick as he used to be.

Harak feinted and then stung Brauk's spine with the flat of his blade, right where Sula had kicked him. "Sa jin," Brauk cursed. He staggered and then countered with a blunt strike to Harak's chest. Harak met that with a slice to Brauk's calf that drew blood.

Kol let out a ferocious bray and galloped to help his Rider, but Brauk waved the stallion off. If he accepted help, even from his beast, the showdown wouldn't count as a victory. It had to be equal, one versus one. Brauk lifted his songsword, creating a zinging whine, and cracked it against Harak's arm, cutting deep. "You're getting slow, old man," Brauk taunted.

"Yeah? You couldn't beat a one-armed monkey," Harak jeered.

Brauk answered with a resounding blow to Harak's shoulder.

The Headwind reeled, but countered with a strike to Brauk's ribs. Rahkki's brother leaped and spun. The two parried up and down the courtyard, their swords clanging.

Harak stumbled and Brauk pressed him, hooked Harak's blade, and sent it spinning away.

As his sword clanged to the ground, Harak kicked, striking Brauk again in the spine. Brauk crumpled into a lifeless pile.

"No!" Rahkki screamed. He squeezed Sula and they plummeted toward his brother.

"Stay back," Darthan commanded.

Lightning lit up the courtyard and his brother's still body. Tears poured from Rahkki's eyes. The courtyard, the soldiers, and the sky—it all smeared into a muddied blur. Harak drew his dagger and leaped onto Brauk's back.

"BRAUK!" Rahkki screamed. Alarmed by the shouting, Tak flapped his wings and shot blue fire into the sky.

Then a fist rose from the crumpled pile that was Brauk. He drove it straight into Harak's nose. Blood burst out and streaked the blond man's face. Brauk rose and shook his head, and Rahkki felt weak with relief. The two men leaped at each other, punching and circling.

Harak dived in low, but Brauk dodged him and then tackled him. They hit the ground, thrashing like crocodiles, and their helmets rolled off. The sword fight had turned into a brawl.

Kol pranced around them, muscles quivering. The men traded blows until streaks of blood, welts, and purple bruises appeared on them both. In a moment of breath, Brauk repeated his demand. "Surrender."

"Never," Harak swore.

No one dared interfere.

Harak lurched forward, wheezing now. Brauk met him and drove his fist into Harak's skull. The Headwind dropped to his knees and then onto his back—motionless.

Stunned silence blanketed the courtyard.

Brauk nudged Harak with his foot. The man groaned and began to blink. Brauk placed one boot on Harak's chest and gazed at his clanmates. His golden eyes were bright and shining against his bruised skin.

Brauk was just about to speak when Harak roused

himself and whistled sharply. His stallion, Ilan, who was hovering overhead, dived down and kicked Brauk in the back, flattening him to the ground.

"Hey!" Tuni roared. And everyone shouted curses at Harak.

Harak ignored them, leaped on top of Brauk, and flipped him over. Brauk had lost his wind and was struggling to breathe. The blond Headwind leaned over and their eyes locked. Brauk's jaw muscles fluttered angrily. Harak leaned closer still, his gaze flitting over Brauk's sweat-sheened skin, swallowing every inch of his enemy. Not a person in the courtyard moved or breathed. "Brauk Stormrunner, you are under arrest, yeah," Harak snarled.

Rahkki gasped. "That's not fair!" Harak had used his stallion to help him win; everyone had seen it. "Tuni?" he cried.

Just then the wild pinto mare—the one that had twin foals—flew by Harak, coasting like a feather on the breeze. She was the only creature in motion and all eyes turned to her. As she glided past Harak Nightseer, she kicked him soundly in the head. Harak crumpled, knocked out cold.

Everyone gawked at the pinto. Tak chortled, sounding very satisfied.

The mare landed and folded her emerald wings. Her arched neck and quizzical expression seemed to say, "What? Someone had to do it."

Brauk pushed himself to his feet, having regained his breath. "Sun and stars," he said to the wild braya. "Thanks for that."

Brauk gripped Harak's arms and yanked him upright. "You are under arrest, yeah," he said.

A cheer erupted from the rebels and the villagers. But the joyful noise ended as fast as it began. Lilliam's private guards threw open her doors and shot arrows at the soldiers holding Harak.

Brauk and the others threw up their shields. In the confusion, Lilliam's guards yanked Harak from Brauk's grip and carried him away to the queen's quarters. Then they slammed and locked the doors.

"*Sa jin huruk*," Brauk snarled, but quickly regained control of himself. "Harak and Lilliam are trapped," he shouted. "It's time to drive the weasels out!"

The villagers and rebels surged forward, cheering "Down with Lilliam!" The remainder of Harak's army gathered in confusion.

Rahkki blanched. Things were suddenly happening

too quickly. He guided Sula away from the fortress toward I'Lenna. They had only moments to get her mother out of the fortress before the mob reached her.

Rahkki urged Sula toward the drainage ditch as thunder rocked the sky. He hoped he wasn't too late.

36

TRAPPED

"**THERE YOU ARE,**" **I'LENNA CALLED WHEN SHE** saw him. Worry lines etched her face, and Rahkki's heart twisted.

"Sorry it took so long," he said. "The rebels won. They're on their way to arrest your mother. She and Harak are trapped in her room."

"We have to hurry!" I'Lenna whirled and unlocked the grate.

Rahkki faced Sula and Firo. "We'll be back," he said to them. Sula nickered and Rahkki hugged her neck, quick and light. Then he and I'Lenna plunged into the draining water.

Tak tried to follow them. "No," Rahkki commanded. "You stay." Facing Lilliam and Harak in her chamber would be like confronting tigers in their den. Rahkki had no illusions that he and I'Lenna would receive a warm welcome, and the effort of keeping Tak safe would be a distraction.

The young dragon flew closer, flapping his wings in Rahkki's face.

"Stay here!" Rahkki repeated, holding up his hand. Then he and I'Lenna swam into the bowels of the fortress.

Behind them, Tak glided in circles, exhaling angry puffs of blue smoke. The wild mares kicked off the muddy soil and flew back toward their herd. Rahkki hoped that his hug had not been his and Sula's final good-bye.

They traveled up the tunnels and climbed out of the water. "This way," I'Lenna said. She took Rahkki's hand. Her palm was cold. When they arrived at the hidden door that led into Lilliam's chamber they heard voices inside.

An argument had erupted between Harak and Lilliam. I'Lenna's sisters, Rayni and Jor, were weeping.

"Move it, Lilliam," Harak shouted. "Brauk is right behind me, yeah. Your guards won't hold him off for long."

Lilliam's response was quieter. "Shh, you'll wake the baby."

Harak's boots paced. "Brauk fought with a songsword and I recognized it. It belonged to his mother."

Silence.

Harak raised his voice. "Where did he get it, Lil?"

More silence.

Harak stopped pacing. His voice went cold and flat. "Darthan sent us a question through one of my soldiers. He wants to know who you burned on Reyella's funeral pyre. So do I, yeah. Who was it, Lil? Why would Darthan *even* ask that if it wasn't his sister?"

Rahkki and I'Lenna stared at each other, hardly daring to breathe as they eavesdropped.

There was shuffling and the sound of wood creaking. Harak's voice, much closer now. "Tell me the truth," he snarled. "You failed eight years ago, didn't you? Admit it! You let Reyella get away."

Lilliam burst into tears. Rayni and Jor cried harder. I'Lenna clutched Rahkki's hand and squeezed it as the past reared up like a ghost.

Brauk must have arrived outside Lilliam's interior chamber door. From their position in the tunnels, Rahkki and I'Lenna heard him pounding on it.

"We need to get your family out of there," Rahkki whispered, nudging her. "Now, I'Lenna. Open the fireplace."

She wiped her nose and took a breath. "Yes, okay." With shaking hands, she tripped an unseen lock using her blackstone necklace, not bothering to hide her actions. So the necklace was a key, Rahkki realized, though he still didn't understand how it worked. I'Lenna hadn't inserted it into anything, just slid it across the stone. The secret door popped open, and the two stumbled into Lilliam's massive, ash-covered hearth.

Lilliam jerked her head toward them. Her lips parted in shock. She wore a long blue cloak over white riding breeches. Harak was leaning over her, his bruised face red with anger. The baby slept in his cradle and I'Lenna's sisters were huddled in the corner.

Harak fell backward at the sight of I'Lenna. He hadn't seen her during the battle outside. He still thought the dragon had eaten her. "Deathlifter," he whispered to Rahkki, crediting him for bringing I'Lenna back to life, as he'd seemingly done with the giants.

Press your advantage; let your legend bloom, the blood of the Pantheress runs through you. Rahkki stepped out of the hearth. "We've come to save you," he said to Lilliam. He refused to acknowledge Harak.

She sputtered and grimaced. "What?" She had the desperate eyes of a trapped animal.

I'Lenna rushed past Rahkki to gather her sisters. The baby boy squirmed in his cradle, asleep.

Outside the chamber, Brauk and the rebels battered on the door with something heavy.

Lilliam stared past Rahkki at the yawning hole that was once the back of her fireplace and nodded, finally understanding how Reyella had escaped eight years earlier.

"There are tunnels back there that lead to the jungle," Rahkki said, pointing. "Go, before my brother breaks down your door."

Harak crept toward his knife. "Don't move," Rahkki barked, and Harak froze. I'Lenna bundled her sisters into their rain cloaks.

Lilliam stood up, as straight and proud as her daughter. "I have nowhere to go."

"We can live in Daakur," I'Lenna said.

We? Rahkki's gut seized. He hadn't considered that I'Lenna would go *with* Lilliam. His eyes searched her face, but I'Lenna didn't meet his eyes. "Hurry," she said. "I told Brauk about the tithes. The clan is furious. They'll kill you."

Brauk rammed the wooden door again, and it cracked.

Lilliam crossed the distance to I'Lenna in one stride

and slapped her daughter across the face. "You *told* on me?"

I'Lenna's hand flew to her cheek. Tears gushed from her eyes. She glanced at Harak. "Reyella did escape that night, and she had a child, an heir. Feylah Stormrunner is outside right now. You aren't the queen, you never really were. This"—she waved at the chamber—"is over!" A red handprint outlined the side of I'Lenna's face. Her breath came in fast gulps.

Rahkki glanced from mother to daughter. This wasn't going well.

Harak gaped at Lilliam. "You lied to me," he rasped.

Brauk slammed the chamber door and it finally broke.

Harak lunged for his knife. At the same time, Brauk charged into the room.

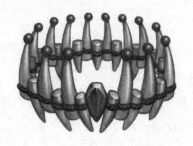

37

THE LAST DOSE

LILLIAM RACED FOR THE DOOR AT THE SAME time Harak flung his knife at Brauk. It spun across the room, glinting and flashing.

I'Lenna's face melted in horror.

The dagger missed Brauk and struck Lilliam. She dropped to the floor and Rahkki rushed to her side, turning her head up. "Lilliam!"

Her eyelids fluttered, her lips pursed. I'Lenna raced across the chamber and knelt beside her mother. "Don't close your eyes! Don't go to sleep," I'Lenna cried.

Darthan and Brauk fell upon the woman, feeling her pulse and assessing the wound.

Horrified, Harak did not resist when Thaan and Tully snatched him by his arms.

"I need cloth," Darthan said. Rahkki grabbed a baby blanket and Darthan wrapped it around Lilliam's wound, staunching the flow of blood. Darthan glanced at I'Lenna.

"Is she going to be okay?" I'Lenna asked.

Rahkki doubted that Lilliam was going to be okay. Her lips had already paled to a bluish hue. Her eyes were losing focus. As if they were her last words, Lilliam mumbled the answer to Darthan's question, "The body I burned on the pyre, it was a pig."

Then Rahkki remembered something. "Where is the Queen's Elixir? We'll give Lilliam the last dose."

I'Lenna wiped her nose. "I gave it to Brauk, remember? He drank it. It's gone."

Rahkki grinned. "No. Ossi has another. We got it in the Wilds."

I'Lenna's lips trembled. "Fetch her!"

"No time," Darthan said. "We have to take Lilliam to Ossi!" Darthan lifted I'Lenna's mother into his arms and they charged out of the chamber.

When Rahkki and his family burst into the courtyard, carrying the pale body of Queen Lilliam, they found soldiers and clansfolk milling about, waiting. The wild herd had gathered far from the rest and stood together, nickering. All heads turned toward Darthan. All conversation halted.

"We need help!" Darthan shouted. "Ossi! Where's Ossi Finn?"

Ossi shoved through the crowd, a look of shock on her freckled face. "Me?"

"We need the spider venom," he explained, holding out his hand.

Ossi reached into her belted carrying bag, still confused. "This is all we have. It's Feylah's dose now. Are you sure you want to use it on Lilliam?"

Feylah swept her dark hair off her face, her golden eyes round with worry. "Yes, she needs it."

The clan noticed Feylah then. Her helmet was off and she faced the crowd, unmistakably a Stormrunner. The silence that rippled through the courtyard was deep, all-encompassing—it was awe, reverence, and disbelief.

Rahkki edged closer to his sister. "Put on your crown." It was time for Feylah to take her place as queen, now, while they had the upper hand and before anyone got any other ideas.

To the shocked stares of the clan, Feylah reached into Drael's saddlebag and withdrew her crown. Crafted of bone and yellowed dragon's teeth, helmed by a gigantic black scale, and tipped in luminescent sea pearls, this was authentic. This was the original Fifth Clan headpiece, fashioned by the ancient Sister who'd founded their clan. It was Reyella's crown, an artifact Lilliam had claimed to have burned on the funeral pyre. More proof of her lies. Feylah lowered it onto her head and the Fifth Clan understood: this was their true queen.

Rahkki glanced back to see that Lilliam had swallowed the healing venom. Darthan ordered her moved back into her chamber, under a team of guards selected by him. Harak was also put under guard, and then Darthan joined Rahkki, Brauk, and Feylah.

At the sight of the Stormrunners reunited, the Fifth Clan rose to their feet and cheered. Darthan raised his hands to speak, but he was interrupted.

A horse and rider galloped through the open iron gates and skidded to a halt in front of them. Rahkki gaped at the rider, a woman in a long skirt and no shoes, with disheveled gray hair. Her cheeks were bright red. It was Brim Carver.

"Giants!" she yelled. "The giants are here!"

38

THREE HORDES

THUNDERING STEPS RATTLED THE GROUND AND Rahkki whirled. From the jungle lands south of Fort Prowl, saber cats leaped out of the trees and landed, blinking in the sun. Their teenage riders snarled, flashing their short tusks and waving their long spears. Elephants trotted out behind them, trunks raised and trumpeting.

And then huge dark shapes emerged, the adult Gorlan warriors. They were barefoot and draped in skins. Bulging muscles corded their legs. The three princes followed, one astride an elephant, one aboard a giant fanged cat, and the other walking with a flight of flame-breathing dragons circling his head.

Rahkki and the others sucked in their breath. His

people rushed to close and lock the iron gates. Tak darted toward the sky, and the wild herd flew up the fortress walls to watch. Brim clamped one hand around the medicine satchel she'd brought with her.

The three Gorlan armies marched right past the Kihlari training yard and headed straight for Fort Prowl.

"Riders up!" Brauk cried, and whistled for Kol.

"No!" Rahkki roared, shaking his head. "Stand down!"

Brauk cocked his head.

I'Lenna grabbed Rahkki's hand and peered up at him. "What are you doing? We can't lose the clan *now*. We have to fight."

I'Lenna's sacrifices rushed across her face in waves of grief. She'd toppled her mother and thwarted her grandmother—she'd risked her own life and livelihood so that the Fifth Clan could live free of the Second. They'd just won, and now they stood to lose everything again. Rahkki hugged I'Lenna tight, crushing her against his chest. "We won't lose the clan. Don't worry."

Rahkki leaped onto an unused wagon so everyone could see him. He lifted his hands. "Don't fight the Gorlanders," he said. "We cannot win a battle against three hordes and all their animals."

His clanmates didn't deny that. At least fifteen

hundred giants stood outside their gates, three hordes working together. It was unprecedented. It was an impossible battle to win.

Prince Daanath spotted Rahkki and roared. The noise concussed the air, like an ancient tree falling, shocking Sandwen ears and rattling their brains.

"Granak protect us," I'Lenna breathed.

"You lived with giants, right?" Feylah asked, breathless. "What do they want?"

Everyone crowded closer and Rahkki found himself standing in the center of a huge semicircle—tame steeds, Sandwen warriors, and his sister—each staring at the boy who had escaped the giants.

His eyes bounced across his people. "They want their ancient land back, and we're going to give it to them."

No one argued with Rahkki. In the face of three Gorlan armies, the land no longer seemed very important.

About fifty Gorlanders stormed toward Fort Prowl's iron gates carrying a massive tree trunk.

Rahkki's scalp tingled. "It's a battering ram!" he shouted.

"Stinkin' giants!" Brauk grumbled, spitting over his shoulder.

The Gorlanders carried the tree to the massive gates

and swung it backward and then forward, ramming it into the iron. The gates shook and the people inside the courtyard flinched back.

"Hold steady!" Rahkki hollered. He approached the gates. Sula dived off the fortress wall, landed, and walked beside him. Rahkki touched her shoulder, grateful for her presence.

The giants rammed the gates again. Prince Daanath's blue eyes met Rahkki's through the iron bars.

"My people won't fight you," Rahkki signed.

"Good," Daanath replied, flashing his tusks.

Rahkki grimaced. *"We have a new queen. She's my sister."* He pointed at Feylah, who was still wearing her dragon-tooth crown. *"She will honor our bargain. She will share soup."*

The prince peered hard at Feylah. She met his gaze without wavering and Rahkki felt proud of her. Then Daanath returned his attention to Rahkki. *"It's too late."*

"It doesn't have to be," Rahkki signed wildly.

The giants rammed their trunk again and Fort Prowl's metal gates screamed like dying animals as they parted and fell, striking the soil. Sula flared her wings and Rahkki gripped her mane, ready to leap aboard if they had to flee.

The giants dropped their massive battering ram. It rolled down the hill, across the Kihlari training yard, and crashed into the stable, tearing down a section of the wall, where it shuddered to a halt. The Gorlanders stood on one side of the broken gates and the Sandwens stood on the other. They stared at one another for a heartbeat.

Then the Sandwens lunged for their weapons. The giants snarled.

"I said stand down!" Rahkki screamed.

Feylah leaped onto a large wagon. "You heard my brother. Stand down," she commanded her people, and the Sandwens stilled.

Rahkki remembered words Brauk had once spoken. *I'm a warrior, Rahkki, and I'll die someday; but when it happens, it won't be some stinking giant that does it. It will be something much grander.* A vision of Brauk lying dead in this very courtyard flashed across his mind. His brother was right! It would not be a giant that killed him; it would be three hordes of giants if Rahkki didn't do something! His gut thrashed. He'd caused this—somehow he had to fix it.

"*We surrender,*" Rahkki gestured. He hoped that his clan's refusal to fight would disarm the giants. They wouldn't massacre helpless Sandwens, would they?

Brauk strode across the courtyard. "Giants don't believe in mercy, Rahkki. If we surrender, we die."

"We've been wrong about the giants more than we've been right," Rahkki argued, and Brauk had no response to that.

Sweat dribbled into Rahkki's eyes. His silly trick with the hot pepper in Granak's mouth and the darts treated with sleep medicine had won him some respect on both sides of this skirmish, but he doubted it would last long.

With his blood singing, Rahkki spoke to everyone in Sandwen and Gorlish at the same time. *"My mother had a dream that Sandwens and Gorlanders could live in peace."* He swallowed. *"I believe in this dream too."*

Rahkki pointed to the fallow farmland his clan used for Gatherings. "That land is sacred to the hordes," he told his people. "Their founding king, Lazrah, made the first soup there and formed the three hordes. They will not rest until this land is returned to them."

Rahkki turned to the three princes. *"There is no reason to fight. Let's make peace."*

The Fire Horde prince set his jaw. *"No reason to fight? You ruined our soup, you've weakened my horde. I say, no more Fifth Clan!"*

The other hordes roared their agreement. Even the animals responded, the saber cats snarling and the elephants trumpeting as if in approval. The giants encircled the weaponless Sandwens. The Fire prince flashed his tusks. *"Your blood will appease our ancient king."* His eyes turned cold.

Hot anger shot through Rahkki's veins. A lifetime of getting chased, dunked in pig slop, teased, robbed, dragged by his ears, and pushed around by kids—and adults like Harak—coursed through him. The giants were just bigger bullies! Rahkki had had enough.

He roared and beat the courtyard's stone pavers. He did this three times. If the giants understood anything, it was a Gorlan fit, and Rahkki had learned how to throw one from a master—the young giantess named Miah.

The three princes gaped at him. Sula reared, alarmed.

Rahkki gestured in huge exaggerated hand movements. *"I have shown mercy. I saved your prince from the snake. I woke your fallen warriors. You have not shown me the same. Let my people go or I will destroy you all!"*

The Great Cave Horde prince snorted. *"You can't."*

Rahkki worked his jaw. It was true. He couldn't. The giants had him and his clan right where they wanted him.

Rahkki had lost, but he could not accept it. Angry tears collected in his eyes. He stared up at the sky and called on the guardian spirit of his people. "Granak! As a bloodborn prince of the Fifth Clan, I command you to protect us!"

Brauk sighed and shook his head.

But Rahkki believed in Granak. Why did his people feed the huge lizard if not for his protection? *Please*, Rahkki thought, *hear my call!*

His people glanced toward the jungle, as though Granak might appear. The giants flexed for attack.

And then Rahkki's plea was answered.

❧39❧
WATERBRINGER

A THUNDEROUS CRACK RESOUNDED FROM THE north.

Brauk startled. "What's that?"

"It's Granak!" someone cried.

But it wasn't the dragon. Instead, Rahkki heard a wall of water come rushing toward them. He smiled, having recognized the huge noise. "Our guardian spirit broke Darthan's levy!" he shouted.

Rahkki met I'Lenna's sharp glance. They'd seen the levy after she'd fallen into the River Tsallan. It was bulging then, barely able to hold the raging monsoon waters. Today's rain had strained the levy too far, and the soil was too wet to soak up another drop. Every Sandwen knew what was coming next. Flood!

The village, the horse arena, the Ruk, the Kihlari stable, and the fallows would soon be doused in water. The fortress stood on a hill, so the Sandwens were safe. But the giants were not. The bulk of the Gorlan forces and animals were spread across the valley below—and giants couldn't swim!

Rahkki reached out his hands. *"Big water is coming,"* he signed. *"Because you refused to show us mercy."*

The princes scoffed at him. One glanced up. The rain had skidded into a light drizzle. A few sunrays poked through the dark clouds. They could not imagine where big water would come from.

Then the floodwaters appeared, rolling across the soil. They crashed through the valley, pushing down trees, sweeping up debris, and racing toward the giants. The first few Gorlanders spotted the water and rumbled in terror. It sped toward the lowland fields. Horror rooted the giants to the ground.

"RUN!" the three princes signed, adding sharp roars and chuffs, inflaming their hordes. They rushed down the hill to help their hordemates.

But it was too late. The floodwaters plowed into the lower valley and swept all the giants off their bare feet. Saber cats snarled and screeched. Elephants skidded across the terrain, their trunks reaching for the sky. The giants shrieked in alarm, choking when their mouths filled with water.

Brauk whistled for the Kihlari Fliers. They came and the Riders leaped aboard and flew toward the giants, attempting to rescue them, but the giants were too big.

The floodwaters flowed deep, reaching the giants' chests and tumbling them. They floundered and sputtered, trying to swim, not realizing they could stand. They pounced on debris that sank under their weight, reached for hanging branches that snapped in their clawed hands, and sucked huge mouthfuls of water.

The elephants braced, some holding their ground as the waters split around them, others floating with the current. Saber cats struck out, swimming powerfully and furiously, their jaws hinged open, lips curled back. Some leaped onto the backs of the elephants, which caused more furious trumpeting.

Rahkki's heart hammered as the waters reached their crescendo and then ebbed, spreading across the vast lowland valley. The giants lay fanned out in spluttering, heavy clumps, like beached whales. Sunbeams stretched from the sky, further confusing the hordes because they didn't understand where the water had come from.

Prince Daanath pushed himself out of the mud, but remained squatting, disoriented. The Fire and Great Cave princes wobbled to their feet and lumbered to join their counterpart. The three horde armies choked and gasped all around them, the fight gone from their eyes. They turned their attention to Rahkki.

He was still angry at the Gorlanders for being unreasonable. He used that anger now. Leaping aboard Sula, Rahkki flew down and hovered above the princes. *"The thousand-year war ends today,"* he signed. *"The sacred land is yours, always was yours."* He waved his hand over the balance of the Fifth Clan territory. *"And this land is ours. You will not destroy it. You will not raid us. You will not hurt my people. If you do, I will call the water back."*

Rahkki glanced at his brother, who soared nearby, and they each smiled. *Let your legend bloom* remained the best and worst advice Rahkki had ever received from Brauk.

The three princes consulted. After some furious gesturing, they faced Rahkki and nodded agreement. Prince

Daanath made a special signal with his hand, and the hordes repeated the motion. It was a clenched fist and then four fingers pointed down. Rahkki blinked, confused. That gesture was also the sign of the Sandwen rebellion. He'd seen General Tsun use it before he died.

I'Lenna had boarded Firo and she flew up beside him. Her dark eyes shone when she smiled. "General Tsun borrowed the signal from the giants. The gesture means *peace* in Gorlish," she said. "But it also means *family*. Giants use the same word for both, and General Tsun felt it suited the purpose of the rebellion."

Rahkki's eyes stung with relief. It had taken Granak's spirit, or perhaps very lucky timing, to terrify the Gorlanders into making peace, but it was done. He'd done it! He'd forged a lasting truce with all three hordes, the dream of his mother. He closed his eyes, turned his face to the peeking sun. *Remember, you have your mother's blood in your veins*, Darthan had said, and Rahkki felt Reyella now, smiling upon him from above. *Rahkki the Clever*, her voice washed over him like wind.

He clasped I'Lenna's hand and then Brauk's. Brauk reached for Feylah, and Feylah reached for Darthan. They created a chain. "We're stronger together," Rahkki said.

Darthan grinned, eyes glimmering. "Your mother's words."

Sula nickered to him and Rahkki paused, dreading what he knew would happen next.

"It's time to say good-bye," I'Lenna whispered.

∾ 40 ∾

HOME

ECHOFROST STUDIED RAHKKI AS HE BROKE FROM his family and ran to her, hugging her tight. She rested her head on his shoulder. Rahkki inhaled and his body shuddered.

"One last flight?" he whispered.

Echofrost felt his pulse thump harder and knew what he wanted. She slid her wing aside and Rahkki unbuckled and removed her bridle, saddle, and armor. Then he threw his leg over her bare back and settled behind her purple feathers. She didn't understand how the Sandwens had made peace with the giants, but they had done it. Brim was with the Gorlanders now, brewing tea to relax them after the near drowning. The Sandwens had also overthrown Lilliam and the Fifth Clan was at peace. Echofrost pressed her forehead to Rahkki's, proud that Storm Herd had helped his clan, but it was time to go. She sensed that Rahkki understood.

"I'm taking him up," she nickered to Hazelwind.

He nudged her. "Go on. We're not leaving here until Dewberry convinces at least one mare and foal to come with us."

Dewberry had flown to Darthan's barn and collected her twins. Now she stood with the Ruk steeds and Fliers, nickering and fluttering her wings as she spoke about their ancestors, their legends, and why they should join Storm Herd and live wild. Windheart and Thornblaze played beside her, rearing and ramming each other.

Redfire interjected with stories of his own, and the calm, handsome stallion was winning the tame Kihlari over faster than Dewberry. Several Fliers and Ruk steeds charged forward, quickly followed by more, eager to join Storm Herd and raise their own families. Echofrost counted breeding stallions, brood mares, foals, elders, and warriors who'd recently lost their Riders. The sight of the foals and elders bolstered her good mood. They would be a real herd, not just a stranded group of young refugees from Anok.

Others, like Kol and Drael and Rizah, chose to remain with the Fifth Clan. The giants had brought Tuni's mare with them and they released Rizah after the flood. Now the golden pinto stood with Tuni, reunited, and their bond was as powerful as any herd bond. Echofrost had ceased judging the foreign pegasi for their attachments to Land-walkers. Had she been raised with Rahkki from foalhood, she might not leave him either. The tame Kihlari were *choosing* to stay, and in that regard, they were free.

Hazelwind arched his neck, peering at her through his thick forelock. "We have a future now," he nickered.

Happiness swept through Echofrost as she whinnied and lashed her tail. "Yes, a future together!" She kicked off the hard stone and spiraled toward the parting clouds.

"Yah, Sula!" Rahkki cheered, leaning over her neck.

This was their final flight, but Echofrost was no longer worried about leaving Rahkki a Half. Her cub had never been more whole! His clan was free of Lilliam, his brother could walk, and his sister was home.

She spun higher, making Rahkki so dizzy he laughed. Then she evened out and flew to the highest altitude his small body could tolerate. The Realm stretched below, a sea of green leaves and valleys, bursting rivers, and engorged lakes. She spied herds of deer and buffalo. Far to the south, mountains stretched toward the sky. Storm Herd would cross those peaks in the coming moon as they traveled toward their new home.

Echofrost dipped and rose in sudden starts, surprising and exciting her cub. He patted her silver neck, encouraging her, so she broke into a free fall, diving straight down. He screamed with delight as they glided faster and faster. She tucked her wings. The Realm rushed toward them, the trees growing larger, the land broader. The sky shrank behind them. Rahkki squinted, a happy grin on his face.

She snapped out her wings and lifted her nose. They sped parallel to the trees, her hooves grazing the uppermost branches. Rahkki sat tall and spread his arms, as if he were flying too. Tears rolled down his cheeks. He didn't bother to wipe them away.

Echofrost spotted Leshi Creek and sank toward it. She touched down so lightly that it took her cub a moment to realize they'd landed. She dropped her head and drank while he lay across her, hugging her neck. "I love you," he said, crying harder now.

She arched her neck and pressed her forehead to his. He calmed and inhaled her warm breath. Then he slipped off her back, his hand lingering between her wings. He stroked her shoulder. "I'm sorry about this," he whispered, tracing her brand.

She sensed his sorrow and shook her mane. Rahkki should be happy. Everything had worked out for him, hadn't it? She dipped her feathers into the creek and splashed him.

"You didn't!" He splashed her back.

She reared and stomped the water, soaking him.

He ran behind and pulled her tail. She whirled and chased him. They trotted through the jungle, hiding and catching each other. They darted around trees, leaped out of bushes, tangled each other in vines. It turned into a game of tag, and Echofrost was surprised he knew how to play her foalhood game. They were each "it" many times. She nickered when he leaped out of a tree and missed her, landing on his face. He laughed when she reached for him and caught air as he swung away on a vine.

Echofrost had missed playing! Most of her life had been spent fighting and hiding and fleeing—in Anok and here in the Realm. She halted suddenly and gazed south—her longing for her new home swelled hard within her, catching her off guard. Rahkki bumped into her and settled, catching his breath.

They stood together for a long time, their hearts

beating the same rhythm. This cub had taught her to trust him. Of all the pegasi in Storm Herd, she was the least likely to trust *anyone*, let alone a Landwalker. With a burst of feelings, Echofrost understood how far she'd come since their first days together—how far she'd come since fleeing Anok.

She'd been stubborn, selfish, bitter, and afraid. She'd kept her friends at wing's length. But somehow, this boy had squirmed into her heart and created a space for himself. She hadn't wanted him there, had fought hard against his imposition, but he'd believed in her—he'd believed in them both—and they'd become friends.

Echofrost nuzzled Rahkki as the sun's warm rays stretched toward them. The crickets began their song in anticipation of evening, and the birds flew with furious joy that the rains had ended.

With nothing but affection between them, the Pair turned and walked back to Rahkki's home. She would leave him there, with his family, and then fly south to start a new life, with hers.

ACKNOWLEDGMENTS

THANK YOU, DEAR READER, FOR TRAVELING
through the Realm with me! It was challenging to write
a series starring three groups of creatures—pegasi,
humans, and giants—who all speak different languages,
but it was also very rewarding. My characters worked
hard to understand one another's languages and cultures
in order to come to peaceful terms. This series might be
shelved under *fantasy*, but fear and misunderstanding
of others is dangerous in all worlds, real and fictional.
I enjoyed watching my characters learn and grow and
slowly become friends.

If you haven't read the Guardian Herd series yet, I
invite you to do so! There you will meet a special black

foal named Star who is born unable to fly but is destined to inherit great power. This makes him a threat to the five herds of Anok and causes the leaders to unite against him. With his best friends, Morningleaf, Echofrost, and Bumblewind, and a few brave adult pegasi, Star must try to survive to his first birthday. For more information about Riders of the Realm and the Guardian Herd, please visit www.theguardianherd.com. There you can play herd games, view the characters, read interviews, view fan art and fan pets, and take quizzes!

Finally, I'd like to thank my primary editor, Karen Chaplin, who has worked on all seven of my pegasi books! Her clever insights and thoughtful suggestions have been invaluable in shaping these stories. And to the entire team at HarperCollins Children's, led by the incomparable Rosemary Brosnan, thank you for bringing these manuscripts to life with art, distribution, marketing, sales, printing, and your passion for books! Special thanks to David McClellan for producing all the interior art for both series and the gorgeous covers for the Guardian Herd, and to Vivienne To for her dramatic Riders of the Realm covers.

To my readers, if you'd like to help each series soar, please write reviews of the books online and request your local libraries to carry them. There is no better way to support an author than to spread the word!

For my family, friends, and the series' fans, thank you for dreaming with me.